BOOK 1

IS WHERE THE FEAR BEGINS...

FEAR IN FLESH

HESHAM N. ALI

REX SCRIBES

Copyright © 2016 - 2019 Hesham N. Ali

All rights reserved.

ISBN: 9781095300893

2nd Edition Published by Rex Scribes in 2019

1st Edition Originally Published on: 29th July 2016

To all the apocalyptic zombie-thriller fanatics out there!

ACKNOWLEDGMENTS

A special thank you to Mahmood Al Khaja for yet another brilliant book cover illustration.

In this dying world you can either swallow your fears or allow them to devour your flesh. Which will it be...?

PROLOGUE

THE FIRST COMING

Varied ideas about humanity are what turns some demonic and others into conquering heroes. The world has settled on the presumed principle of homogeneity of mankind, granting no place to those contradicting their notions of "reality". What prevailed was guided by eons of sinful deeds all leading to a singular event, catastrophic enough to annihilate the very fabric of mortal, flesh, and blood.

Long before the modern civilization became festered with intensified greed and regulating bodies constraining them, there grew among in the core of the thriving world a suppurated village. It grew in isolation from the richness of the beauty that lay beyond. Many broke free of its confines realizing the ugliness that settled there among them.

Hunger had its reins free in this village, it burgeoned into malevolence. All dressed in ragged clothing and battled endless struggles with death every day. Such a punishing habitat to raise a child in, it was. No matter, children survived and grew to father and mother children of their own, until the baleful day came when this village became the realm of a queer-looking boy who went by the name of "Rot".

Originally named Angster, was born by a loving mother but, the merriment of his childhood was short-lived as he lost her to a dreadful fever. The village folk infamously called her cause of demise as the *"Death Sentence Plague."* Angster was six years of age when his mother went to an early grave. The fate of his father, who had been torn to shreds by a pack of mountain lions during the harvest season, he didn't know. *"He is too young to learn about the ugliness of death. I must retain the innocence of his mind and give him hope"*, the mother had told herself over and over, so she herself, could learn to make this lie a reality in her mind.

Angster often wondered about his father's whereabouts, and his mother would tell him, "Father is busy dwelling up there." She'd point towards the sky. "He's flying over the clouds with his great wings, keeping the evil monsters at bay. One day, when he's stopped them all, he will come back and fly us with him over the clouds, so high up that you'll touch the blue of the sky." His face would lighten up, with a beaming smile plastered across his face whenever he heard those comforting words from his mother.

The orphan lived all by himself in a cruel village where none had the heart to foster him. All of this fear was of the unknown, for a certain alien feature that the boy possessed kept everyone away from him. Children of the village refused to play with him. They would always flee at the first sight of him, Angster's heart bled at the sight of such forbiddance for him. Parents counseled their children, "Keep away from Rot." They called Angster by that menacing disease of a name, because of a green glob with a moldy semblance he was born with on one side of his temple.

The mold spread as the time went on. It became swamped with thick black burgeoning veins that resembled thorns. It claimed one side of his head, where it devoured his shaggy silvery curls and then slithered down like green roots over one brow of his face, turning the blue of his eye milky white. It made the poor boy appear monstrous with only a few wisps of hair remaining on his head.

"Rot is the harbinger of death, never stand alongside him," the village folk warned, "or you will suffer the same fate his foolish mother did when she turned a blind eye to his malady." They thought Angster was the bearer of the "Death Sentence Plague" that, by merely getting too close to him they would be infected by the scalding fever and prematurely, embrace the bitter arms of death. Everyone feared what was an inevitability of life.

For a time being, the plague set a number of villagers—older and younger bodies—to burning with fever till death cooled them off in the stone-cold earth while maggots feasted upon their decaying flesh. Meanwhile, Angster still lived in the village's mucky streets, where he slept among a colony of rats, which were largely dispersed among the population of the village folk. He dined upon them, as he barely found anything else to fill the hollowness within his increasingly growling belly.

One day, the heartless villagers reached the breaking point of their patience with Angster and decided to get rid of him once and for all, they chased him with pitchforks, knives, and meat cleavers, hurling stones at the frightened, feeble child who ran shoeless with his stick-thin legs.

"Away with you and this rotten disease you brought upon our village!"

"Yeah, why must you make our lives miserable?"

"Kill, Rot!"

"Let's wipe this scourge off the face of the earth!"

Terrified and alone, he had tattered clothes on his body, the pockets of which held dead vermin. Breathless, with toes bloodied from running on hard land with sharp-edged gravel, he came to a stop at a place where the worst fears of a child manifested especially, when alone at nighttime.

Ghostly mists scoured the grisly plains where Angster discovered himself lost. This place made him feel even more fearful than the angry mob that was after him. It was a place where soulless bodies dissolved to bones far below the surface of the earth, a graveyard. He could barely make out the shapes of the ruined and the shattered tombstones that were strewn across the ground, swallowed up by the dense, eerie fog. Though in the midst of his angst, he could hear bone-chilling murmurs clearly, echoing across the cemetery.

Ghosts, he feared, for the sounds that traveled through the mists were inhuman, moaning and wailing. Angster was determined to appease the source of this unkind sound, as a means of finding a temporary safe haven, rather than risk falling back into the arms of his pursuers. So he took a few shaky steps forward, sinking into the eerie white vapor. "H-hello? Is anyone there?" Angster's voice sounded exhausted and frightened as the chilling moans chased his feeble steps. "I'm not here to bring anyone harm. Sorry if my disease was the cause of you being here. I didn't mean to infect anybody. It just happens, I swear it! I didn't ask to be the bearer of this plague. I don't want it! Please forgive me. Don't let the bad people hurt me. I'll be good, I promise! Just make these people go away. My legs can't run anymore."

How far he walked, Angster was not sure. The misty yard seemed endless and began to feel like a troublesome maze. He was, without a doubt, lost, both in his physical surroundings and in his mind from the terror of the unknown. The boy finally tripped over a stone and fell face first, dead rats spilled out of his tattered pockets. He lay there for a while, whimpering as the moans around him rose in magnitude.

Cold as death, were the bony fingers that coiled about one scrawny arm of Angster lifting him back to his feet. He stared in absolute horror. Gazing back at him was a pitch-black void, hidden beneath a shadowing cowl, as dark as night. A long robe disappeared into the fog that concealed its lower half. Hands and fingers were fleshless bones. One held a scythe as tall as a full-grown man, the other released Angster's arm and then gently touched the glowing green mold on Angster's face with his finger. "You are the one they call, "Rot". You cursed child." It spoke hoarsely and sounded ancient. "Sobs will do you no good here, little one. Remain that way and you will soon join those who slumber deep beneath the earth you stand upon. Would you like that to happen?"

Rendered speechless, Angster did not move. The fear shaking his body faded away as if he could no longer sense his former self. His voice was caught in his throat, and he fixed unblinking eyes upon what could only be what all saw when dying. The one they called the "Angel of Death" or, sometimes, the "Grim Reaper." Whichever dreadful name the faceless skeleton bore, his sudden appearance in such a foul place with a scythe, that could easily slice the small boy in two, did not bode well.

"What is the matter, cursed child? Did one of your vermin prey claim your tongue or has fear bid you to swallow it?" Following another lengthy pause, the Reaper added, "'Tis a pity to take a soul that could hold such power. Cursed, you are, child. That does not mean you ought not to live, however your time shortens with each passing moment of your silence. Doom closes its tendrils around you. Do you wish for maggots to feed off your rotting corpse? Or maybe you'd wish to deliver justice for the sorrow those people brought upon you."

"Justice," Angster managed to wheeze out, with a hint of a tremble in his voice from the chill.

"Justice can be granted at the cost of *blood!*" The creature extended the answer.

"B-blood? N-n-no … no, no, I wish no harm to come to anyone, no matter how much they hurt me! All I want is to be away from them, forever. My disease has brought much gloom to the villagers." Angster dropped his marred head low. "Including my own mother, you see. You must neither touch me, nor get too close, or you too will get sick with the fever!" Angster backed up a few steps to keep some distance between them.

"I am the Claimer of Souls, who mortals fear. I am the One who separates a being from its mortal form in this world and reincarnates it in the one hereafter. Thus, they could serve as soldiers to the lord of the kingdom above the clouds or of the one below the earth. No plague can cause harm to *me*. I'd end it with a swing of my scythe."

"Can you truly end it? Can you rid me of my disease and bring an end to this plague?" asked Angster wondrously. "Maybe then the villagers would accept me, and children my age will let me play with them."

"If I to do that Cursed Child, then I would end you entirely."

"Why do you keep calling me a 'Cursed Child'?"

"You are a child cursed with this—what you call a 'disease'—that drove the villagers after you. You can choose a path to make use of this curse and turn it into a blessing—it is not too late."

"No blessing has it ever brought upon anyone here. It only causes death. I told you, *it killed my mother* and more villagers than I could ever count! It is nothing but an *awful* disease!"

"*Insolence!*" The Soul Claimer's roar echoed throughout the cemetery. The tombstone closest to Angster shook and the ground beneath his toes rattled. In the blink of an eye, the void beneath the cowl was immediately before him again. The cold hand of the Reaper rested atop his mold, and the sharpness of the scythe's curved point touched the boy's quivering neck. "Resume your foolishness, boy, and you shall soon enough fear my second coming when I arrive to take your pitiful soul." Angster was shaking when the scythe left his neck. A trickle of blood slid down his neck. "I do not desire your soul yet," the soul claimer admitted. "'Tis your power I hold precious to my cause, not your tears of sorrow or your youthful innocence."

"W-what power?"

"The immeasurable power which your curse holds is of great value. What they deem a plague, that exterminates the living, is in reality, a *cure* to bring the dead back among the living. Those vermin that lay dead at your feet are what caused the plague from the beginning, not your disease. It was the habitat that those impudent villagers built their lives around that brought forth this pestilence."

"I ate many of those rats when I had nothing else to eat. Why wasn't I infected?"

"The gift of the curse, they did not possess to shield themselves, against the plague, as it did you. But you lack the wits to wield its true power."

"Bring the dead back among the living? How could that come to be?"

"The answer to your query shall come, and you will witness a living proof before your very own eyes. However, if you seek to obtain this knowledge, this secret of power beyond comprehension, you *must* heed my bidding, Cursed One."

Angster nodded, his wide eyes fixed on the death-wrought creature counseling him.

"You must bring me the souls of those who torment you, and you shall have access to the curse's power to do so. Is that understood?"

"Yes," Angster spoke gingerly. "You will teach me how to use the power of my mold so that I can take revenge against the bad villagers that will come after me."

"Call it as you wish, so long as you proffer their darkened souls to me. As for their physical forms, you do with them as you please. You could fulfill your long-time wish and have them become your "friends". Though, they will neither speak nor play as they do now. They will however, obey you loyally. They will always stand guard over you and bow their heads at your command."

"Friends! You will get me friends?"

"They, Cursed One, you will now have." The scythe rose toward the blackness of the night sky, and the fog faded to reveal a vast circle of tombstones and corpses around them. The corpses moved and groaned as worms gnawed through their naked bodies, exposing a hardened layer of tissue and rotted flesh that still clung to their bones. Eyes were as pale as clouds and as dead and cold as the graves they rose from under. They were moving closer to Angster in a limping trot surrounding him in a great ring.

The boy retreated to the safety of his shadowlike guardian. "W-will they hurt me?" Angster asked.

"All they seek to hurt are the creatures seeking to hurt their master. And their master must know no fear of them, or anything else. Prove yourself to be worthy of wielding the curse's power, to control the undying spawn of the underworld, to will them to protect their true leader. They will serve you loyally, as you serve me. As I once served *my* makers. Eliminate your fears, Cursed Child, and your army of undead shall grow to take kingdoms beyond your wildest dreams under your rule."

"Dreams?" Angster felt the word alien on his tongue as he heard that it could be a hopeful summons for him. "I always dreamed of my father's great white feathered wings flying me high up to the blueness of the sky. How I wish my mother had not died so that when father would have returned, all three of us would have been a family once more and flown together. Mother always said so."

"And look what has become of your mother now." Bony fingers touched Angster's chin and turned his head towards one approaching corpse garbed in dirt and oozing maggots with eyes most unnaturally white. But her face was still recognizable, as is the face of every loved one.

"Mother!" the boy wailed. He wanted to run and embrace her, though his wits urged dread over compassion. "I can't see her this way, she's in pain. Put her back down!" he commanded.

"'Tis, not my pursuit to harm the mortal forms. This scythe I hold is the mouth that feeds on the souls of the dying, and I, the black wings lead the spirits to their unfortunate paths. Your mother and all those who stand rotting before you are neither human nor spirit anymore, they sense no form of pain. They are the living dead. Soulless abominations brought back to life for the sole purpose of protecting the bearer of the mark." The chilling skeleton hand once again laid an open palm on Angster's green glob. "The mark that brings life to death, a mark that feeds on life till there is nothing left but *rot*. The villagers didn't realize the true meaning that your derogatory name held."

"Will they do whatever I tell them to? Even mother?"

"So long as it involves bloodshed and feasting upon the living flesh, all you need is to utter only a single command."

Meanwhile, in the not-so-far distance, various torch fires shone like small orange moons gliding in the surrounding mist of the graveyard. Angster could hear the furious murmurs from afar. The villagers had come. They had come for him and would find him. -*If they find me, they will surely kill me,* he apprehensively thought about that. "Will you stay here and help me?" he asked the Grim Reaper.

"I have helped you as much as I deemed essential. 'Tis time you handle the matters as yours and my intentions orient unanimously to serve our superior purpose. Obliterate your fears to gain power over the strong and the weak alike. Make them fearful of your rising, fearful of your arrival, fearful of your mere existence! The hour grows near. They are here. Show no mercy. If you allow your fear to build, you will weaken. You have stared into the face of Death, spoken to it, and yet you still breathe to speak of it. You are now the apprentice of Death itself, Rot. You are one of the four horsemen: You are the physical manifestation of Conquest and Pestilence, among the four horsemen they will rides alongside you and reside within you. You shall inherit many dread-inducing names as you spread terror and ruin until you become known to the world as the *Fear in Flesh*." The empty black cowl didn't waver. "I must depart now. Farewell, cursed one, and let us both hope for your sake that we never choose separate paths. Once we conquer this world, we shall create a race that will obey and forever bow down to the four horsemen and none else."

FEAR IN FLESH

Titanic black wings burst from the back of Death's cloak, his aura carried melancholy. The wings spread wide and swept down as the fourth horseman departed towards to the sky. Raven black feathers rained down on Angster and his army of groaning corpses. He saw the tombstones tinged with a dampened orange hue because of the torchlights. He could see the pitchforks and the knives carried by barbarians far uglier than his corpse army—but he did not feel as intimidated now, he reflected.

"W-what is this sorcery?" One man said whose masculinity wavered at the sight before him. The enraged mob drew close to Angster and his newly recruited protectors.

"*Monstrosities*," a woman wielding a knife declared. "Look at the bestialities he bore! *Kill him!*" her hands trembled as she said so. None dared to take a step forward though, fearing what those groaning roamers shielding the boy might do.

"You all are the barbaric savages, not them, they are my friends. They will protect me from you monsters! I never did anything to harm you. I was not the bearer of the plague. It was the rats, I swear it!"

"*LIAR!*" a voice bellowed.

The groans of the undead army around Angster grew vicious due to the crassness of villagers against their master. The bodies of the villagers quivered and forced the ones standing in the front to take a few hesitant steps back, their resolve faltering.

Devilry resides within the human nature. Angster drew pleasure from the fear of these people, and the child flashed them a crooked demonic smile. Darkness dominated his sense of eternal helplessness. "My friends sound rather hungry. I believe it's because they can smell fear in your flesh. I would like to find out. And since you dogs are very fond of following me around, maybe you *should* become my loyal followers as well." Angster aimed a dirt-encrusted finger at the ignorant mob that stood before him and announced, "I think I've kept them waiting long enough … *FEAST!*"

Ghastly hands rose up from under the ground that the villagers stood upon. They undead army had risen to avenge their master. Some were pulled down screaming, others were used as leverage for the corpses to heave themselves out of their graves while crushing the bones and lacerating the flesh of the villagers. Panic and indecision swept through the mob. Should they flee and abandon those in torment or should they stay unyielding to try to nip the evil in the bud?

The screams of the vanquished villagers rang in Angster's ears and throughout the otherwise silent surroundings as anguished melodies. Screams were chanted from the teeth whose fleshes were being relentlessly gnawed at and their bones crunched to the marrow. The brutal fingers burrowed into their bellies and ripped them open to haul out the slimy and miasmic innards.

The villagers fought back with whatever weapons they had, but no matter how many times they struck the corpses down, the creatures got back up painlessly and punished the villagers by biting chunks off the very limbs that wielded their weapon in. One after the other, the villagers fell while the living dead increased, for the villagers rose again shortly after their demise and opened their eyes that possessed a milky haze, waking up to an oblivion, groaning and limping they became, as their predators.

Anger is an all-consuming entity, it makes sure to bring ruin in its wake, and an unceasing satisfaction if one acts on it. Angster's former self had caved in, dominated by the protection that anger brought him. The wails of agony surrounding him were music to his ears. The spillage of gore made his mouth water for a red feast for himself, as he was the boy who ate vermin for his survival, gore was his "normal" and the blood ... oh, the blood. It was red and moist and as it dripped down it reminded him of the wetness of his own tears he shed in isolation, with no one to provide him any solace. It filled his entire being with a crazed wrath and an agonizing melancholy. He realized the death of his childish innocence at the hands of humanity.

From that night forth, Angster the Cursed was dead, and Rot the Fearful prevailed like a menace. His atrociousness rivaled that of Death's, his counselor, as this youthful king of the living dead swept through a myriad of nations, conquering rich realms and spreading carnage and malady wherever he stepped. His name struck fear even into the hearts of the realms that lay thousands of leagues away. He was an unstoppable force.

Conquest and Pestilence marched their great army of the undead against what remained of the united realms, allowing them to open the ancient door, which had been withholding his fellow horseman War from entering, eventually it paved the way for their chief horseman Death to arrive. It culminated into a cataclysmic event in the human history. At last, the Apocalypse came to put an end to all the kingdoms, especially the one over the clouds and the one embedded in the earth, the Great War was waged to decimate the world of all the living souls.

However, the might of all kingdoms combined prevailed and tore through the horsemen's undying soldiers till they got to the fearful Rot himself, astride his undead white horse. And thus, the Apocalypse was no more. The greatest war in the history of the mankind had ended. With the fall of the mortal Conquest, the undying army crumbled, and War was locked back in its delicate cage like the resolve and the nature of humanity itself. Death retreated to his eternal duties of claiming dying souls for the armies of the supreme kingdoms flourishing in the great beyond above and the lands camouflaged below.

Though the body of Conquest perished, the green mold—Pestilence—refused to fade to nothingness along with its host. Instead, it buried itself thousands of feet deep, beneath the earth. Centuries passed, as civilizations rose and fell atop his long forgotten tomb.

All memory of his malicious existence faded from history, undiscovered until the day came along when the actions of humanity culminated into their doom.

1

UNDERGROUND

NIGHT 1

Violet felt as if she was suspended in the darkest end of space and time. The hue of her creamy white hands seemed to lose its existence in this agonizing darkness that prevailed around her. She couldn't hear anything other than her own rapid breathing. The concept of time seemed to hold no significance here, for a few seconds felt like an eternity. She stood static as if the slightest misstep could lead to dire consequences. She felt stuck and lost, the darkness felt overpowering. Finally, she managed to say one word in a tentative voice, "Hello?" Maybe, it was this display of courage on Violet's part that the darkness started to fade away. The blurry edges of the scene shifted and took the form of a busy New York street. She found herself standing in the midst of the street, rather befuddled. Quickly, she ran towards the sidewalk, where dozens of people were walking by in a hurry wearing a stern expression.

Violet looked around at the familiar scenery spread before her eyes. Her spine tingled as the world went eerily quiet, all of a sudden. She saw the faces of the people around her morph into a petrified expression. It was after that when she heard the echoes. They sounded wild, angry. They grew in frequency until they became deafening. Violet then felt the earth shake. She saw the ground rupture in front of her eyes. She ran, in the chaos unfolding around her. People screamed while utter mayhem had ensued. Violet then saw the familiar structure of the comic book store which she loved. It exuded safety to her. She ran towards it, thinking it could protect her. The ground shook harder now, she turned around and saw the buildings around had cracks in their foundation. A realization dawned upon, she turned around quickly, and she saw the comic book store that she so relished tearing apart. It was then that she saw those cracks creeping towards her and before she could make a deliberate move, she was swallowed by the very ground she stood upon.

Violet opened her eyes, with her heart thrumming wildly in her chest. The darkness faded away as she gasped for air, panting. She felt a gentle pat on her back. "There, there, sweetheart, you looked a little flustered in your sleep. It was only a bad dream that you saw. Here, drink some water." An old woman wearing a yellow trench coat, whom Violet vaguely remembered sitting next to on the train when she first got on, offered her a bottle of water.

Violet's green eyes grew wide in confusion and she stared at the old lady. Adjusting to the reality unwinding around her, overriding questions went through her mind. *What's going on? Where am I?* Once she came to her senses, she blinked, shook her head a little, and said, "No thanks, ma'am. I'm fine." She flashed the lady a smile of gratitude for her act of kindness.

The woman smiled back and said, "You looked very uncomfortable in your sleep."

"Well, I *was* sleeping on a subway train. I don't ever expect good dreams in here."

"I thought about waking you up, but you started talking. Couldn't quite catch what you were saying. So, I figured maybe it was one of those important sleep talks that people have sometimes," the old lady said with a laugh.

Violet laughed along with her and then she asked, "How long was I out?"

The old woman looked at her watch and said, "About ten minutes." Violet's train trip should last only twenty so, ten minutes were left before she would finally reach her destination.

Violet Turner had good reason to be exhausted that evening, after having a fierce one-on-one wrestling match against a larger female in an actual squared wrestling ring with ropes and turnbuckles her muscles were sore. She remembered the fiery fans cheering or booing all around them.

It was 7:30 pm and Violet was making her way back to Cliffroyce Bay. It was a moderate-sized town off the east coast of Manhattan Island, between the borough itself and the East River. Cliffroyce Bay was well known for its port business and forested hunting grounds.

Violet, at twenty, was a part-time professional wrestler who participated in small, independent wrestling events around New York City and nearby areas. She stood five-foot-five and was a slender young woman, but her body supported far more muscle from her intensive training. Her velvety dark brown hair reached a couple of inches past her shoulders. Her hair framed her creamy complexioned face dusted with freckles. Violet's most beguiling feature were her alluring green eyes which sometimes flickered like a wildfire. At the moment, she wore a white hoodie that had *I Love NYC* on it with baggy blue pants and white lace-up sneakers.

When the train came to Violet's stop, she once again thanked the old woman and said, "Good-bye, enjoy the rest of your evening," to her.

The old woman waved back and said, "You too, darling. Take care of yourself."

Violet felt a slight rumble in her belly the moment she got off the train and remembered that she hadn't eaten anything since her match. She dug around in her backpack, looking for some snacks that she usually carried with herself but today there was nothing. She looked around and saw a vending machine. That made her happy so, she extracted a dollar from her bag to buy some potato chips. She inserted the dollar into the machine but was startled when she heard a loud, shrill scream coming from the east side of the subway tunnel.

Worried—and curious—Violet took several steps towards the tunnel but stopped. She hesitated moving forward when the screams began increasing in number and volume. She stood stock-still for a second, and then she jumped a little when she felt a hand grasping her right shoulder. It was a police officer with a thick mustache, holding a flashlight in his left hand. "Miss, we are authorized to clear the area for an emergency shutdown. I'm going to need you to head to the staircase and walk out of the station immediately."

"Sure thing, officer," Violet said and obliged to the command. She jogged up the stairs just as a SWAT team ran down. When she reached the top, she looked back down, wondering what could possibly be happening. Violet stepped out of the station's gate to see a yellow police tape already going up, to prevent the bystanders from entering. Just like a crime scene in the movies, only there weren't any dead bodies lying around. Violet spotted three police cars and two SWAT vans parked on the sidewalk, next to the stairway gate. The rest were parked on the road, blocking the right lane. Cars were at a standstill, honking and pouring out the exhaust. Violet had a moment of déjà vu but it was ephemeral. She sucked in some of the air congested with smoke. There was no space for fresh air in this town. She then shoved both her hands into her hoodie pockets and walked away from the frenzy that transpired almost every day from the vehicles. On a happier note, she wondered what her father might have cooked for dinner tonight. The mere thought of food appeased her stomach for some time.

As she was walking back home, she passed by the local comic book store that Violent was so fond of, Comic Books Daily. Immediately, the strange dream she had sprung into her mind. The memory made her skin prickle. She was staring at the window of the store reminiscing when the man working inside the store glanced at her. He smiled when he saw her and waved her in an inviting gesture.

Marvin Conley was the name of the twenty-eight-year-old man who co-owned the comic book store with his friend, Richie. Slightly tubby, his ginger hair was pulled back in a slick ponytail. He also had a bushy beard covering his face which had a color similar to that of his hair. His face was adorned with circular-framed glasses and he often wore oversized superhero themed T-shirts. Tonight he was sitting behind the counter with a box of donuts next to him.

Violet and Marvin had been good friends for more than two years. Violet made it to the store once or twice a week and loved engaging in heated discussions about the comic books—mostly about the best and worst superheroes and villains. Occasionally, they would go out to watch the movies together, but their relationship was completely platonic.

"Hey," Marvin greeted Violet and asked, "What brings Vicious to Cliffroyce's busy streets this fine evening?"

"Vicious" was Violet's wrestling name, inspired by her aggressive moves within the ring, though it could also have described her nature of arguing ferociously about the comic books with Marvin and other comic book geeks that visited the store.

"Fine evening?" she mocked, pointing at the honking wars taking place outside the store. The noise of those horns was exasperating and could spoil the mood of anyone subjected to them.

"No, seriously," he said. "You know that we won't have anything new until tomorrow. Don't tell me you came all this way just because you missed this?" he said that while rubbing his bushy beard.

"Uh-huh, don't flatter yourself, Ginger Claus." Marvin had acquired this name not only because of his appearance but also for his generous gift-giving powers and of granting Violet discounts. "As you saw, I was walking from the other direction. Walking *back* home, not from it, idiot."

"Where were you walking *back* from?"

"The subway station, I just came back from a match in Brooklyn."

"Aha, I bet you got your butt kicked 'cause you didn't tell me about any matches booked for this week."

"No sir, *I* was the one who handed out the butt-kicking tonight, thank you very much." She stuck her tongue out at him.

He rolled his eyes at her, and then a sudden realization dawned upon him. "Wait a minute ... you came back from the subway station?"

"Yeah," Violet started to get a little apprehensive when Marvin asked that.

His eyes widened at her affirmation. "Really! It's all over the news! That place is being heavily guarded by the cops, watch!" He directed her attention to his twenty-inch flat-screen TV on the counter next to the cash register. "They are saying that a bunch of deranged, unstable tourists is attacking people down there. Did you see it happen?"

"No, I was going to when I heard a scream, but a police officer stopped me and told me to leave. Did they say who it was? Or why these people are attacking?"

"Not yet. The police are still investigating, I guess."

* * *

Meanwhile, back at the subway station, gunshots were being fired rapidly at targets that looked barren of life, they were moving at a slow pace and were completely unresponsive. It was a massacre. Quickly the situation reached an alarming level when two officers rushed outside the station's gate to call for backup and a medic. A news reporter immediately pounced on the opportunity on seeing the police.

"Officer, can you let the public know what is going on down there? Is it another terrorist attack? Is it linked to the series of attacks that took place this past week in other states?"

"Get that freakin' camera off my face!" the officer snapped, shoving away the cameraman while trying to cover up his bleeding left arm. The cameraman noticed the bleeding and zoomed in on it to reveal that something had ripped through the officer's uniform sleeve and gashed his skin terribly.

* * *

"That's the cop who asked me to leave the station. The one with the mustache," Violet confirmed. "What the hell happened to his arm?"

"Looks like a knife cut to me, maybe," Marvin guessed.

Violet was getting a little uneasy so, she decided to divert her attention and look around the store. Then she suddenly remembered, "Where's Richie tonight?"

"Right behind you," a gentle voice said.

Richie Morey was another close friend of Violet's. He joined Marvin's and Violet's weekly discussions and occasional movie outings. He was also Marvin's roommate and of course, business partner. Unlike Marvin, he had messy black curls and preferred a clean shave. He looked generally fit, not muscular but not too skinny. In his arms, he juggled paper bags stuffed with groceries.

Violet turned around and said, "What's up, Richie? Where've you been?"

"Doing some grocery shopping." He hoisted the paper bags a little higher as if to demonstrate. "Wait, what are *you* doing here? New comic books don't come in until tomorrow."

Violet closed her eyes and sighed. "You don't say."

Marvin jumped in. "She just came back from a match, which she didn't even tell us about."

"Ooh, so were you booked to lose a match?" Richie sounded surprised.

"Of course not! *I* was the one who pinned my opponent all the way to three, after reversing her power-bomb attempt, landing her face first onto the mat." She glared at Marvin ferociously.

"Wow, there you have it. Precise details always get Vi the win, whether it's in the ring or arguing with you, Marv. Congrats, Vicious," Richie said.

"Thanks, handsome."

"Say ... did you guys hear about what went down at the subway station?" Richie asked.

Marvin answered, "Yeah, man, it's all over the news right now. How did you find out about it?"

"I overheard a guy talking on his cell phone about it on my way back here."

"Looks like some sort of an attack by 'deranged tourists' according to Marv," Violet said.

"You'd often hear 'terrorists'. But they said 'tourists' on the news just before you walked in." Marvin defended his statement.

"Anyways, unlike him, I was down there. I heard some screams. Then a cop asked me to leave, and just moments ago I saw him on TV with a bloody arm."

"Did they say what was happening down there? Or at least confirm the crazy tourist-attack story?"

Both answered, "Not yet," at the same time.

Violet's cell phone rang. "Hello? Oh hey, Dad."

"Violet! Where are you?"

"I'm at the comic book store. What's up?"

"Oh ... thank God. I thought you were still stuck in the subway station!"

"So you heard about it too, huh? No, I got out as soon as the cops started to shut the place down."

"They say people are biting each other down there. Did you see any of that? Some form of cannibalistic attacks. I ..."

"What?" Violet interrupted. "We've had the news on the whole time. They didn't say anything about people biting each other or ... cannibals!"

Marvin and Richie became slightly worried, on hearing Violet's last words, but they were still skeptical about their authenticity.

Violet's dad said, "I wasn't home when they reported it. Your brother told me."

"Dad, c'mon. Billy's seven, I'm sure he misunderstood."

"I know ... but ... just a little while ago, the same thing happened in our own neighborhood—in the Carlson's house."

"What do you mean 'the same thing happened'? Did someone—"

"Listen, sweetheart, me and your brother are packing enough clothes and food for all three of us. Then I'm coming straight to the comic book store to pick you up."

"But, Dad, what—"

"Violet, I'll explain everything when I get there. But until then, *do not* step a foot outside the store till I call you again, understood?"

"I won't."

Violet's father hung up, but she kept staring at the phone. The unpredictability of the situation and unanswered questions bothered her. She mulled over her father's words. *What the hell happened in the Carlson's house? And where does Dad wanna go off to?*

"What was your dad telling you exactly?" asked Richie.

"That I should stay inside the store till he gets here to pick me up," she answered, still sounding confused and a little unnerved.

"What for?"

"I don't know. Just something about ... cannibals, I guess, he was really spooked out about it."

"We must've missed that part on the news, then." Marvin jutted in while reflecting on this whole ordeal.

2

NEIGHBOR DRAMA

NIGHT 1

Earlier the same night ...

Not far from the comic book store, in a small beige house in a cul-de-sac, on Second Avenue, lived Gavin Turner, a forty-six-year-old single father of two—his daughter, Violet, and son, Billy. He was also a well-known, successful realtor. Gavin had just finished cooking dinner and was headed up to the living room to see what his seven-year-old was up to.

Billy looked a lot like his older sister, except his hair was lighter and his cheeks were so big and round that they looked like they were stuffed with marshmallows. "Hey, pal. Aren't you supposed to be getting your homework done instead of watching cartoons all night long? It's almost time for supper," Gavin said.

"I'm waiting for Violet to come back home, so she can help me with my math problems," Billy confessed.

"Well, she should be here soon," Gavin assured his son and sat beside him on the couch. "Can you turn on the news for a second?" Billy clicked away on the remote obediently, until they came to the news channel and saw the words *Breaking News* scrolled under a subway station clip with authorities swarming the gate. Gavin immediately felt a chill run down his spine, and his heart started beating loudly in his chest.

He knew that his daughter was supposed to be arriving from that station. Fear took over as he imagined one worst-case scenario after another, a hostage situation, a terrorist attack, or a murder. The possibilities seemed endless. The news coverage didn't seem to distinctly say anything about what was going on down there. *Whatever it is, it must be bad*, Gavin thought.

"What's happening, Dad?" Despite his age, Billy sensed that something might have gone terribly wrong.

"I have no idea, Billy. But keep watching while I go call your sister and see if she's still in there." He got up to get his phone when suddenly, the doorbell started ringing frantically. Whoever was on the other side of the door was pressing the bell in urgency.

Gavin rushed up to the door and opened it to see her neighbor, Pamela, looking rather distressed. "Gavin, we need your help." She said instantly in quick breaths. "It's the Carlsons, something's happened. There were screams coming from inside the house. Their daughter Kelly ran out of the house, crying and not making any sense of what happened in there and—"

"Whoa! Whoa! Slow down, Pamela. Am I the first person to hear about this?"

"No," Pamela answered. "Some of the neighbors are already inside the house. They told me to round up more men from around the cul-de-sac until the police get here."

"All right, Billy, stay right where you are and keep watching the news. I'll be back soon."

Gavin and Pamela ran to the house and saw a bunch of women, mothers, and wives, standing outside the front door. One of the women had the Carlsons' sobbing daughter Kelly embraced in her arms. The girl was no older than Billy was.

Gavin went inside to join the men. The front door was open, so he walked into the living room, but no one was there to be found. He heard footsteps right above his head, so he went upstairs to find the men scattered throughout the hallway.

One was on the phone, giving details about the house address. Another was peeping through the keyhole of the room at the end of the hall, and two others were aiding a man sitting on the floor with a bleeding leg.

"What the hell happened to your leg?" Gavin asked Shockley.

"I'll tell ya what the hell happened, it's Carlson. He went nuts!" Shockley said.

"Is he the one who did this to you?"

"That bastard bit me! When I was trying to pull him off his wife, he turns around and bites my leg, in a boiling rage, all of a sudden!"

"He ... bit you?" Gavin asked, horrified and confused. Carlson had always been a good neighbor.

"Turner, you gotta come and see this for yourself," encouraged the man at the end of the hall. He was still staring through the keyhole. When Gavin went to look, the man told him, "You won't be able to see clearly from here. You go in quietly and just don't touch him."

Gavin took his advice and opened the door quietly. He immediately found Carlson on the floor, kneeling with his back to the door and making loud crunching noises. Like someone was biting through rough meat with their mouth open. "Carlson?" Gavin called.

The crunching noises came to a halt as Carlson turned his head slowly to stare right at Gavin with his foggy eyes. His hands were painted red with blood. Pieces of flesh were hanging from his mouth, and a fleshy piece of meat was stuck on his blood-stained mustache.

He started to climb slowly to his feet, struggling with balance. Gavin looked down at the floor and saw Mrs. Carlson. It was hard to recognize her with half her face gone. *She* was the rough meat Carlson was crunching on.

Gavin placed one hand over his mouth to stop himself from vomiting then and there, and ran out of the room, heading straight to the toilet next door. The neighbor who'd encouraged him to go in slammed the bedroom door shut before Carlson even managed to get fully back on his feet again. Gavin kept his head over the toilet, vomiting, unable to get rid of the revolting images in his head, the blood, chewed-up flesh and the scattered flesh in places it's not supposed to be in—such a gruesome and disturbing scene it was.

When he'd finally emptied his stomach, he suddenly remembered his daughter. *Have to go call her and make sure she's safe.* He flushed the toilet and pulled himself up to the sink to rinse his mouth. When he walked out of the bathroom, one of the men asked how he was doing after having seen it up close.

"I'm okay," Gavin said. "Listen, the cops will probably get here any minute now. I have to go call my daughter. She's supposed to be coming back from the subway station that's on the news. Cops are surrounding the gate. I don't know, why, just yet. So … excuse me."

Gavin returned home, and no sooner had he entered the living room than Billy jumped to his feet. "Dad! On the news … they're saying something about people biting each other down there in the station!"

FEAR IN FLESH

Gavin's mind went blank and he just stared at Billy. "Dad, did you hear what I just said?"

"Ye-yes, Billy, of course." He shook himself out of his paralytic state induced by the events surrounding him. "Now listen carefully to me, son. I'm gonna need you to go up to your room and put on a jacket and shoes. I want you to pack some clothes inside your biggest backpack. Then stuff as much food and drinks as you can grab in plastic bags. I'll go call Violet and then do the same."

"But why?" Billy asked.

"I'll tell you all about it later in the car." He gave Billy a kiss on his forehead. "Now, hurry."

Gavin went up to his bedroom, grabbed his cell phone, and dialed Violet's number, praying that she'd answer her phone.

3

A NEVER-ENDING TRAFFIC

NIGHT 1

It was past 9:00 pm. The comic book store was well past the closing hours, and customers were long gone. The only people left inside were Violet and the store owners, Marvin and Richie. They were still waiting for the arrival of Violet's father, after hearing his claims about the cannibalistic attacks in the neighborhood. They were all perturbed by what they had been hearing from Violet's father and the news reports that both, the police and the SWAT had been engaged in a battle against the attackers using their teeth in aggression down in the subway station tunnels. Eventually, the Special Forces were left with no choice but to open fire on the attackers, while one officer retreated from the station during the shooting after sustaining an injury on his right shoulder.

Marvin and Richie figured that the best thing to do was to stay put. After closing the store, they locked themselves inside and decided to sleep in, till the roads became less congested with panic-stricken people and the whole situation calmed down.

"Ugh!" Violet was frustrated after hanging up the phone with her father for the second time since he'd originally told her not to leave the store. He was still stuck in traffic, and Violet's belly was rumbling even louder than when she'd left the station. "Hey, Richie, can I have something else to eat, please? The potato chips you gave me earlier didn't do anything, but make me hungrier."

"No can do, Vi. You're gonna leave soon, and we're going to need the food in case we have to stay here longer."

"C'mon, at least one small chocolate bar," she pleaded.

"You don't get it, Vi," Richie moaned. "The grocery shopping I did is supposed to be our food supply for about two weeks. But now, I have to go buy more every nine or ten days, thanks to Ginger-Claus's weekend appetite," Richie explained.

"You can't blame me," Marvin protested, "You're the one who got me hooked on watching *Friday Night Stand-Ups,* and you know I can't watch comedy without food."

"If I stay here any longer without food, one of you will end up as my midnight snack, and the other, dessert," Violet said, looking at Marvin with a devilish stare. Her cell phone rang. "Please be here," she said and answered the call. "Hey, Dad, you here yet?"

"No. Listen, I'm still stuck in traffic at the moment, but we are just a few blocks from the comic book store. Right next to the Italian pizza place. You know where it is, right?"

"Yeah, that's close enough. I'm on my way."

"Violet, wait."

"What?"

"Can you ask one of the guys if they can escort you to the place? I don't want you walking alone outside tonight."

"No problem, Bye." She hung up the phone without allowing her father the chance to say another word. "All right, guys, my ride's here. See ya later."

"Did he say where he's taking you?" asked Marvin.

"No idea. I guess I'll find out when I get to the car," she replied as she started walking towards the door.

"If the car's far away, I can walk you there if you want," Richie offered.

"No thanks, Richie, I'm good. It's only next to the pizza place. I'll manage. Take care now, dorks."

"Right back at ya," Marvin said.

"Call us when you get there. So, we make sure that you're safe," Richie added.

"What are you my dad now?" she teased and walked out without waiting for a response.

Richie exhaled. Marvin looked at him and mimicked his voice, "'I can walk you there. Call us so we make sure you're safe.' How desperate are you, man?"

Richie's sole reply was an extended middle finger.

Violet was heading to the Italian pizza place when a man ran past her in the opposite direction, muttering on a phone, "Don't worry, baby. Just stay calm. I'm on my way to you, right now!"

"*Hey!*" a voice shouted from a car nearby. "What kind of person leaves their car in the middle of the road while there's a traffic jam?"

Violet assumed he was shouting at the man running the other way but she ignored the situation and kept walking. She dove into the midst of the congested road once she saw the pizza place on the other side. She walked among the unmoving cars, scanning for her dad's vehicle as she reached the pizza shop, but when she couldn't find him she pulled out her phone and called him again.

FEAR IN FLESH

* * *

The phone rang, and Gavin immediately glanced at the pizza place that he'd passed moments ago when the traffic started moving for a few seconds. "Billy, stick your head out of the back window and wave to your sister, so she can find us." Gavin then answered the call. "Violet, I see you back at the pizza place."

"Where are you? I can't find the car."

"We just went ahead a little bit. You'll see Billy waving to you from the window."

A moment passed.

"Do you see him yet?"

"Not yet. Oh, wait, there he is!" Violet hung up the phone and sprinted to the car. She slipped into the front seat and said, "All right, Dad … start explaining."

"First of all, are you okay, sweetheart? I didn't see Marvin or Richie with you. Thought I told you to get one of them to escort you?" Gavin asked wearily.

"I'm fine, and there was no need for anyone to help me cross the street, I'm not an old lady. Now, could you please tell me what happened with the Carlsons? And where are you taking us exactly?"

"I don't want to talk about what happened to the Carlsons. Now's not a good time." Gavin lowered his voice. "Especially, it's not appropriate to talk about it in front of Billy. And we're off to the airport. By the looks of this traffic, everyone decided to do the same thing."

Violet's eyes lingered on her father, as she struggled with what to say. Billy jumped in. "They probably got bit, just like the people down at the station, didn't they?"

"There's gotta be something more to it than just getting bit, Billy," Violet argued. "It must be something really bad if dad's refusing to tell even though he promised to, once I was in the car."

"Billy's right about the biting thing. Let's just leave it at that," Gavin said.

Violet continued, "But, Dad, if this is an actual evacuation, don't you think we have the right to know what we're running away from? I'm assuming it's from something you mentioned earlier, something about cannibals. What, did one of the Carlsons turn into a zombie or something?"

Gavin just sat there silently trying to avoid answering Violet's questions.

"So … were the Carlsons victims of cannibalism?" she asked one more time. "Or something worse than that happened?"

Gavin sighed. "Only one of them was."

"Who was it?" Violet and Billy both asked at the same time.

"It was Mrs. Carlson. She was on the floor, with … half her face chewed off. And there he was, her husband, sinking his teeth in her like she was a Thanksgiving turkey. There. Happy? I said it. Now you both know the Carlsons' tale of terror."

Violet and Billy sat, in stunned silence. They were both imagining the carnage in their minds. They'd been good neighbors for years. Till suddenly, a man snapped and ate the mother of his children, on a night when people were terrorizing the city.

"What about Kelly? Is she all right?" asked Violet.

"Other neighbors were taking care of her. The poor girl was terrified," Gavin answered. "I'm clueless as to why Carlson would go off like that. I'm not even sure if *it* was really him."

Violet noticed her father's stress on "*it*" like he wasn't referring to Carlson as a human being. "What do you mean by 'it'?"

"Well ... for starters, his face was covered in blood. The scene was so bloody! The floor was soaked with blood, all around him and his wife. What got to me the most was when I called his name and he turned around and looked right at me with his eyes—those inhuman eyes! I didn't know if he could even see me. His eyes were almost completely white. Like he had them turned inside out."

"Did Mr. Carlson really turn into a zombie, Dad?" asked Billy, astonished.

Gavin took a second to remember what had happened after seeing that awful scene, and all he could remember was his own vomit. He decided to skip that part. "No, Billy, there are no such things as zombies. Your sister was being sarcastic." Gavin gave his daughter a warning look, for her seven-year-old brother was getting anxious, but he was also curious to hear more.

Can it really be zombies? Violet thought to herself. She wanted to tell her father about the cop in the station, that she saw him with a bitten arm on the news. She tried connecting the dots, but she was still absorbing the story about Carlson eating his wife.

"You shouldn't be worrying about zombies, Billy." Violet tried comforting her little brother. "They eat brains. Since you have none, you'll be safe, even if they ever come." She turned around to flash Billy a wide-eyed teeth-baring smile. "What are all those bags for?" she asked when she saw that the backseat was overcrowded.

"Billy and I bagged most of the food from home. If you're hungry..."

Violet did not wait for her father's permission to start digging into the bags. "Great, I'm starved!" she said, thinking, *zombies are only real in movies, video games, and comic books.* But her father's story sounded as if it were taken from one of those three main zombies featured originators. *Why else would he be acting so strange and anxious all of the sudden? Leaving town in such a rush, ignoring the fact that Billy has school tomorrow ... and his job too! Something spooked him and it must have been really bad.*

"Since we'll be stuck here for a while, I suggest you guys go ahead and eat something, but just a little portion. We'll need the food in case we can't catch a flight when we get to the airport."

Violet had a sinking feeling that they would need the food for a while.

4

FROM DUSK TILL DAWN

DAWN 1

A few hours later, Violet opened her eyes from a nap she hadn't planned to take. Sleep had overpowered her. Her father was snoring, his head resting back on the seat. She looked back to see Billy curled up in the backseat, hugging his dinosaur action figure to his chest. She shook her dad's shoulder. "Dad, wake up." But all he did was snore louder.

Dawn had begun to break, as she looked out of the window. The light revealed that they were still backed up in traffic as if the car had not moved since she embraced sleep. The only difference was that the honking had completely stopped. It was quiet ... too quiet.

Violet noticed a man, in the car next to them, was also fast asleep at the wheel. She got out of the car to take a look around, only to find other people in the cars all around them sleeping soundly. Violet caught a slow movement from the corner of her eye. She turned her head quickly, but it turned out to be nothing more than her own shadow, cast by the steadily increasing light.

She turned around and gazed upward. Her green eyes captured the vividness of the rising sunlight. She stared, eyes not even blinking, mesmerized by the breathtaking view of the large orange ball sitting low in the sky alongside the tallest tower in town, standing as a guardian over the congested streets of Cliffroyce Bay, famously known as the business district.

Suddenly the reflection in her eyes shifted from bright orange to the fierce colors of fireballs, when the sun exploded midair, releasing a massive force of hellfire raining down on the tower and all the smaller buildings beside it. Glass buildings, windows, and windshields shattered from the first wave of heat. Buildings were engulfed in flames within seconds. Fear broke through Violet. The enormous tower emblazed with fire was shrinking as it sank to ground level and collapsed with a quaking effect, unleashing a storm of dust that spread with the speed of an avalanche. Violet jumped back inside the car and closed the door. Seconds later, she could see nothing but massive clouds of dust devouring the street around them.

Gavin and Billy were still sleeping as if they'd never heard or felt the sun explode and the towers collapse. Violet drew closer to the window, trying to see if something was visible beyond the cover of dust. Her face was only an inch away from the window when a hand drenched in foul black blood slammed against it. Violet jumped back, letting out a shriek. The hand slowly slid down the window, leaving its bloodstained print on the glass. Violet again, hesitantly, edged closer to see who the bloody hand belonged to, her heart thumping in her chest. She finally got close enough, but only to jump away again with a horrified scream when four more bloody hands came slamming onto the window with a cracking force.

Cracks formed in the glass and it was getting frail by the second as Violet yelled, *"Dad! Dad! Wake up!"*

No response.

FEAR IN FLESH

The window was almost fully broken, and it became more difficult to see through with all the cracks and the bloodstains. Violet turned in her seat to see her little brother. "Billy!" Her voice was almost a whimper. He too remained cuddled up with his dinosaur, eyes closed and mind caught in the void of the dream realm.

A great cracking sound stunned her completely. It was the windshield. One of the bloodstained hands broke through the windshield and grabbed hold of Violet's hands and clothes, tugging her through the shattered pieces of glass. She pulled back with all her might, but the hands were too strong. She closed her eyes shut for the darkness to engulf her.

Violet opened her eyes and found that she was still inside her father's car, which she felt was rocking slowly. No bloody hands. No shattered glass. No collapsing towers or exploding sun or clouds of dust outside. Cars were backed up in traffic and honking endlessly. A soft grip on her shoulder was gently shaking her awake. "Violet, come on, you have to wake up." The voice sounded like her father's.

With a parched throat, she replied, "What is it?"

"The plan's been changed. We're not heading up to the airport anymore," Gavin said. She stared at him incredulously through her sleepy haze. He continued, "Just a few moments ago on the radio, they announced that the airport is being forced to shut down because of several 'deranged individuals attacking people on board on the arriving craft'. Some even made their way inside the airport, causing a lot of ruckuses, they say."

"Oh, crap," said Violet, banging the back of her head softly against the seat, exhaling a shaky breath while a chill tingled down her spine. *What the hell, was that dream all about! I can't remember any of it, but I can't shake off this bad feeling in my gut.* Last time her fingers and legs trembled like this was after when she had woken up on the train where she'd had another bad dream she couldn't really remember. "What's the plan now?" she asked her father.

"On the radio, they said to stay at home and to shut the doors and the windows. But there's no way for us to go back home with the car." Gavin pointed out the front. "See that gap over there? That's an alley. Once we get there, I'm parking the car, and we'll head to Lake Valley on foot. It's close by. Way closer than the house."

It was now past five o'clock in the morning. The sun would be rising soon. Dawn was upon Cliffroyce Bay with loud traffic still raging in the streets. Violet was very tired but she tried to fight off sleep the best she could. She needed to be alert for the walk to Lake Valley, though she didn't bother to ask her father what they were going to do once they got there. She believed she already knew the answer to that question, Dad owned a boat there. *If air travel is not available, traveling by water might still work. He just wants us to get away from the city ... far away. Lake Valley stretches out to the East River, after all. Is he thinking about isolating us down there for a while?*

Gavin parked the car in the alley and then woke Billy up. "C'mon, buddy, time to get up."

Billy sat up, eyes sleepy as ever. "Are we there yet?"

"Not the airport, Billy," Violet answered. "We're gonna walk to Dad's boat in Lake Valley."

"What for?" asked Billy, sounding disappointed, as he rubbed his eyes.

"Well ... because many people have already gotten to the airport by now. It's a bit crowded there, and all flights would probably be booked too," Gavin explained, avoiding the truth so as to not scare him anymore.

"Why don't we just go back home?" Billy complained.

"Because we're much closer to Lake Valley than we are to the house. Going there will not only keep us safe from those dangerous people, but we will no longer be stuck in traffic, and I can finally get some sleep." Gavin yawned.

"But ... how long are we gonna stay on the boat?" Billy asked.

"Yeah, Dad, I was meaning to ask you the same thing myself," Violet added.

"To be completely honest, I'm not sure. Hopefully, the radio connection I have on the boat will keep us updated about the situation here. But until then, get your backpacks on, grab three to four bags, and let's head to Lake Valley."

5

NEW COMIC BOOK DAY

DAY 1

Marvin and Richie both fell asleep in the store's back storage unit after Violet left. It was past six in the morning when the sun's first glow shone lightly. Richie was lying on a wide bean bag chair on the floor. Next to him was Marvin who looked surprisingly comfortable asleep in his wheeled computer chair, facing a blank screen. On the computer desk was his only-for-emergencies shotgun loaded and displayed.

Loud thumping sounds coming from the front door woke Marvin up. Out of the two, Marvin was the light sleeper. He picked himself off the chair and glared down at Richie, who was half humming, half snoring. He heard thumping at the door again, except louder and faster, and a voice cried out, "Is anyone in there? Please, let me in!" It sounded almost like a child's voice.

Marvin bolted to the front door, where he found a young teenage boy, a regular who shopped in the store every week. His face and body strained against the glass door while two women, one on each side, sank their faces into his shoulder blades. Blood was squirting out of his shoulders, spraying the glass red. The teenager screamed in agony as was he forced down to his knees in deep pain. Marvin ran back to the room and grabbed his shotgun from the computer desk, spun around, and tripped over Richie on his bean bag chair.

Richie woke up with a deep gasp. "What the hell, man!" he said, startled. Marvin didn't stop to say anything. He just climbed back to his feet with the shotgun in hand and sprinted out of the room. When he got to the front door again, all he found was the boy's bloodstains on the glass door. What was left of the teenager was on the ground. Marvin was only able to see his feet twitching from where he stood. He moved closer with Richie behind him.

"What's going—" Richie couldn't finish his question when the red glass door caught his eye. He stood behind Marvin, gaping wordlessly.

Marvin moved closer to the door and got a view of the teenager's body lying flat on the sidewalk while the two women preyed on his flesh like a couple of lionesses feasting on a freshly hunted gazelle. One was tearing the skin off his neck with her teeth, baring the tissue while the other was digging her hands deep into the hole she'd bit into his shoulder, grabbing a handful of red chunks and stuffing them into her mouth.

Aghast and sick to his stomach, Marvin realized that this scene was exactly what the news channels had been exploding from, from the night before. Richie was standing, as still as one of the many superhero statues that were displayed around the store, behind Marvin, and speechless.

It can't be, Marvin thought. *No, not zombies!* Had the living dead finally broken out of the fiction realm to take over the world, as a few paranoid people had claimed was possible? It was right there, happening in front of him, and as a strong believer of the fictional world, he could not think otherwise. Marvin loaded the shotgun, unlocked the door, and pushed it open while taking aim. "*Hey!*" he shouted, unsure of how the attackers would react. He wasn't even a hundred percent sure that they were zombies. He could've been dreaming all this.

The two feasting women didn't respond to Marvin's shout, their mouths still full of human flesh. So Marvin approached the one on his right. He yanked at her from the back of her blouse and tossed her roughly onto the edge of the sidewalk. Then he went for the other one and grabbed her, but he failed to pull her off. This one had a tighter grip on the boy's neck, clenching him with her blood-covered teeth. "Give me a hand over here, Richie!" Marvin demanded, struggling with one hand because he was unwilling to release his shotgun or use it.

Richie didn't respond to Marvin's cry for help instead, he stood staring at the mayhem taking over the streets. People were running everywhere, leaving their cars behind or climbing on top of cars to stay out of reach. He saw a fat man wrestle an old woman down after she failed to strike him hard enough with her walking cane, a little girl being yanked by her ponytail by a red-headed man whose clothes were stained with dark red blood. He could no longer hear any honks by the cars over the metal thuds a bus was making as it rammed through the cars in the frozen traffic. People were panicking, crying from the horror that had befallen them.

"*Ahhhhh!*"

"*My God, they're eating her!*"

"*Aiieeeeeee!*"

"*Help! Get him off me!*"

In the midst of all the cries of pain and fear, he finally heard his name. *"Richie!"* He turned to Marvin. "Get your ass over here and help me!" Richie shook his head briskly and then rushed to aid the fallen boy with Marvin. Together they managed to pull the second attacker off and throw her next to the first woman. When they looked down at the boy, they knew it was already too late to save him.

Before they could even look up or turn back. The two women were getting up with such a sloth-like motion, sounding as if they had a sore throat, groaning eerily. They glared at Richie and Marvin with their dead-bleached eyes, extending their arms straight forward, and slowly they started limp-walking towards them. One was walking ahead of the other, the one that Marvin pulled off first with the flashy blouse. He aimed the shotgun at her finally deciding to put it to some use. "Let's see if you two really are zombies." He said edgily.

"Raaaghhh!" The two women shot back.

"Let's get back inside, Marv," Richie urged.

"I'm not going anywhere until I do something about these two," Marvin said.

"I don't think they even understand what you're saying. It's not safe out here, everyone's getting attacked or … attacking!"

"Then I'll make them understand." Marvin fixed the muzzle of his shotgun and aimed it just a few inches below the groaning woman's neck.

6

LAKE VALLEY

DAY 1

After ten minutes of walking, they reached Lake Valley's front gate. Inside Gavin had anchored his boat, which he usually used for fishing and occasional cruises with friends and family. Never had he thought that he would seek refuge on it from the people of his own city.

The place was very quiet. Only the faint murmurs of traffic from the highway were audible. It was pretty desolate, not only because it wasn't yet six in the morning, but also because nearly every resident, in utter panic, was fleeing the city.

Gavin spotted his boat, sitting on the piercing blue water alongside dozens. It was a white boat with its name, *Cliffroyce Fishers*, emblazoned on both the port and starboard sides. "C'mon, let's hop on board," Gavin said eagerly.

As they were heading towards the boat through the vast field of grass and concrete walkways, Violet stopped and said, "Hey, carry my bags for me. I'm going to go to the shack to get us some more snacks and drinks."

"Okay, you need money?" Gavin asked.

"Nope, I already got some in my backpack. You guys move along,

I'll be right there."

Violet made her way to the west side of the valley along the walkways, entered the shack, and began picking out a basketful of snacks and drinks with the latest expiration dates. This would help them last for at least a few weeks, she figured, not knowing how long they would be staying on the boat. The snacks and the drinks, plus the bags of food they'd brought from home, would hopefully keep hunger at bay until everything got settled down. And if they ran out of supplies, there was always her father's fishing pole and bait in the boat's cabin.

She approached the counter and placed the basket on top of it, ready to pay, but the clerk behind the counter did not seem to be conscious of her presence. He had his elbows resting solidly on the counter and was holding his head in both hands as he coughed violently. Violet backed away from the counter, a bit, covering her mouth and nose with a palm. "Umm ... are you okay, dude?" she asked warily. The clerk didn't answer her. He only coughed harder until he coughed up a little bit of blood on the counter that splattered onto her shopping basket.

Violet was just about to move near the counter, to check on him, when a wave of screams hit her ears, freezing her where she was. The screams were coming from outside—louder than in a mosh pit at the most popular concert—only these screams weren't out of excitement or amusement. They were the screams that were uttered when someone visualized death, and it felt as if they were coming from as many as a hundred pairs of lungs. Violet opened the shack's door to find a storm.

One moment it was peaceful and quiet, not a person in sight or noise to disturb the harmonious nature, but then came a gale of loud people, blowing through the beautiful green field of Lake Valley, stampeding towards the boats in the lake, and the small shack.

Violet jumped into the havoc, on sudden confrontation with uncertainty. She ran so she could reach her father's boat. Mere seconds in the screaming crowd and she was overpowered by the agitated mass around her, she was bumped and pushed until she tripped over a body. On the ground, she got stomped on a couple of times, and when she managed to sit up, yet another person bumped into her, making her curse at him.

That was when she noticed that the man she had tripped over, had a fixated gaze on *her*, crawling on all fours like an animal towards her. The running crowd neither stomped on him nor bumped into him. Everyone seemed to keep their distance from him. As the crawling man dragged himself closer to Violet, she noticed his eyes. Very … abnormal, was her first impression, and very white. The color of his eyes had a homogeneous tone, a foggy white that obscured the pupils and irises. She watched him, frozen, as he slowly grabbed her foot, opened his mouth wide, and lowered it to her shoe. Violet immediately gave a solid kick to his mouth, knocking out, one of his front teeth.

She got back up on her feet and again ran towards her father's boat, pushing and squeezing through the crowd. Only seconds after her encounter with the milky-eyed man, she slammed into the back of a large bald man. He turned his head to face her, and she saw a huge chunk bitten off his left ear. Again, she gazed fearfully into the discolored eyes of a madman. Hesitantly, Violet backed away, and at the same time, the bald man extended his arms to make a grab for her. Violet dodged and ran back, right into the grasp of the crawling man.

Luckily she was fast enough to stomp on the back of his head before he could fasten his teeth onto her leg, smashing his face into the concrete floor. She broke away just before the giant man with the bitten ear could make a grab for her again.

She ran out through the gate that she and her family had entered through. *Try avoiding the crowd and find another way to Dad's boat.* Once she was on the highway just outside the valley's gate, it was complete and utter chaos. No different from Lake Valley, except there were more of those milky-eyed madmen with blood-splashed clothing, dragging people out of their cars, wailing, taking down runners in their path, ultimately making the screaming victim's clothing as blood-soaked as their own.

"It's really happening," Violet whispered to herself. "They *are* zombies." She said with certainty.

Trying to catch her breath, she failed to notice that she was already being stalked. Too small to spot in the rampaging crowd, one of *them* was almost upon her. She came—a little girl, parallel to a corpse, barely reaching Violet's bellybutton in height, eyes white and hungry for human flesh. Violet might have ended up with a deeper hole than her bellybutton was if it hadn't been for the interference by a man in a biker's gear, who slammed his massive boot to the side of the little zombie girl's head, shoving her against an abandoned car's tire.

"Come with me." He pulled at Violet's wrist.

"No!" She pulled back. "I can't. My family's waiting for me on the lake. I have to go back."

"It's not safe there any more than it is over here!" said the man. "I have a bike I'm struggling to get started." He pointed to his vehicle only a few feet away. "I need you to keep a lookout until I can get the clutch unstuck. Then, I might be able to get you back to your family. Just help me, deal?"

Violet accepted the helping hand in this time of crises and waited for him as he repeatedly stomped his motorcycle's clutch until the engine roared back to life. The man had handed over his helmet to Violet as he tried to work on his bike, she used that very helmet, to fight the same little girl she had encountered before. Violet only had to bash her over the head with the helmet a few times to keep her down. Finally, the bike started functioning and Violet hopped behind the man. For a moment, the bike's engine was the loudest sound she heard in her perimeter. As the biker wheeled his motorcycle towards Lake Valley's gate, however, Violet's ears began ringing with an awful metallic shrieking from above, nose-diving with a speed enough to annihilate any object in its path.

The man, she was with, did not hesitate a second when he saw their doom, shaped like an airplane plummeting from the sky towards the highway, north of Lake Valley. "Hold on!" he shouted and immediately wheeled the bike back around, tires screeching and smoking as they left black tracks on the road. *We have no other choice.* Violet thought through the buzzing shriek of engines. *I'm abandoning Dad and Billy.* The bike cannoned along the gap between cars, away from the valley's gate.

Buildings were ripped in half as easily as an ax splitting a stump of wood. Road signs, light poles, street rubble, and cars went airborne in clouds of smoke and flame. And whatever living or dead may have been down there were flattened as the plane landed with a thundering KABOOM!

7

DAILY COMICS DRIVE-BY

DAY 1

BAM! Marvin pulled the trigger.

Shots pierced both the stalking women. Their bodies flew to the edge of the sidewalk again but this time with large holes blown into their chests. They lay there on their backs with their legs, arms, and heads twitching in a petrifying maneuver, the spasm for the briefest moment made their body movements brisk, a feat they could never achieve while walking.

Richie started retreating back into the store. Just as he was one foot away from the doorstep, he heard an engine racing towards them from his right-side. Astride a motorbike was a man with a helmet shielding his face and Violet clutching his waist. As they rode along the sidewalk, terrified runners got out of their way, but one refused to step aside, forcing the driver to swerve and smash into a wall so violently that the engine shut down. Violet was hurled a few feet into the air and landed on her backpack, rolling along the sidewalk.

"Violet!" Richie rushed to her.

Marvin turned his head at the sound of the crash, shifting his gaze from the twitching women climbing back to their feet. Distracted, he felt a sudden wrenching force on the shotgun. One of the women had managed to get a grip on the front of the gun, pulling it, and Marvin along with it closer to her. He quickly wrenched back, pulling *her* to him. *Not good,* Marvin thought. In both cases, she was getting closer, relentless, unwilling to let go. The creature drew closer, her red-stained mouth open. Marvin noticed the other one still struggled to get back up, though she was halfway there. It was only a matter of time before one of them managed to get a grip on something other than the shotgun he was holding. Something with meat!

Violet's head was spinning, as blood trickled down the left side of her brow. Pain radiated through her whole body. She was able to catch only a glimpse of the bystander who'd intercepted them, causing them to crash. Wearing a police uniform, biting the biker's gear, the zombie cop bore a thick mustache dyed red with blood. Her poor helpless savior, whose name she never came to know, lay there shrieking as more zombies joined in on the feasting. Violet was unable to react as she was hastily carried off to the store. She heard a blast being fired.

BAM! Marvin fired another round, and the dead woman was left standing there with her upper torso obliterated and her lower half still a bit twitching as "life" struggled to depart from her, until her body finally collapsed. The recoil of the shotgun jerked Marvin backward, off his feet, sending the shotgun far from his reach. He froze when he lifted his head and saw half a dozen more limping dead, heading his way.

"On your feet, Marv, hurry!" It was Richie, heaving Marvin to his feet and bolting towards the store. Marvin grabbed his shotgun before running in, slamming the door shut, and locking it.

Zombies swarmed about the front door thumping lazily on the glass, groaning and gathering around the teenage victim and finishing off what remained of his limbs and inner organs until the boy woke up as one of them. Then they let him be.

8

LOCKED IN

DAY 3

Two days had passed since Violet, Marvin, and Richie had locked themselves inside the store. For two days the teenager lay flat on the sidewalk in a pool of his own blood just outside the store. His legs were reduced to mere bones, and his entrails were scattered around him in ribbons of gore. His ribcage was exposed, with flies swarming around the small pieces of flesh still hanging from it. His face was covered in dried dark blood. The poor boy kept on clenching his teeth endlessly, while a foggy haze took over his eyes, too. He groaned constantly, along with the other half a dozen moving beside and over him.

The three survivors inside became accustomed to the groaning sounds outside their safe haven, as if it were a grim song being played over and over. Those two days felt like an eternity, for fear was clasping them by the throat, refusing to let go yet refusing to smother the life out of their lungs, keeping their minds paralyzed.

With deep sorrow in his eyes, Marvin looked at the devoured victim he'd failed to rescue, through small gaps in the barricaded glass door. It was the first time he'd been able to gather enough self-control to take a good look without feeling the need to retch. He sighed mournfully at the sight. "Sorry I couldn't save you," he muttered to no one. "I should've acted faster."

"Stop blaming yourself, Marv." Richie came up behind him. "At least you actually tried saving him instead of standing there, like a statue, crapping your pants!" He was referring to himself disdainfully due to a momentary lapse of sanity on the sight before him, in his moment of shock, he watched everyone flee for their lives while being viciously attacked by people who showed no regard for human life. They looked as if they'd lost every ounce of humanity they'd had in them, with all the blood their teeth had spilled. All knew with lucidity now, what *they* were. There was no question now that this was the rise of the living dead: zombies. Everyone had seen them on a television screen or in a horror house, and some presumed fanatics had even predicted their rise. But believers and unbelievers alike were equally shocked. The unbecoming events had marked the commencement of an apocalypse led by the undead. The sand was pouring from the hourglass for humanity each day. One by one, either each victim was killed completely or took on the pale eyes of the undead, strengthening their legion.

Marvin sighed again, turned away, and walked through the empty store with Richie by his side. All the wooden shelves containing the comic books and graphic novels had been used to barricade the glass door, so they could hide from the gaze of the creatures roaming the earth now.

They went to the storage room, where they had been sleeping since the outbreak and where all their food was kept. They'd laid cardboard boxes flat to make beds and used folded bubble wrap as pillows. There was also a bean bag chair, generally occupied by Violet for the past couple of days. Her body sank into the soft comfort of millions of tiny Styrofoam beads, but she hadn't found any mental comfort after being separated from her family. She feared that she had abandoned them to die. Barely sleeping or eating, she sat there with her dead cell phone, wondering if her father and brother were still alive after the plane had crashed. Had they sailed off without her before the air behemoth had descended on earth, or were they still waiting for her on the lake?

Numerous times, she tried to contact her father, using her cell phone, Marvin's, Richie's, and the store's own landline, but to no avail. Gavin never answered nor did he call back, and Violet's insides were tied in knots of fear. Fear of the unknown consumed them all. That, combined with the knowledge of what awaited them outside, kept them locked in, temporarily away from the sickness that had befallen men, women, and children everywhere.

It was a sickness that took people in and turned them into these vile creatures—senseless, without remorse, craving living flesh as the sole purpose of their "life". Their state of disorientation had left them wobbly and slow, but no less dangerous. No matter where the three friends stayed in the store, the groaning never ceased. A song of agony beat against their eardrums day and night, sleeping and waking.

"I can't take it anymore!" Violet snapped. "I have to get out of here and find them and shoot the mouth of every zombie I hear groaning out there!" She got up and headed for the exterior exit door from the storage room that leads to a back alley, which they had cautiously been using as a toilet for the past few days since, running water was gone.

Richie sprinted to intercept her and grabbed her shoulders to spin her around. "Are you insane?" he said brusquely. "We have to stay inside and wait a while longer until help arrives. You heard that news reporter yesterday on TV ... more than *half* the town was overrun in just a day!"

"Yeah, and then the idiot reporter got bit in the neck when she didn't move quickly enough. I'm fast and they're freakishly slow. I can outrun them."

"True. But you're forgetting the broadcast about the U.S. military moving through the city, rounding up all the survivors to take them to an evacuation camp. New York's huge, it could take a while before they find us, and we have food here to last us for weeks if we're careful enough," Richie said.

"Find us? How? How the hell will anyone be able to see us if we're so perfectly hidden in here, Richie?" Violet lashed out, unwilling to wait for a military force to come to rescue them, God knew when.

"I ... don't know. Maybe they'll see the ... the ..." Richie was struggling for a justification, not quite sure what solution he was about to offer.

"The what? They're gonna see the barricades from the inside and *assume* that there are still survivors in here?"

"Yes! We have no other choice but to wait. The only weapon we have will run out of bullets way before we can get near Lake Valley," Richie said. "And you can't actually believe that you can outrun *all* of them, now, do you?"

Violet exhaled softly and crossed her arms, looking down at the floor in utter hopelessness. "I'm scared," she admitted. "Not from the zombies so much, but as to what might've happened to my dad and Billy." Her eyes began to water. "The worst part is ... I'm starting to doubt if they're still alive at this point."

Richie didn't know what to do or say. This was the first time he had seen Violet actually expressing her emotions. After all, she had never been your typical girly-girl, talking about her feelings or involving unnecessary drama in her daily life. Those were the things that did not mix well with her persona. This situation, however, gave her a full right to be dramatic, if not hysterical. It was agonizing not knowing whether someone you cared for and loved was dead or alive—well aware that if they *were* still alive, they might still be in grave danger. Richie thought about going for a hug but turned to look at Marvin first, who was sitting on the floor leaning against the wall, eyes gazing at the ceiling, probably not even listening to the argument. Richie turned back to Violet and found her rubbing her eyes dry, fighting back tears.

"It's okay," he said, patting her on the shoulder. "I'm sure they're perfectly safe. You said it yourself, those zombies are incredibly slow and unable to walk straight, let alone swim to your dad's boat!"

She looked at him with no signs of either grief or relief on her face, just an emotionless stare. "Two more days, no longer. That's as long as I'm willing to wait," she said, putting up two fingers for emphasis. Then she lay back in the beanbag chair with her dead phone pressed against her chest, eyes closed, praying silently for her family's safety.

As for Richie, he just stood there in the middle of the room between a depressed twenty-eight-year-old man and a grumpy Violet. All he could think about now was his rumbling stomach and the plain bread buns he was planning to have for dinner in a couple more hours. He prayed as well—prayed for positive updates on the news and for the military to come knocking on the door before another forty-eight hours passed. Or he would be forced to reveal a solution just across the street that he and Marvin had kept hidden from Violet.

9

NIGHT IN

NIGHT 4

A deep snort woke Violet up from her slumber. She closed her eyes once more to fall back to sleep but opened them again when another snort interrupted the silence. It was Marvin who was snoring so loudly.

The storage room was semi-dark, no lights were turned on but the door to the left was kept open, it let in the rest of the store's light, which made everything in the room faintly visible. Violet could easily recognize where she was when she opened her eyes and immediately spotted Marvin still leaning against the wall in front of her, next to the door. She struggled a little to sit up on the beanbag chair she'd been sleeping on, getting used to this would take time. None had ever expected that they would be living here long-term—having sleepovers in the Daily Comics store seemed an inconceivable idea before.

As she sat up, something slid off her chest and fell into her lap. It was her cell phone. She retrieved it and tapped a button, but nothing came up. No light. No picture. No sound. The screen remained blank. It'd be another day of waiting for a call from the store's telephone. No matter how many times she dialed her father's number, results came in exactly the same each time, as when she tried it on her cell phone until the battery died on the first day—zero answers.

Unsure of her family's safety and life, being unable to check the time after waking up in a place that was not her bedroom made the situation even worse. Doubt was like a small parasite nesting in Violet's mind, eating up all of her thoughts and filling her mind with apprehension, fear, and misery.

What could've happened to Dad and Billy that Dad can't even answer his phone? He probably lost it ... or maybe he's been facing the same problem I've been facing, a dead battery. Yeah, that's probably it. Although, I'm sure Dad was smart enough to have a phone charger on his boat or at least carry a travel battery around with him. He always did. His career depended on his phone. A lot of people were running towards the boats that day on Lake Valley. I hope none of the zombies managed to get on Dad's boat.

Doubt kept Violet distracted as she imagined several terrible circumstances Gavin and Billy could have ended up in. Finally, she came to her senses and realized that she was only making things harder for herself. She got up and walked out of the room to see how Richie was doing and to ask about how the situation was developing in the outside world. Thus, she willed herself to take a temporary respite from the parasite of doubt playing with her mind, pushing her into an abyss of despair.

Unfortunately, Richie was fast asleep on a chair next to the barricades. *Poor guy must've taken the responsibility to keep guard over us all night.*

Yes ... night. Violet peeked through the glass door between the barricades and found no trace of sunlight. The surroundings, outside were somewhat visible, though, thanks to the gleaming light of the pale moon and the light poles on the sidewalks.

Strange, she realized that the environment was quieter than, what she had heard the past few days. No longer were there, sounds of futile groaning and clumsy footsteps disrupting the peace. She peeped through the gaps again to check for any signs of life. Not a single soul was she able to track through the gaps. Not even the munched on body of the teenage boy.

That gave her an idea, a crazy idea, but an opportunity to sneak out the back door unnoticed. And if luck was on her side, there wouldn't be an encounter with any of the town's dead roamers on her way to Lake Valley. *Sorry, Richie, but I think I'm gonna have to break my promise tonight.* Doubt had been gnawing at her mind like the undead with the human flesh, for days. She couldn't wait a day longer in distress.

The store's telephone was right there in front of her on the counter as she turned back to the storage room. Violet stopped for a second. *I should call him one last time before making this decision. But if he doesn't answer for the hundredth time ... then I'm left with no choice but to take the risk.* So she picked up the receiver and dialed her father's number. Her fingers shook, and she almost forgot the number. One would think after calling the number repeatedly, she'd be able to dial without even looking. Then again, she was nervous each time she picked up the phone and was mostly used to pressing one or two buttons on her cell's contact list, not dialing digit by digit. *Three ... nine ... zero ...* Violet completed the number.

Oddly enough the phone kept on ringing for quite a while, which was surprising because if Gavin's phone had suffered the same fate as hers, it should go straight to voicemail. No matter, it was still ringing. Just as she was lowering the receiver to hang up, the ringing stopped, and a man's voice muttered, "Hello?" in such a low register that she barely heard it.

Violet froze in utter shock, staring vacantly down at the receiver without bringing it back up to her ear for a few moments, "Is someone there?" the man's voice asked. "Who is this?"

Violet slowly raised the receiver and, with a hint of a tremble in her voice, said, "Dad?" She wasn't even sure that it was him on the other end. His voice sounded weary and far off like someone who hadn't spoken in days.

"Violet, is that you sweetheart? Where are you?" This finally sounded like his normal voice, reassuring Violet that the man she was speaking to was indeed her father, Gavin, at long last.

"Where have you been all this time not answering my phone calls?"

"It was a complete mess down here! I'm sure you saw it. I jumped into the crowd looking for you. I wanted to squeeze my way to the shack to find you and bring you back to the boat, but … I couldn't leave Billy alone on the boat, people were trying to get on! I tried calling you while I was down there and got knocked over so many times, I lost my phone."

"And now you found it, and its battery's still alive!"

"No time to explain how and why, okay? You have to move now and get here as fast and quiet as you can. Those—I wanna say … zombies—left the valley a couple of minutes ago. The coast is clear for you to sneak in."

"But that's impossible. How the hell did your phone battery make it all this time?"

Silence met her question.

"Dad? You still there?"

The call had been disconnected. Violet hung up and redialed once, twice, again and again. No use. Gavin's phone was no longer receiving her call. Maybe the battery had finally died in the middle of their conversation. Now she wondered what was happening. *Why are the zombies leaving, both here and from Lake Valley? Where is it exactly that they're heading to?*

Her own father's request made her feel more obligated than ever to get back to Lake Valley and sail with her family to East River. As for Violet's two snoozing inmates, suppose she woke them up to join her, would they agree to come or would they restrain her? They might not believe her or might be unwilling to take the risk of leaving their sanctuary. Violet was caught again in an overwhelming decision that involved abandoning people she cared about, during desperate times.

So, Violet came up with a hasty excuse to head out on her journey so, she could reunite with her family. Although "abandonment" sounded harsh, Violet promised herself to counteract her broken promise to Richie by doing whatever it took to convince her father to come back for her friends by using his car parked in the alley, which was not far away from Lake Valley. Only Gavin had the keys.

Without a second thought, Violet snuck out of the back door, gently tip-toeing from the narrow alley to the front sidewalk, where, not long ago, hungry zombies had been limping about, waiting patiently for living meat to cross their path so they could savagely carve through skin and flesh with their brutal once-human teeth.

10

NIGHT OUT

NIGHT 4

The entire business avenue district was still packed with cars, all motionless. Most had collided against one another, toppled over, with doors left open and windshields shattered. Broken glass was scattered everywhere and it sparkled under the dim light. The best thing about the chaos that ensued was its resultant lifelessness. Not a being was in sight nor a sound heard except the echoing of Violet's own shoes hitting the concrete as she walked to the front door of the comic book shop, where she saw nothing of the inside through the barricades.

She stood on dried blood that she thought had belonged to the chewed-up teenager. But where was he? He had been in no condition to ever walk again. Besides coming back to life, did zombies possess some sort of a superpower to grow back body parts? Regenerating a new set of legs and then disappearing with the rest of the wandering dead? *In a world where people are hunting and devouring each other, expectations of comic-book-like powers are almost practical*, Violet thought wryly.

The distance to Lake Valley was lengthier from here than from where she, her father, and brother had started after enduring hours of traffic. Nonetheless, Violet kept on walking, bypassing countless empty shops and vacant cars, unwilling to use any of them fearing that someone might jump out of the backseat and startle her. Violet was never a fan of jump scares.

She stopped by one store that seemed too bright with all its lights on, only to pick up a cold bottle of water to quench her thirst and keep her body hydrated during her long walk in the humid weather. Silently she walked until only one more road lay ahead between her and the valley: the highway where the plane had crashed. It had twice the wreckage of any other road she'd come across. And just like the previous ones, she was the only one that walked.

As Violet crossed the highway, squeezing through narrow openings in the piles of wreckage, she heard the sounds of other footsteps. Either other people were nearby, or Violet had grown a couple more legs. She came to a halt in order to listen better—making sure that the sounds weren't just in her head. Louder and louder, the feet kept on stomping. She could even track from which direction this stampede was coming as the sounds drew closer. Ruined cars and other rubble blocked her view of the surroundings, but she soon heard the all-too-recognizable abnormal noises: sounds of pain and death, noises people made when suffering through agony.

No, they're supposed to be gone. Violet thought with a shiver, catching a groaner's gleaming pale eyes as it limped through the rubble, a pack of ten was en route to where she stood. Violet hid in the first car she saw with the door open, gently closing it most of the way. She lay low so that she'd be able to see the undead pass by without their noticing her, she hoped.

Once the coast was clear, Violet leaped out of her hiding place and marched on, only to halt right away when she met a pair of ghostly dead eyes. This time they belonged to a little girl, who'd fallen behind the pack. It was the same girl whom she had fought off with the biker's helmet before the plane crashed, Violet knew. A staring match began: the vine green of Violet's eyes versus the pale whiteness of the dead girl's. *She saw me there's no escape now,* Violet worried. *I must stand my ground and fight, and then run before the others can get to me.*

The dead girl seemed not to be reacting to Violet's presence, especially considering that she stood no more than five feet away, easy attacking distance. Violet held her breath and sucked her core in to try to control her shaking body. Not letting fear take charge, she readied herself for combat, quietly clenching her right fist. She was mostly worried about the noise that would result from a face-off, which might cause the advancing pack members to turn around and pursue her.

Closer and closer the girl got, her strange eyes gleaming. So close that Violet could feel the girl's heavy breathing tickling her neck. Violet got goosebumps and accidentally clenched her left hand, the one that held the water bottle. The soft sound of plastic drew a reaction from the little girl, her eyes widening. The tone of her groan shifted more to a growl, as she sensed a physical presence before her.

A quick thought surged into Violet's head, and she let the bottle flow out of her grasp and hit a car with just enough force to cause a solid thump. It lured the dead girl away from her path. Violet quickly weaseled her way through the ruin's belly to the valley's gate and exhaled in relief once she got there.

She peered around every corner before advancing just in case there were any more of the undead limping around stealthily. It was completely empty she couldn't even tell there had been a massacre here a few days ago. It appeared as though the pack she'd crossed paths with was the last one of them to leave Lake Valley, for a reason that yet remained a mystery.

All the boats were gone. No surprise there since most of the crowd had been running towards them for a sanctuary that day. But there was a single boat floating, it was attached to the dock, bearing the words *Cliffroyce Fishers*. Violet's heart bloomed with happiness on seeing the boat. This whole time they had waited for her return, to reunite and survive this catastrophe together.

Violet hastened towards the boat. On the grass field, she stepped on what appeared to be a cell phone with a severely shattered screen. She immediately recognized it as her father's cell phone from the cover: an NBA cover with Gavin's favorite basketball player's signature. Violet had given it to him for his birthday. *Is that why the call got disconnected?* Violet's heart filled with anxiety.

Just like that, happiness shifted back to sensations of fright. Violet boarded her father's boat, looking to the stern, but neither Billy nor Gavin were in sight. She pushed open the cabin's door to find no one there either. Finally, she looked to the bow, where they were standing at the edge. Gavin had his arm around Billy's shoulders, and both were facing the rippling waters that reflected the glow of the stars and the moon.

"Dad! Billy!" Violet blurted out excitedly, moving forward with open arms. They turned around, and Violet got her hug. What a shockingly hollow hug it was. She was the only one that had her arms wrapped around them. Violet sensed the awkwardness and released her family from the embrace. She felt a stab through her heart when she finally laid her eyes on them. A flood of tears almost instantly came to her eyes when she perceived their hideously decaying faces. The left half of Billy's face was disgustingly peeled off, only fragments of skin remained. His lower lip was entirely gone, a full set of yellowed teeth were exposed from his mouth's lower region. His neck was tainted red from all the blood, spread down from his exposed jaw. As for her father, most of his face was just tissue without skin; between his teeth, a small chunk of meat was dangling, the torn lower lip of Billy's.

Gavin's jaw dropped open. Billy's lip fell to the floor with the tiniest *splat*, and then teeth burrowed into Violet's skin. The bites were agonizing—unbearable—but only for a second. Violet closed her eyes and opened them again to find herself back in the storage room, sunken in the cozy beanbag chair next to Richie and Marvin, who were sleeping on their cardboard beds.

Nightmares haunted her whenever she fell asleep now, showing her terrible omens that she could not remember when she woke up. All she knew was that she was facing death in them every single time. And all that she felt afterward was the rapid pounding in her chest and beads of sweat dripping from her forehead, filling her with dread.

11

TOSS AND RUN

DAY 4

As soon as morning came, Violet was straight out of the back door, and into the alley. The sun was up and shining meekly, hovering above the white fluff of clouds in the blue sky. The weather had been cloudy for over a week now, windy during the day and chilly at night. On this fine day, no birds were chirping, no cars were honking, and no people were chattering. Only the grunts and moans of the undead were heard.

Death was lurking around every corner, literally. The zombies were spread out across the whole avenue, sounding more dreadful than ever, now that Violet was closer. From afar, they looked partly human if you disregarded their loopy movements and deathly noises. Up close, their eyes gave them away instantly: bleached white, hollow as death.

Violet didn't give another minute's thought to the action that she had already decided to take and soon in the morning, stepped into the opening of the alley with two empty glass beer bottles which she had collected from their trash. She needed them to experiment with the idea, playing around in her mind that noise could draw in the zombies, based on the attacks she had witnessed on the first day. She was going to use the glass bottles to make a noise that would lure them away from her path. She sized up the avenue, eyes glancing east and west. Her plan was to retrieve a handgun that had fallen off a man who was trying to defend himself days ago but failed. Violet needed to draw away the horde swarming around the front door, where the gun lay. Before doing so, she thought it would be wise to draw the attention of the bunch that was closer to the alley away, towards the congestion of the cars on the road, and plotted her moves carefully.

She started by roughly tossing one bottle towards the middle lane. It made contact with an SUV's back window, causing a loud shattering that sent a flurry of undead feet limping towards the car, in the river of unmoving vehicles. Even some of the ones lingering beside the store were able to hear the clatter and limped their way through, towards the noise.

The coast was nearly clear. She made her way to the store's front, slowing her pace to catapult the other bottle high above the street, without even looking or aiming at an exact target. It crashed on top of a yellow taxicab squashed between the middle and right lanes. The crash caught the attention of the small bunch that stood yards before her faster than it did the first group. It cleared the path for Violet to move forward and retrieve her prized weapon. Now she could move on to the next stage, which she had not quite planned yet.

Finding a car that still worked was out of the question. Even if that was somehow possible, it would limit her movements too much, given the jam-packed streets, especially when she would reach the highway across Lake Valley. Before turning to her next stop, Violet wanted to check how many shots were left in her newly acquired gun, but she knew nothing of how to open the magazine. Making a noise where she stood was the last thing she wanted to do, so she decided to enter the closest empty store she could find, and do it quickly.

Unable to overlook the spoiled body of the teenager left behind, so desperately trying to crawl towards the noise the bottle had made, she hesitated. It wasn't paying her any mind, as if she were not even standing there. She aimed the gun at the teenager's skull, yearning to pull the trigger and end his misery. But she dared not to do it. "Look, I'm not sure whether you're still in pain or not," Violet whispered so he wouldn't notice her. "But I can't kill you without making noise, so … I'm sorry."

She lowered her gun and spun away, coming almost face to face with a corpse closing in on her hurriedly, most likely responding to the first shattering bottle. It seemed as though the walking corpse did not notice Violet right in front him. He bumped right into her shoulder with his ripped-open chest, skin, and clothes sloughing off in ribbons, and then stopped.

The groaning began to increase dreadfully. Milky eyes fixed on where she stood just inches away from him. Violet raised the handgun. The moment his groan picked up in volume, his mouth was struck with the backend of the gun's magazine, dropping him on his back to the blood-ridden and filthy sidewalk. Then, in a flash, Violet rushed away from the scene.

Violet took shelter in a small abandoned antique shop, only three shops away from the comic book store. Panting for her breath, she had chosen the smallest shop whose interior she could see from the outside to make sure that no one was inside. She went in to deliberately plan out her next move without being chased down by hungry groaners.

Luckily for Violet, every item in the store was breakable. Mounted on the wall behind the counter, was a huge sign that read, *Fragile! You break it, you buy it.* It was a gold mine place for thieves with extravagant taste in antiques or nosey kids that enjoyed poking around weird artifacts. *Anything you break, you don't have to buy anymore. You can also take whatever you like without having to point this gun at anyone.* Violet mused playfully.

Violet, still shouldering her backpack, looked around for tiny breakable items that she could store easily alongside the portion of food and water she'd carried back from Richie's bought food supply. Preparations for more toss and run operations.

Oddly enough, Violet found the technique to be quite thrilling, similar to being inside a survival-horror video game she had been so fond of playing with Billy, who was less jumpy than his older sister during surprise-attack scenes. For a boy of seven she didn't think it was normal, but at least he was brave enough to cheer her on and keep her company throughout the gameplay. Now, he might be playing his own survival-horror reality, like she was, and there was no *restart from last checkpoint* option to bring them back to life. They'd either be dead for good or come back to life and contribute to the horror, as the hunters of living.

It was truly a man-eat-man world out there. Violet needed to be brave and clever, acting cautiously in every move and every decision.

The majority of the uninfected survivors, Violet included, were unaware of the main cause of the infectious disease exterminating humanity. As she was breathing rapidly to draw clean air into her lungs, it came to her, *Air ... what if it's the air that's toxic, turning people into zombies! Toxic fumes from different factories merging to create a poisonous vapor.*

Violet had been out there since day one of the outbreak, breathing in the fumes of burning fossil fuels most of the time, and yet she hadn't felt the slightest hint of illness in that time. Her body was functioning normally. Her brain was working competently. Human meat was still not on her menu. Extra precautions must be taken, however, no one could be too sure.

She kept on stuffing her bag with the tiniest items she could forage: teacups, lids, glass coasters, anything that could be broken in a fall. And the best part was that she wouldn't have to pay for any of them. As she took an old Chinese kettle from a table, she noticed an elaborate handkerchief, ornamented with flourishing red and white orchids, big and small. Immediately realizing its potential, Violet tied it around her face, covering her mouth and her nose. Just in case. Then she wore her backpack on her front, with the zippers opened halfway, so it would be easier for her to reach the delicate items when needed.

Violet could clearly hear her bag rattling on her way to the exit. "Crap," she cursed. With a gun in one hand and a bag on her shoulders, Violet was already worried about the disadvantage of moving more slowly. Now that she had a bag full of noise-producing items, her movement was bound to be slower and noisier. Violet wrapped her free arm around the entire bag, pressing firmly against the contents to prevent the rattling from increasing when going back outside.

The motionless river of traffic wreckage, with living corpses meandering through it, was Violet's next obstacle to beat, unnoticed and alive. She dove into the hectic street, paying no mind to the gentle rattling sounds her bag was making when moving. She kept her eyes and ears focused on whatever was moving or groaning closest to her. Her muscles warmed up for running and were ready to throw an antique whenever she needed to lure the noise-chasers away from her track.

Once she had finally made her way across, she scurried into a wide alley that looked ten times larger than the narrow one alongside the Daily

Comics. Violet had anticipated—hoped—that the alley would be less infested with zombies, keeping her out of sight and earshot, shrouding her movements and leading her to a shortcut to Lake Valley's highway crossing. After several moments of walking safely in the alley, Violet set the gun down and took off her bag, relieving herself of the extra weight to stretch out her muscles and pour some water into her mouth. She thought she was the only shadow moving in the alley, but footsteps were already approaching her when the bottle was halfway to her mouth. She saw a man armed with a baseball bat walking towards her from a northern opening of the alley. She put down the bottle and went straight for the gun, but in vain, as it was already covered by a blue-laced shoe of a fellow who'd snuck up behind her. Threateningly, he tapped a crowbar repeatedly in his bony palm.

12

DOUBLE TROUBLE

DAY 4

In the isolation of shadows and walls, Violet now had a reason to look out not only for the undead tailing her to Lake Valley. "Well, well, what have you got there, doll?" asked the man with the baseball bat. Violet didn't like him calling her *doll* "A present for us, perhaps?" he cooed.

"Looks like we have us a cop gun here," the crowbar-wielder said as he picked up the firearm to examine it. "Now, I'm no expert, so could ya teach me a thing or two about that, cutie?" Violet was not flattered to be called *cutie* either; the expression on her face showed as much.

The men had cornered her against the wall. The one that had taken her gun was a thin young man wearing short sleeves and skinny jeans, looking as if he didn't weigh any more than Violet, but he made up for it in height, for he stared down at Violet with black eyes that matched his long stringy hair.

"I doubt that she has even the slightest clue of how to fire that thing, much less the details," the man with the baseball bat predicted. He didn't look quite as much the bad boy as he was pretending to be. He was wearing a wrinkled white T-shirt under a button-down—the worst for wear—sticking out of his trousers covered in dust like he'd been sitting on chalkboards all day. He was not as tall as the younger-looking one, but he was wider than him.

"It seems like I know as much about guns as you two do," Violet shot back with a barely visible grin.

"Is that so?" the messy but somewhat formally dressed man retorted, clapping one palm against the baseball bat.

"She talks," said the taller one. "But was it just me, or did her voice sound a tad boyish? Say something else." Violet glanced at him with one brow raised. *Great, just what I needed: two loons that grow a set of balls when there are no zombies around.* "Alrighty then," he said after Violet silently refused to utter another word.

"The gun will do us good. But shooting it will cause noises ... very *loud* noises." The speaker pointed his baseball bat in the direction of the street. "We don't want *them* to hear us now, do we?"

It seemed that the troublemakers had some knowledge about the infected. Violet wondered whether any useful data could be extracted from them. "What else do you know about them, other than them being sound sensitive?" she asked casually.

"Well, I only found out that they're 'sound sensitive' after causing a lot of noise that lead to the death of two people I know," he said bitterly. "A friend of mine got bitten by one of them when he was laughing out loud about the way they walked. Ironic, huh? Couple of hours later, he was gnawing on my girlfriend when he heard her yelling at me. And I was right there, sitting next to him. He just got up, completely ignored my existence, and attacked her! He turned into one of them. I had to kill him ... hit him over the head till I heard his skull crack. My girlfriend was dead. When we went to bury her, she woke up in the middle of us shoveling dirt on her. Her eyes had ... had turned ... white!"

"I'm sorry. That must've been tough for you to witness."

"Nah, she had it coming. Cheating on me twice and having the audacity to yell at me when I confronted her about it."

"Oh ..."

"Would you like to be my girlfriend? Of course, you'll have to take that napkin off your face so I can make sure the rest of your face is as pretty as your eyes." *Such a sweet talker. Too bad I don't date idiots that could probably be named after private body parts.* Violet wanted to tell him just that but decided to tread lightly.

"Look, guys, aren't we all supposed to be on the same page here? We should help each other out. Instead of looting one another, we oughta work together." Violet tried to think her way out of this dilemma. "I have people in danger right now. They need saving, so please ..." Violet leaned over to reach for her backpack.

The bat poked her in the shoulder, stopping her from proceeding. "Whoa! Hey, now. What's the rush? Do I look like I care about your super-girl wannabe act? You haven't even answered my question yet, which I was polite enough to ask in the first place. I mean, come on ... all I need is that gun, you, and whatever's useful there in your backpack." With a snap of bat-guy's fingers, the skinny man began pawing through her backpack.

"This whole situation is bad enough as it is. Why make it worse? People are already hunting us down for our flesh! You can have the gun, for all I—" She stopped in the middle of her protest as his fingertips started combing through her hair. Violet smacked his hand away. "Don't touch me," she said irritably.

"C'mon, we can go find a place where you can scream as loud as you want and no one will hear you." He rubbed his greasy slicked hair with his blackened fingertips.

Violet's aggravation turned to fury. When he reached out for her a second time, she grabbed his hand, squeezing his wrist. "Don't!" she warned and then pushed him away. *That might've been a mistake.*

"You know you want to, and I wasn't asking." He edged closer and yanked the handkerchief off her face. "Hello, beau—" But before he could even lower the handkerchief, he came to know that this maneuver was his last strike. Violet gripped his wrist tightly, pulled forward with unexpected speed, and rammed his nose with her bony elbow. She then delivered a roundhouse kick to the back of the other man's head before he could even stand up, putting her professional wrestling abilities to good use. But the one with the broken nose was surprisingly persistent and yanked her by her hair, starting to pull her backward. Violet was faster, though. She turned around before he could pull her back all the way and kicked him in the crotch. He squealed from the pain and untangled his fingers from her locks so that he could protect his delicate area.

She made a grab for her backpack and this time succeeded. Violet started to run but failed after the first few steps when steel came bouncing sideways against her spine with enough force to knock her over. The crowbar thug had hit only enough to immobilize her, planning not to cause her any fatal injuries just yet.

"Sit her up!" the beaten one snarled with rage, scrubbing blood from his nostrils. Violet's captor followed orders and wrapped his skinny arms around her elbows, sitting her up straight, legs stretched out on the ground. She didn't even bother to struggle, as pain radiated throughout her body by the blow to her back.

He walked up to her, one hand still covering his crotch, the other carrying his bat. "You like to play rough, don't you? I'll show you rough." He unzipped and loosened his trousers.

The adrenaline rush had died out, and suddenly she was terrified, more so than when facing zombies even. "What are you doing?" "*No! Someone, help!*" she yelled out.

He clasped one hand around her mouth, shushing her. "Are you crazy? You'll lure them here!"

"That's the plan," Violet said when he removed his hand, then swore at him and added a short but loud scream: "*Aiieeee—*" Then her lights went out with a smack over the head from his bat.

Everything was blurry then. She saw and felt the man forcing himself on her while his accomplice pinned her down. Then everything went black again.

Violet woke a short while later. Her vision was blurry as her head swam and throbbed. She blinked once and then twice to clear the fog, and was able to hear gut-wrenching groans narrowing in on them from a different opening to the alley.

"Muuuhhh!" "Gaauuhh!" Followed by many other terrible symphonies.

"They're getting closer," one of the thugs cried. Violet wasn't sure which one. "We can't take on all of 'em. I'm bailing, man." Violet turned to the side and saw the skinny fellow collect both the weapons and run the other way.

She only then noticed that her pants were halfway down to her ankles, and there was a massive weight on top of her with a palm pressing down on her mouth. No point in that, as the undead had heard her the first time. Violet's vision cleared. The guy's face was the first thing she saw clearly: reddish nose with a mustache of blood, and sweat dripping down his forehead. This was hardly the time or place to be committing such vile acts. He was not only crazy: he was absolutely—a hooligan with his eyes closed, lost to his sickening pleasures.

Violet clawed his eyelids, burning red lines all the way down to his cheekbones, scrapping off flecks of skin beneath her nails. He rolled off her and wailed in agony. She heaved herself up, pulled up her pants, and grabbed her backpack, hightailing it away from the marching army of the dead, leaving her aggressor as bait for far more pain coming *his* way this time.

The pain couldn't be compared to a kick in the crotch or a broken nose or even scrapped off skin. It was far beyond hideous! The wailing had stopped. He wanted to scream but was not able to. His first assailant clenched a firm jaw around his throat, constricting airflow while pints of blood splashed out. His Adam's apple was quickly torn out, along with portions of neck tissue. The rest of him was ripped open in seconds as soon as the others joined the feast. Intestines were pulled out and munched on greedily like strings of sausages. Body organs flew everywhere, and not a single one landed unnoticed. The zombies were keen on not leaving an ounce of his flesh uneaten, leaving only the smallest flecks for the flies.

A part of Violet wanted to run into his skinny associate to get back the gun, and even shoot him in the process. The other part of her was worried that if she *did* run into him, he'd use that gun on her. She had reached a dead-end. Blocking her path was one brick wall, maybe twenty feet high, with a dumpster standing next to it. It seemed possible to reach the top of the wall using the dumpster. Violet adjusted her pants and wore her backpack properly. Up the dumpster and then to the top of the wall she got, not daring to jump down to the other side, for his eyes had already targeted her before she spotted him. Flat on his back and moaning in pain was the other assailant. Even with his height advantage, the clumsy fool had landed poorly, breaking one knee, which she could see by the bone trying to punch its way through his jeans.

Violet landed evenly on both feet next to him. She felt not an ounce of empathy or respect for this man who'd held her down for his accomplice to assault her.

"Please, help me … O God, it hurts so bad!" he sobbed. But Violet simply reclaimed the gun, along with the crowbar that was no longer his, in silence. "Please, don't leave me here like this."

Violet turned to him with a spiteful look in her fiery green eyes. "Can you even stand?"

"No," he replied in tears.

"Good." Violet clenched her jaw and continued forward, leaving him to wail in agony until the undead found him.

"No, don't go! Just kill me at least, please! Aaaahhhhh!" His voice died out in echoes as Violet put distance between them, making her way through the remainder of the alley.

13

ABANDONED

DAY 4

Eyes scanned every inch of the store for Violet or any evidence that would lead to her whereabouts. With everything stacked up in one location, a free space was left between the counter and the door, and books formerly residing on shelves now displayed themselves along the superhero carpeting. No one was there except for Richie.

No place to hide other than the back room or behind the counter.

No one was hiding behind the counter, and only Marvin was asleep in the back room. Violet was not to be found anywhere inside the Daily Comics. *Maybe outside? The alley!* Richie hurled himself to the back room and swung the door open. *Not out here either.* Disappointed, he went back in, closing the door and locking it behind him.

Violet was not the type of person to up and abandon her friends without a word. She had her reasons—strong reasons—but still, she'd promised to wait a few more days for the prospect of help arriving. If it didn't, they'd leave together. And just like that, the day after she'd made her promise to Richie, she left behind his back.

Marvin woke up after hearing the door being closed and the lock clicking. "Back from the can?" he asked.

FEAR IN FLESH

"Violet's gone," Richie said drily, like a part of him had suspected this would happen. "She took her backpack with her and a very small portion of our stash too."

"Where'd she go off on her own like that?"

Richie frowned. "Where else other than Lake Valley, Marv?"

"And now you wanna go after her," Marvin said.

"What choice do I have? I gotta get to her before any of the zombies do. That is ... *if* they haven't already." Hope was striding away from Richie's strength of character to face the merciless beasts and to bring Violet back. To what purpose, though? If she was still alive, and he managed to catch up to her, it wouldn't be a rescue mission so much so as forcing her back. He assumed that, no matter how small of a pro wrestler she was, Violet would not be easily forced. He'd seen her in action against men and women twice her size. She always gave her opponents a run for their money. Richie would probably end up flipped on his back or be forced himself to go along with her to Lake Valley before he'd manage to drag her back to the store.

"All right, we'd better get moving if we want to catch up to her," Marvin said.

"Wait ..." Richie stopped him as Marvin reached for the shotgun. "You're coming with me?"

"You'd be stupid to think I was gonna let you go after her alone."

"But I was planning on using my new bike," Richie explained. "I think it'll be for the best if you stay here and keep an eye on the place. Keep it locked up."

Marvin sighed, understanding that Richie meant he would slow him down. But also the bike would only be able to carry one of them until Violet was found. "Fine, then. When you get back, I'm gonna need you to honk twice so I know it's you out there. And I'm sure when you do find Violet she'll be thrilled about your new motorbike. You know … a nerd riding a badass bike without manual pedals." Marvin was trying to lighten the mood, and it worked. Richie smiled.

"Let's hope I can convince her to get *on* the bike after what happened to her that day."

"Let's hope you can convince her to come back with you willingly," Marvin added. He handed Richie the shotgun with a shoulder strap to support it while on the motorbike.

Richie burst out of the back door into the narrow alley. To get to his new motorbike, he'd need to get across to the other side of the road, where it was kept at a place called Pauli's Garage where he recently purchased the bike and convinced the shop owner to park it inside during work hours, safe from harm's way.

He'd intended to reveal the bike to Violet on new comic book day, which should've been the day after that day when all hell broke loose. No one had mentioned the bike in front of Violet during their first days of living in the store, as everyone was preoccupied in their own thoughts. And now she was out there on her own.

Richie jumped from car to car, staying out of reach of the zombies with agility as if he were in a thriller movie chase scene. In truth, he was the one being chased down. Noise echoing from every step he took alerted groaners to his exact location as they followed. He didn't plan out how he could draw them away from him as Violet had done. Richie was terrified, yes, more terrified than Violet was when she embarked on her dangerous quest, but he was as recklessly brave as she was.

Thump! Richie landed on top of the car parked nearest to the opposite sidewalk. Beside the car, on the walkway, three pairs of extended arms waited to carve out the flesh of the victim causing this racket. All three mouths slobbered hungrily with a mixture of saliva and dried blood. Richie measured the distance of the jump. He leaped. Right knee extended in midair, drop-kicking the slobbering fiend to his left, forcing it down on top of the other slobbering mouth that stood behind it. Both tumbled to the pavement as Richie stood steadily on the sidewalk.

Two down, one to go, not counting a couple of dozens heading my way. The thrill was starting to shift into a panic; he had Marvin's shotgun for protection, but using it now might put him in a vulnerable position later when the horde of corpses would become bigger and he would have lesser room to run.

The third slobbering mouth belonged to an old woman, who was drooling all over her flashy yellow trench coat, groaning hoarsely. She grasped his hoodie from the back with both her hands. He threw his forearm against her neck, keeping her reeking mouth away from his face. The other two were making an effort to stand up again. More of them were not far away from the sidewalk, getting closer by the second. Richie needed to do something other than holding the old lady back—and fast. There was no room for pity or respecting his elders at a time like this. She had probably been nice in her old age as a human, but as a zombie, all she wanted to do was rip Richie's guts out for a drink and crack open his skull for a fresh meal of brains.

Richie spun the old lady back against the car, repeatedly smashing the back of her head onto the windshield. Back and forth, her head cracked the glass till it shattered on the fifth blow. Richie was off the sidewalk in a flash before the others surrounded the car. Two would have gotten him if he hadn't raised the shotgun and blown their heads off with a single blast.

* * *

"C'mon, Richie, where the hell are you?" Marvin stood impatiently just outside the store, waiting to see Richie reach the garage safely and make it out of there alive. He couldn't see Richie running anywhere. Marvin started to worry and wanted to go after him, but he didn't.

Pauli's automated garage door was rising, as Marvin could finally see. A roaring engine rocketed out of that door, swooping down the sidewalk. Richie, on his green bike, raced along the street. On his head was a massive green helmet with black zigzag lines. The engine kept roaring, not slowing down for any limping creatures on its course. On its tail, a stream of Cliffroyce's infected inhabitants followed sluggishly.

Marvin went back inside when he'd made sure Richie had escaped in one piece. The first thing he did was turn on the television. Nothing had been airing regularly since the day after the sickness exploded and the general public panicked. One short news update had broken through two days earlier, randomly airing on local channels for a very limited period, saying that the US military was rounding up survivors all over New York.

Another update suddenly broke through as Marvin surfed the channels. It was a frenzied scene, and he was unable to tell where it was being shot from. The camera was focused on the reporter, but behind him, the space was crammed with people.

The reporter began to speak: "We are back on air for another short segment of news. As you may already know, these creatures are highly contagious. Stay away from them. Despite the fact that they are incredibly slow, they are highly dangerous. We have learned that they are completely blind and respond only to sound and body heats, like snakes, do in the wild. But that does not make them any less dangerous. *Do not* engage in close combat. The slightest bite could kill you in mere hours, if not minutes. Survivors have been, and still are, gathering in the Royce Pentagon Arena off the west side of the business district on Tenth Avenue. We advise any survivors who are still out there to try to join us as fast as possible. Especially if you are anywhere near midtown or the Cliffroyce business district, where we've just received news that an airstrike will deploy to in less than thirty minutes. They will fire on the streets reported holding the highest rates of infection in the city. We will do our best to broadcast more announcements in the near future, but for now ... may God be with us all."

The news report concluded, and the screen went blank as if someone had pressed the *off* button. Marvin clenched the remote in his hands while staring numbly at the screen, and sighed. "I should've gone with ya, Richie."

14

LAST STOP

DAY 4

Violet made it all the way past the airplane crash site and entered Lake Valley's gate. The pandemonium outside the gate was not much different from what she had experienced in the business district. Well, except for the part where the two debauched humans delayed her journey. Violet had found her way out of that cursed alley with a great bump on her forehead, a reminder of her awful encounter with the other survivors.

The swollen bruise ached worse and worse as she proceeded on her way. The further she got, the wearier she grew. If not for the power bar and energy drink she'd taken from the store's stash, Violet would most likely have passed out in the middle of a street and ended up as a meal for the groaning vultures.

The crowbar she had seized was lodged in her backpack. Too lengthy to fit all the way, it stuck up between what was left of the breakable antiques and the snacks. Its curved head was poking out the top of the bag, peering in whatever direction Violet was running during her toss-and-break spells. These eventually got her to where she was standing now: Lake Valley.

Near the dock, one boat floated on the lake—no other boats in sight.

FEAR IN FLESH

That last boat bore the words *Cliffroyce Fishers* on each side. Violet's hopes and wishes were true. They *were* still here awaiting her return, and she had finally made it. All that was blocking her way now was the undead: not as many as out on the streets, but still an overwhelming number strewn about the green field, highlighted red with gore. The concrete pathway was covered with leftover limbs: masticated arms, fingers, legs, and toes, as well as splinters of bones, spit out. They served as hurdles along the path leading to the shack. Worse, an open field meant that there were no places to stay out of sight. With only three breakable items left in her backpack, Violet's odds of survival were short to none. She needed to move with extra caution, as quiet as a roach if she was going to make it.

Two glass coasters and a teacup remained. Violet had to make every throw count. Into the air flew the cup. It twirled above the concrete, landed and broke into multiple fragments. Despite how small it was, the shattering sound it caused was picked up by the, half a dozen infected roaming closest to the pathway. It kept them busy long enough for Violet to get closer to the shack.

The first glass coaster hit the shack's front steps, fracturing into an ornamentation of glittering dust. Creepers both inside and outside of the shack went to investigate as Violet crept ever so slightly closer to the docks.

The second coaster and the final breakable item were already in tiny pieces, crushed beneath the weight formerly atop it. What to do now? So close to the dock's bridge, all she needed was to derail the five infected standing guard so that she could make her move. It might not be a bright idea to finally test the gun out, which might only draw them after her. Plus it would waste a resource as valuable as water, which was the equivalent of throwing her life away. But she was *so close.*

There was not much time left. At any moment, the ones she had already distracted, finding no fresh bodies to carve into, would regroup and cross the field once again.

Think, Violet, think! She erratically grabbed the curved head of the crowbar and felt an instant surge of energy as an idea clicked. *Steel on concrete ... loud noise! I'd be losing a valuable weapon here, but ... I have to do it. I can't stand here till they notice me!* Violet drew the crowbar out then flung it forward, over the pathway.

The crowbar bounced off the concrete a couple of times with a loud clanking sound that echoed. Then the noise-chasing groans dove straight after it. Violet quietly slid away to the docks, crossed the bridge, and climbed aboard her father's boat.

Her eyes narrowed as she searched in every direction, nervous and excited. Her facial expression was frozen, neither frowning, because she couldn't find Billy and Gavin the minute she boarded, nor smiling from the anticipation of seeing them again. She noticed bloody handprints on the cabin's wall. "Oh no," she said to no one. She tilted her head down and saw blood tracks trailing to the bow. "No." Her voice was almost a whimper.

And just like in her dream, though she couldn't remember it, Gavin was present on the bow. Only this time he wasn't standing at the edge staring at the lake with his arm around Billy's shoulder. Instead, he was on his knees, both hands busy holding up a hunk of liver he'd been gobbling up like a juicy hamburger. His right side was turned to Violet, as he knelt beside an unrecognizable corpse bathed in its own blood, staring blindly at the sky. Its belly was open, organs everywhere, still inside and all over the body. Violet's mind jumped to the worst, but no, the corpse did not belong to Billy. It was too big for a seven-year-old, but not big enough for a full-grown adult.

The father fed as the daughter watched in repugnance, feeling an overwhelming flood of tears welling up. No, not tears. A sickening feeling in her stomach from the shock of witnessing her own father wolfing down human liver with blood leaking down it. Violet could not hold it in much longer; the nauseating feeling crawled up her throat. Her mouth opened to allow the contents of her stomach out, and ... nothing came out. Just a loud burp and a choking sound, for her stomach was partially empty.

That sound, however, made Gavin stop shoving his recent kill's liver into his mouth. He just held it in there, crawled on all fours, and pushed on the floor with his hands to stand up. "Muuurrphh!" Gavin's gaze was fixed on where Violet stood. She aimed the gun shakily at his color-faded eyes, not yet daring to pull the trigger.

"Dad, if you're still in there somewhere, please stop. Fight it, whatever *it* is, don't give up!" Violet pleaded. No use reasoning with him, she knew. He was a full-fledged zombie. Her pleas only made his limping pick up in pace. "Don't make me do this," she begged of her no longer a rational father.

Gavin opened up his arms as if meaning to embrace his daughter. Violet had her finger trembling on the trigger. *Pull the trigger now and end it all; there's no reasoning with him anymore,* Violet argued with herself. But how could she? Her own father, the blood that ran through her veins, the man responsible for her having a life. She *was* his own flesh and blood. Now he lusted for her flesh and blood to feed upon.

No more emotions in Gavin's hollow eyes and needless groans. Craving human flesh was his true nature now. His human instincts, empathy, and compassion were no more. Everything had been erased: his vision, his mind, and his memories. Gavin Turner's humanity was as dead as the corpse he had been devouring. Now all he wanted was to make a grab for his own daughter and rip apart one of the two lives he had brought into this world.

Still hesitating to pull the trigger, she sidestepped to avoid his grasp and get a better aim at his head. The gun was ready to fire, but all it did was whack Gavin across the head. The hunk of liver dropped from his jaws as he stumbled into the cabin's front wall, preventing his fall and keeping him up on his feet. He went back for more. No matter how blind he was, he somehow sensed Violet's physical movements, knowing exactly where she took her next step, and he went after her, forcing her to retreat.

Moving backward without looking where she stepped, Violet was busy whacking her father away each time he made a move, not yet ready to kill her *own* father. She slipped and fell, after stepping into a slick smudge of blood. The back of her white hoodie was dipped in red.

Gavin groaned louder after the sound of Violet's fall. "*Raahhh!*" he growled and looked as if he was about to jump on top of her. The gun's muzzle was aimed before Gavin descended. Finger back on the trigger, she finally did what she most dreaded. The muzzle let out three shots: BANG! BANG! BANG!

15

SWIMMING LESSONS

DAY 4

The sound of gunshots traveled throughout the valley. Undead ears caught the echo that directed them towards the boat, surrounding the dock, making their way across the bridge, tumbling over each other. The boat's ledge was not all that high; it wouldn't be a problem for them to stumble aboard. The field empty, the dock's bridge was starting to overflow. Violet was in desperate need of a distraction by now, or she was lunch.

A roar blasted through the valley's ruined gate. Tires screeched along the concrete, leaving their tracks in lines of black. They churned the grass, leaving a mess of brown muck behind them. Living corpse heads rotated towards the accelerating engine heading their way. Richie, on his green motorbike, had his eyes on the dock. *Violet has got to be in there since they're crowding that bridge,* he thought.

The racing bike increased again, in speed, and the engine in volume. Richie had his mind set on clearing a path to that last remaining boat on the lake. Without hitting the brakes, Richie leaped off the bike with Marvin's shotgun and rolled over the grass with the force of a bowling ball. His body came to a stop while his bike drifted along the dock, driving through the bodies barricading its passageway. Off the bridge it roared and splashed into the water, taking down a staggering bunch of the undead with it. The others dove into the lake clumsily, forgetting all about the gunshot from the boat.

That's odd, Richie thought, though he felt relieved that none of the infected remained on the dock—or the entire field, for that matter. All the zombies were struggling to keep standing in the water, trying to get on top of each other for support. But more had followed Richie's roaring bike through the streets and would sooner or later be swarming through the destroyed gate, ravaging the field with their presence once more.

Richie walked towards the dock and stopped when another BANG sounded. The undead wobbled from excitement at the explosive sound, but this set them gargling on water as they groaned and splashed more frantically than ever.

16

FAMILY TRAUMA

DAY 4

Gavin's corpse had sprawled on the cabin's window, splattering it with black blood, after taking three solid shots: the first in his right torso, the second in the chest, and the third just scratching his left ear. He stood again and groaned.

Violet's eyes were squeezed shut as she had pulled the trigger on her corpse-eating father. She heard the explosive shots blast through the muzzle and pierce flesh, her father's flesh. She opened her eyes to see him still unyielding to death. None of the bullets had pierced through his skull to destroy his useless, corrupt brain. It was almost as if she'd meant to miss that wide-open target. But to what avail? It was either her life or her father's half-dead life that he was now damned to for eternity.

As the father rose to pursue his helpless daughter once more, the daughter prayed that there was at least one bullet left to save her. She took a shaky aim. He stepped awkwardly forward. She was on her back, sprawled in a dish of gore all around her. He was salivating, with blood oozing from his ragged, rotting body. Violet inhaled deeply. Gavin groaned carnivorously. *Sorry, Daddy.*

The daughter squeezed her eyes shut as the father descended …

BANG!

His body came crashing down on her frontward-worn backpack, containing shards of broken coasters. The bullet luckily entered through his gaping mouth and escaped from the back of his head, saving Violet's life and releasing Gavin's soul from his tortured body.

The first thing she noticed when her father lay dead atop her was the full set of bite marks that ripped his clothing and pierced deeply through his left shoulder blade. Then, her nostrils filled with the odor of decaying body parts and bloodshed. It made her nauseous again; her face was dotted with splattered blood that belonged to her father. Violet did not hold back her tears, "Please, God, let it all just be a nightmare … *please.*"

When she heaved her father's corpse off herself with weak, shaky arms, Violet sat upright, drenched in blood while the stench of decay emanated from the top of her hair down to the base of her sneakers. Her right hand held the gun that she'd used to kill her father. Her left hand fumbled on the deck and touched something small and skinny. The object resembled her own hand, but smaller.

She held it up; it *was* a hand that was also drenched in blood, with the forearm still intact. It ended in a stump at the elbow. Violet studied it, along with the devoured corpse that lay in the midst of its entrails, measuring the arm against what remained of the corpse's elbows and shoulders. She prayed for the arm to fit, but she knew it didn't. Living palm clasped to dead palm, the size difference was not all that great, but she knew: Violet knew this hand the moment she'd grabbed it. It was the last time she would hold the innocent hand of what remained of her little brother.

17

CLEANING TOWN

DAY 4

After sacrificing his precious new motorcycle, Richie boarded the swaying boat to witness a devastating sight that punched his gut like a fist. He felt a little dizzy but stood strong when he gazed at the dead body he recognized as Violet's father, Gavin Turner, and beyond it; the remnants of an unknown victim. In the midst of all that slaughter, Violet sat, holding a lacerated arm in one hand and a gun in the other.

So she was the one who had pulled the trigger. Richie struggled to speak, fighting back the urge to gag. *And that shot was meant for her dad!* Richie finally found his tongue. "My God ... V-Violet, w-what happened here?" Richie couldn't keep the repulsed look from his face.

Violet averted her sad eyes from Billy's hacked arm to stare up at Richie when she heard his strange, yet familiar, voice. Her mouth was in a straight line. Her eyes flooded with tears, sliding down her cheeks. She grimaced faintly and started talking. "Dad was eating a body when I got here." She glared at the prey's demolished corpse. "Then he turned to me." Violet turned her head to face Richie again. "So I had no choice; I had to do it. I pulled the trigger, shot my dad *three times,* and he *still* came at me, groaning with those unblinking white eyes, clenching his teeth at me like I was some delicious treat. It was either me or him. He was probably suffering. I shot him in his mouth ... hopefully, putting him out of his misery."

Violet smiled bitterly as she finished telling her story. "But lately, I've been having these strange awful nightmares, where I wake up shivering and can't remember a thing. This could be one of them. It's taking me a while to wake up, but I could be dreaming *all* of this. And when I finally wake up—Dad and Billy could still be alive, and there will be no more zombies. Everything will be back to normal, Richie, and I won't have to miss new comic book day," she said, in tears.

A quick glance back at the dead bodies, though, seemed to confirm that this was no dream. Not one of those awful nightmares: it was a nightmare come to life. Violet would have preferred dying in any of the nightmares she'd had if only she wouldn't have to experience this profound reality.

Richie approached her with sorrow, feeling a sick tension in his stomach. He wanted to say a lot to Violet to comfort her, but couldn't. *You have to suck it up*, he told himself, stepping over and around a swamp of gore. *You risked your own life to come to save hers and went against all odds, fighting zombies to make it here alive, without incurring any causality or messing your pants. There's no reason for you to gag now. Not in front of her.* But before Richie could reach down and grab her, Violet pointed the gun at him. He froze.

"Your eyes look normal," she said, "so you're not gonna try to eat me ... or ... rape me, will you, Richie?"

Richie was more shocked by that than the gun in his face. "R-rape you?" he asked, astonished. "No, *no*! Why would you even think that,

Vi?"

"Because someone did earlier today," she answered. "It didn't feel as awful as this, though, and I got to see the man who did it get eaten alive by a pack of zombies." She chuckled eerily at that for a second and then went back to crying, not believing the words coming out of her own mouth.

Richie didn't know what to say. He simply took the gun from her and set it cautiously to the side. Then he took Violet in his arms, despite the appalling smells. Her face rested on his chest, staining the front of his hoodie with her father's blood as she wept some more for this horrible day that would haunt her memories for as long as she survived. "I'm very sorry, Violet, for all that you went through today. I should've gone with you from the start. I'm sorry." Richie paused. "You've done the right thing. Your dad wanted you to pull that trigger. He turned. He couldn't say it to you, but he wanted you to do it. No father wants to be burdened with the guilt of murdering his own daughter. Don't worry; he's in a better place now. You've ended his suffering."

Now it's time for you to bear this lifelong scar, and it's my turn to keep you safe as we survive together. Richie noticed the arm she had latched onto and immediately remembered her mentioning that Billy was dead as well. *That body can't have belonged to Billy: it's too big to be him. Is this arm all that remains of her poor little brother? My God! Mr. Turner ate his own son!*

The boat began rocking on the waving waters instead of the gentle sway. The air filled with deafening engine shrieks, even louder than when the airplane was nose-diving toward earth. Overhead rocketed four fighter jets, flying towards the Cliffroyce business district. Two jets flew at higher altitudes over the two tallest building centered in the towering condominium. They launched what appeared to be missiles—several each. They hit both sides of the tower, and the fifty-story building caught fire, which rapidly spread, causing the structure to collapse and crumble onto the streets.

It didn't end there. There were more explosions as far as Richie and Violet could see from Lake Valley. Midtown erupted into roaring orange flames and black smoke that overtook the cloudy sky with its dreaded toxins. The air jets then whooshed away, back from where they'd come from. The two friends witnessed the annihilation, shaking on the boat as they stared at the jets flying away. When the jets could no longer be seen, reality struck hard. Richie grasped his curly locks with both hands, fingers digging deep. "No!" he cried. "Marv's still inside the store!" Violet seemed deaf to Richie's words, locked in grief as she stared down again at the corpses that remained of her family.

Immediately, after, Violet and Richie heard a CHOP-CHOP-CHOP that cut through the air—less deafening than the jets but in close proximity to the lake. "You two on the boat, wave your hands up in the air if you are still human!" a man's voice demanded through a megaphone. Richie complied, but Violet only glanced up at the helicopter with mournful green eyes, and then back to her deceased father.

The helicopter circled down to land on the slaughter field that was Lake Valley. The speaker had asked Richie and Violet to disembark. Richie took Violet by the hand, fixed her backpack, and picked up her gun. Side by side they went back to the field. Violet did not carry the torn arm of Billy with her. She left it next to her father's body and walked out, still a bloody mess.

Four individuals emerged, excluding the pilot. All were garbed in black SWAT uniforms, and they spilled out onto the open field with their machine guns ready. Bullets flew towards the damaged gate, where a flock of new limping corpses found their way in. One SWAT member sprinted towards Richie and Violet with two other men in safety red-and-white vests, carrying strange looking devices and medical kits. "Sir, ma'am, I'm going to have to ask you to lay down your firearms so that we can proceed with a contagion test." Richie, being the law-abiding citizen he always was, laid down both the guns.

One of the men in a safety vest approached Richie with a black rectangular device and aimed the small circular gap an inch away from Richie's right eye. It beeped with a flashing green light. BEEP, it rang again on the left eye. "He's clean. No signs of infection." said the man with the device. The other safety member did the same to Violet, and she passed as well.

"Do you require any medical attention, ma'am?" Violet shook her head miserably.

The gunfire had ceased. Another SWAT member joined them and said to Richie, "Sir, I'm sorry, but for safety purposes, we're going to have to confiscate your guns until we arrive safely at the disease-free zone."

"Disease-free zone?" asked Richie. "Where's that?"

"Royce Pentagon," a third officer answered.

They all boarded the helicopter as the choppers spun and took to the air. The pilot swerved at times to avoid being swallowed by the black mists, from the explosions, that hovered the north beyond the devastation. Down below, they saw piles and piles of waste that were once buildings, homes, shops, and roads. All were demolished into pebbles and ash from the flames that engulfed the business district, including victims of the infection buried underneath all the rubble.

As the chopper passed over the location where the Daily Comics shop was supposed to be situated, not a trace was left of the store. An enormous black pit of rubble opened up underneath where the store had stood. It gulped down the comic book store and its neighbors, obscuring a quarter of the avenue.

Richie looked down at the vast pit and prayed for his best friend's life. Violet, on the other hand, didn't think of Marvin; instead, she felt like she'd been hit by a freight train as vivid memories of the awful dreams she'd had came pouring back. Her thoughts swam from the puzzle that started putting itself together from top to bottom.

Her latest nightmare was of Billy and Gavin on the boat becoming zombies and attacking her just before she woke up. Before that, the largest tower in town plummeting down over the streets from the hellfire the explosive sun had caused—the recent airstrike on the business district. Last but not the least, the immense destruction that had cracked the ground sucking the whole of the comic book store into its bottomless abyss—in reality, a massive sinkhole that opened up from the earth-shattering missile detonations.

All of it, Violet had seen coming. *All* had been fulfilled this very day, only minutes apart. Her nightmares had breached her reality like psychic visions. What did it all mean? Could Violet predict the future now? Or was it just one disastrous coincidence after another that cost her a friend, a father, and a baby brother?

18

ENDLESS NIGHTMARES

DAY 493

Dark memories prowl through my mind, even after all this time. You'd think I would've healed by now. Physically I'm fine, but mentally ... that's the deeper wound that needs to be stitched closed over and over again to prevent sickness, and that sickness is a weakness. Keep grieving and praying to God to wake up from this torment, and you expose yourself to weakness. In this new world, weakness is a disability. Weakness means as-good-as-dead. After the travesty I went through, I realized how weak I was, still letting those memories get to me this way. But I'm not crazy; well, at least not yet. My mind is strong, stronger than my body even. It was up to me to prove to myself that I'm strong enough to seize control over it. Keep my emotions in check, fight back the fear, let the wounds become scars, drive the dead back, and keep on surviving.

If I had no intention of staying alive, I would've shot myself instead of my dad on the boat that day when his dead eyes had met mine and his red-stained teeth sought my flesh. By then I knew that there was no coming back for him. He was gone but suffered still. So when the choice came between me and him, I chose to end my dad's suffering. Afterward, my mind crumbled for some time, when everything came crashing down on it all at once. Only grief was there to help keep me stable, yet it paralyzed me for a while until it began cutting even deeper. That's when I had to put a stop to it. I had the power to eliminate anything that threatened to weaken my mind, to try breaking me again. I am partially fixed now, but I still don't want any screws to go loose on me, not when we're at war.

    The only challenge my mind still faces, is withstanding the dreams ... those nightmares that come and go. My mind is vulnerable when it's shut down in slumber; otherwise, I would go insane or die of restlessness to try and eliminate those dreams too. When I close my eyes and darkness swarms me, locking me in the obscure recesses of my mind where dreams seize control, I see things—terrible things. I hear loud screams of terror in places filled with blood and torn limbs. No matter where those dreams take me, groaning and gnawing creatures always chase me, making me scream while I run for my life, not knowing where to go. I wake up, and the nightmares are not as foggy as the ones that came true on that tragic day. No. I can still remember them in flashes when I'm awake. I still wake up trembling with goosebumps all over, whether it was me playing video games with Billy or watching a wrestling match with my dad. Whether I was running away from zombies and the earth starts pushing me backward, allowing them to catch up to me, or I'm hanging from a ledge, my fingers slipping, with gravity pulling me down to where hundreds of decaying hands are reaching out for me.

Those nightmares occur so often that I don't worry about them coming to life anymore. I kept recording them in my diary to keep track. A nightmare I can remember is only a normal dream, not a prediction. Those visionary ones, I couldn't remember them when I woke, and when they happened in real life, it was so overwhelming that I thought I was going mad. But after a long period of healing, without any dreams breaching the real world, I figured that it may have just been one big coincidence. Until I woke up today during the ride back to Royce Pentagon Sanctuary, hands and legs

FEAR IN FLESH

trembling, goosebumps arose, traveling down to my lower back, and a hazy memory of what the dream was about, haunts me now.

✳ ✳ ✳

Caught in the thickness of a dark void, alone and unmoving—Violet was surrounded. A swarm of silvery dots was floating in all directions, closing in on her very slowly. Violet, in her shimmering white nightgown, with her dark brown hair flat across her shoulders and back, stood alone in the middle of a dark hive, *trapped*.

Her legs did not work, but her upper body did. She punched and pulled with her arms at her legs, trying fruitlessly to bring life back to her numb legs and run, or at least throw herself to the ground as the slow-moving waves of sparkling silver things got even nearer. Were they the twinkling of stars as the night sky fell? Were they the flickering flashlights of a rescue party? Were they fireflies soaring in the murkiness to show her a path to light? She feared the uncertainty.

"C'mon, damn it, *move!*" Violet yelled at her legs, panicking as the swarm grew larger, flying closer. "What are they?" she asked the darkness around her. *They* got as close as they could get before impact. Violet got a swift glimpse: "Bullets!"

Her hair fluttered and her gown blew back as bullets flew past her, though other passed through her body, flying onward still. In the darkness, the bullets started to disappear. Buckets of blood foamed and spilled from the dark corners of the black abyss that swallowed Violet, she could smell it. Screams of agony followed as blood flowed underneath her icy feet, yet she stood unharmed.

Clear as daylight, puddles, and streams of bright red splatters coursed together to shape a sailboat. She stood in the bow of the sticky red boat, where a dripping red man with pale white eyes tucked a small arm into his mouth. The red man noticed Violet's presence and marched towards her. Still unable to run, Violet fell to her knees, tinting them red.

Clearer than daylight, a circle of pure blinding light flared far above Violet's head. "Violet," a soothing voice called out to her from the circle of light. The red man approached her with a bloated belly; his arms began to swell, and so did his legs. Then his head grew enormous and exploded in splatters, along with his entire body—reduced to the red liquid shaping the boat. Within that new puddle laid a small, repulsive corpse—distorted limbs all tangled up in a heap. "*Violet!*" the soothing voice called out to her more stridently. She responded by looking up again with one hand over her brows to shade her eyes from the blinding light. There was no light anymore. The circle of light was overtaken by a larger storm of sparkling bullets that blotted out the light completely, swooping up like an eclipse and raining down in a shower of blood and death. Violet could not move, and it was only her and the child's dismantled corpse on the blood-dripping boat. She closed her eyes and was yet again lost in the dark.

"Violet, wake up, we're here." The soothing voice jerked Violet awake. "Easy there, just me," Richie said, as she jumped in her seat. "And, of course, those two guys in the back." He pointed towards the backseat, from where he sat at the wheel, with a calming smile. Violet stared with bleary eyes at Richie and the two gentlemen armed with guns and knives in the backseat. She noticed her shaky hands and legs, goosebumps tickling her neck, down to her spine. She rubbed her eyes tiredly with shaky fists.

Her head swam with the images of darkness and blood. It wasn't at all like the nightmares she had gotten used to. She couldn't make any sense of it at all. Too many pieces of a jigsaw puzzle—a puzzle that took charge during her unconsciousness and then left her stranded in thought with many pieces of the puzzle lost as soon as she woke. It filled her with a sense of dread.

"Another bad dream?" Richie asked her with a casual sympathetic smile.

"A nightmare," Violet croaked as the car came to a stop behind four other vehicles, waiting for the Royce Pentagon parking unit gate to open.

19

SCAVENGER RUN

DAY 493

They were back from a two-hour scavenger hunt for essentials, including eatables and drinkables, gas, cooking oil, pharmaceuticals, melee weapons, firearms, ammo, and any cooperative survivors they ran across. Those were the top priorities for the scavenger teams sent out, provided with appropriate weaponry and a sum total of five cars with a quarter tank of gas each. Plus, the loading truck was still on its way, catching up with the rest of the crew waiting at the gate.

Although not even half of what was on the list had been retrieved, the hunt was fairly successful. There were only a few encounters with the living dead, with no fatalities, no injuries, and no loss of weaponry or equipment. They hadn't encountered any cooperative survivors, but neither had they encountered any bandits. They'd retrieved three dozen bags of uncooked rice, around sixty unopened cans of beans, and two vending machines filled with soda, snacks, and water bottles (a very rare retrieval).

All of the two hours' catch was to be added up and divided among the population that had survived within the Royce Pentagon Arena for over a year. The combined might of Cliffroyce Bay's police department and Homeland Security acted as authority figures when finding the first survivors to seek the Pentagon arena as a sanctuary. They had also kept everyone in check and fed them with the help of the few military operatives that made it through their survivor-rescuing operations before the explosions blew out New York City.

They organized systems and laws concerning curfew, usage of toilets and showers, drinking fountains and water filters to provide just enough clean water for everyone to drink at least one full bottle a day. Most of all, they divided the work and ruled that every person old enough must pull their own weight by cooking, cleaning, keeping watch, or serving the community in a number of different positions.

Transport was another major responsibility that fell in the hands of the law enforcers and scavenger hunters they allocated. With quite a number of land vehicles taking a quarter of the parking lot, the rest of the space was reserved for three helicopters that traveled back and forth between Manhattan and across the East River, as a part of the trade agreements with other sanctuaries. They used two of the three choppers to deliver weapons, ammo, and a few pharmaceuticals in exchange for freshly grown fruits and vegetables from Long Beach's quarantine zone. Precious transport fuel was growing scarcer with every mile traveled, though. Therefore, the travel had to be narrowed down to once after every three passing months a year until more fuel was obtained.

As for the third helicopter, it accompanied the scavenger team on their hunts every couple of months, to go ahead of the team and guide them—making sure that they didn't get surrounded by the undead or the bandits. And here it came, hovering above the parking lot, landing slowly and disappearing from the scavengers' sight. "Finally," Violet mumbled. "I'm in desperate need to pee, and I'm not doing it out in public again."

That earned her soft laughs from Richie and the two men in the back. "Look, the gate is opening." Richie pointed. Suddenly, two unwanted guests joined the party, slamming themselves against Violet's side window. She jerked with a sudden gasp. They'd come out of nowhere, pushing their decaying skin, still dangling from the rotting flesh, against the glass. Violet gave them the middle finger for the scare.

"They probably followed the engine noises. Don't worry. Marksman Gunter will put them down," Richie assured her.

Marksman Gunter Waters, the man who'd opened the gate, was signaling with one hand for the drivers to move in. A fifty-nine-year-old ex-military trained marksman with years of experience in hitting targets from long distances and close range self-defense, he was of average height with a squat figure. He typically wore his military boots and cap with sweatpants and a light green shirt. He carried a silencer-equipped rifle, which he took aim with through the scope. He saw the two walking corpses falling behind the fifth car as Richie drove towards the gate. "Waste of bullets," Gunter muttered aloud. "The truck will run 'em over."

VROOOM! The behemoth vehicle's engine revved, as the truck driver stepped harder on the pedal. Then, squelch went the two living corpses limping at a snail's pace. Their bodies were flattened by the six-wheeled tons of metal grinding over them. Bones crunched and guts spilled. One head flew and hit the passenger's side window. The other one burst open like a dropped watermelon. The aftermath looked like human-sized cockroaches had gotten squashed by a giant boot until they were reduced into a big repulsive mess of insect fluids and slimy goo.

20

SCARS

NIGHT 494

Violet stepped out of the shower, wrapped a towel around her body, and scurried towards the lockers for women, which, in the old days, had been reserved for sports players competing in the Pentagon arena in front of thousands of attendants. She hauled out her same old backpack from one of the lockers and extracted her undergarments. Violet slipped on her bra and panties and then folded the towel over her head and around her hair in a cottony capsule to dry it.

She stared at the reflection of her half-naked body, thoroughly examining it from chest to waist. Yes, still skinny, but not anorexic skinny. Her body had been this way even before she started wrestling. Practicing the sport had given her stronger muscles without making them outwardly bigger. She could still see that in her reflection. It made her happy.

Her freckled face grew pale on some days. Today it was not, especially after the refreshing shower she'd just taken. The bags under her leafy green eyes were becoming more visible, however. All she needed was some rest. And Violet was on her way to get it if it hadn't been for the reminiscence of scars she bore, that delayed her movement.

Her neck looked fine, creamy as always. Arms and legs showed no signs of even the slightest bruises or scratches. Her stomach was tucked in nicely but her abs didn't show a "six-pack". There were no scars visible on her body. Not from the outside, anyway. Without blinking she stared deep into her own eyes and remembered the wounds that deformed her on the inside over a year back. In that alley, she remembered how it had felt to be forced down against her will. On her father's boat, she remembered the blast of the gun that she had fired to spill her father's brains out. Then she remembered holding onto the small fragment of her cannibalized younger brother.

Violet shuddered from the memories. She'd lost a lot on that dreadful day: her home, her friend, her family, and more. But she lived on, and she did not do it alone. She had her dear friend, Richie Morey, with her. The thought of him stilled the tremors and made her feel glad of his presence. So she walked away from the mirror to put on a white nightgown. The gown bared her arms completely and hung down to her knees. It shimmered slightly, causing a vague sense of déjà vu.

Then her dark brown locks came tumbling down, like a waterfall of silk, when she loosened the towel that incubated it. It stopped at the center of her back. She gathered it to her left side and brushed it out carefully. A yawn forced itself out. Another girl, changing, noticed.

"You ought to go get some sleep, Violet. Got a long night ahead of you."

Violet didn't even look at her. She kept on brushing her hair and said, "Yep, just readying myself for bed."

"We both know that bed is not *all* you're readying yourself for," the girl said accusingly.

FEAR IN FLESH

Violet responded with a sarcastically shady smile, looking over her shoulder. She brushed her hair until it was straight and glossy from the moisture still being absorbed. She then took out a small black notebook from her backpack and began scribbling with a black pen:

Hands and legs were trembling, goosebumps on my back and a hazy memory of what the dream was about. It was the same damn feeling from just over a year ago ... when everything fell apart. Don't know who else around the world are recording their daily routines and interesting events and changes, but someone in Cliffroyce should keep track of the constant changes in history around here. So whoever might be reading this in the future, in a better world ... know that all that's written here is truly madness, yes, but no lie. How I wish it all were, but none of it is. This is written by a survivor, Violet Turner, on night 494 ... still alive in Royce Pentagon Sanctuary.

21

READY FOR BED

NIGHT 494

Richie turned off the shower and emerged with a towel wrapped around his hips while a smaller one enveloped his hair. He rubbed his head with it vigorously, making a mess of his waterlogged curls. He then scrubbed water off his upper body while his hair fell over his eyes and curled down to his broad shoulders. His fit build had taken a turn for the better over this past year; pecs of steel and ripped abdominal muscles strained his clothes whenever he bent to pick up something heavy. All this came from the hours of training that prepared the brave men and women who volunteered to go out there and salvage tools necessary for survival, wandering the streets with overgrown shrubs, rubbish, tarnished cars, and—of course—man-eating fiends.

The fittest were most likely to survive out there, but one clumsy mistake could lead to an infectious bite, which would then lead to a quick kill by the teammates. That is *if* the bitten was able to escape the monster's jaw at all. The worst fate was to face a slow, agonizing death by teeth peeling the skin off of the body and chewing the flesh piece by piece, limb by limb, till the body was a pile of fractured bones.

Richie was one of the fortunate ones to have made it back in one piece from all the scavenger trips he'd participated in. Now, an expert in a variety of defense techniques, with and without a weapon, he'd lost count of the dozens of corpses he'd sent back to their graves during his time outside the walls of Royce Pentagon Sanctuary.

Richie slapped on some shaving cream on his cheeks and above his lips. With a small razor, he carefully shaved off the little facial hair he had growing untidily as if he'd just hit puberty.

A man strolling into the locker room saw Richie and stopped. "Hey, man. What are you shaving for?" he asked mockingly. "You barely even have any facial hair."

As Richie created another clear path through the white foam, he said, "I know. That's why I'm shaving it otherwise it'll grow thicker and bushier, just like my head. I'm just hoping it doesn't grow as curly and messy. Then I'd have to shave like ... twice every week."

"I gotta tell you, man, having facial hair can be a pain. Especially during the summer, when it gets itchy. Most of the time, you wanna scrap it off with the skin still attached. Trust me, Richie, it's better for you this way. But don't shave too often. By the way, thanks for having my back today—out there when the corpses showed up. I had no problem taking out the first two guys, but that kid, man ... she didn't even look old enough to walk! I just couldn't bash her head in, man. I know it ain't wrong, but ... it wouldn't have felt right either. Sorry, you had to do it instead of me."

Richie stopped shaving. "Look, Elliot, there's no need to apologize. We know how hard it is out there. You just have to keep in mind that *none* of it is right. What happened to those people, that little girl out there ... it's all wrong. None of it is natural. And we have to keep doing what we're doing to stay alive, by whatever means necessary. Think of it this way," Richie went on, "The sickness takes over their brain and turns them into skin-eating, walking decomposing corpses. What if somehow the human part in them is still in there? Inside somewhere, feeling the pain of their rotting body, begging to be killed. And that's what we do. We put a bullet in their head or bash their skulls open to put them out of their misery."

"But what if the scientists up in Long Beach and Washington and … wherever else, figure out the source of this disease and invent a vaccine?"

"This 'vaccine' may help keep us immune from turning when bitten," Richie said. "I highly doubt that it'll be able to save the ones who've already turned. Even if it could imagine how *they* would feel about the way they look, with most of their muscle tissue gone and skin peeled off. Or a missing body part. I bet it'd sting like hell!"

"Guess you're right," Elliot said with a sigh. "Anyways, me and some of the guys are celebrating our successful return today with beer. You and Violet are more than welcome to join us."

"Thanks, man, but I think I'm gonna have to pass on drinking tonight. Need to get some sleep before my shift with Violet starts at midnight."

"Right, you guys are on watch tonight. Looks like you're in for a long one. Night's pretty chilly. Make sure you have jackets."

"You know it," Richie said, wiping off the last of the shaving cream and then dressing for bed. He wore a white, X-large T-shirt with red baggy pants. He then left the locker-room and headed for the stadium.

On his way, he encountered numerous looks and caught some whispers concerning him. A few flashed him smiles, as he walked past them, and a small group of young ladies waiting in line by the water fountain exchanged looks when they saw him. "That's one of the hunters," one said in a not so quiet whisper.

"One of the cute ones," another added. "Wonder if he's single."

Richie put on a sweet expression as he walked away, shouldering his backpack. He passed a group of men, who offered him high fives, thanking him for what he'd done that day in the face of danger. He felt like a celebrity—more of a superhero than the slim nerd he'd always been. Joining the hunting team came with a hero rank and he loved it. *Should have come up with a superhero nickname by now,* Richie thought, with a nod to his nerdy self still kicking beneath his soldier-like body.

When Richie got to the arena, he trotted through the open space filled with yards and yards of camping tents in various shapes, sizes, and colors. The benches weren't as crowded with tents but still, they held additional people. Mostly, people sat on the arena benches or lay across a few with pillows, quilts, and sleeping bags as their primary source of comfort.

The walk among the maze of tents seemed endless. The people's chatter was a tad too loud, but the children's laughter was delightful to hear. People had slowly gotten used to living inside, resuming their daily activities as best as possible, forgetting about the horror roaming outside the walls. Soon a whistle would put an end to the chatter and laughter, indicating the beginning of curfew, which meant that the early morning workers could sleep in peace and quiet.

Richie paused in front of a small blue tent to take a quick peek inside. In there she lay, underneath the zebra-striped sheets. Her dark brown hair spread majestically over a white pillow. Her eyes were closed. He went in as quietly as he could. She sensed his presence anyway and opened her eyes. "What took you so long? I've been so sleepy waiting for you," Violet said while she folded her cover back and gave a yawn of exhaustion.

"Sorry," apologized Richie. "Got caught up talking with the new guy Elliot in the locker room." He dropped next to her under the covers. So close, they could feel each other's body heat. They got even closer and exchanged a kiss.

Violet pulled away after a few seconds of passion. "That's enough for now," she said. "We have to sleep. Only four hours till our shift begins." Then she turned away, and Richie gently held her lean body, cuddling into a spooning position. He gave her one last kiss on her bare shoulder and wished her sweet dreams.

Nothing is ever sweet about them, was what she wanted to say but dared not disturb her drowsy state. "Yeah ... sweet, sweet dreams," Violet said back to him tenderly. Then she closed her leafy-green eyes, submitting her mind to darkness.

22

MIDNIGHT SHIFT

NIGHT 495

The digital alarm clock buzzed at 12:00 am and Violet emerged from her deep slumber and slammed a palm on top of the buzzing clock to shut it up. The same palm went inside her backpack and brought out her diary. Inside, the pen was placed between two pages as a bookmarker. The left page was almost completely full of words and figures; the right page was empty. She added *Day 495 ...* before placing the pen back in the center of the book. Violet tapped, gently, with her fist on Richie's bicep lying across her body. "Time for work, Richie get up," Richie responded with a husky snore. His head was half on her pillow, curly hair all mussed. "Wake up, Richie," she tried again, and he snored back another reply.

With a scoff, Violet rolled her eyes and heaved herself from beneath the hypnotically warm covers, and she did so without being swift or quiet like a ninja. Her violent movement made Richie breath in a snort. "What's going on?" he asked drowsily.

"We're under attack," Violet joked with her normal snarky tone. But Richie's still fuzzy state of mind did not process Violet's joke as such. He kicked the sheets off, grabbed the shotgun, and checked its cylinder.

"Zombies breached the arena?" Richie asked, shocked. He knew he was a heavy sleeper, but not so heavy that he would sleep through gunshots, high-pitched screaming, and loud groaning. After all, Royce Pentagon Sanctuary carried almost half the remaining population of Cliffroyce Bay.

"Sheesh! Easy there, Kill-shot: it was only a joke—and a bad one at that. I was being sarcastic. But I guess your sleepy head didn't quite process that."

"Seriously, Vi?" he asked, astonished.

"Yeah, sorry, Mr. Kill-shot. Won't happen again." She meant it sincerely, but her whimsical smile acknowledged that it wasn't the first time, nor would it be the last.

Richie breathed a sigh of relief and fell back on the pillows again. "You scared the crap out of me," he admitted as he laid the gun carefully aside and snuggled back underneath the velvety soft covers.

"You need to get dressed. Our shift has already started," Violet said as she stripped out of her nightgown, gaining Richie's undivided attention. She then slipped on a pair of jeans, her skin showing through from the thighs down to the knees from the ripped sewing design. She was about to put on a shirt when she caught Richie staring at her from under the sheets. "Hurry up and get dressed, perv," she scolded him.

✶ ✶ ✶

The wind was whistling in the chilly night. Violet's hair fluttered across, in waves, in the direction of the wind. Richie's curls flew across his eyes, partly blocking his sight and covering most of his still-drowsy face. Both sat in lawn chairs atop one of the six watchtowers on the pentagon-shaped stadium walls that overlooked the outside. Both consumed spoons full of canned green beans while flashing a large circular searchlight to bring them a slight view of the west where Cliffroyce business district and midtown was barely visible. This was in an effort to keep the grim memories locked away yet retaining the tenderness of some of them, though maybe not far and definitely not forever, when they stayed up late to watch over the ruin that was once their home.

The Pentagon arena was their home now, and since *that* day, Richie and Violet had barely even spoken of Marvin. Their deepest and darkest secrets found a way of pouring themselves out into one another. Violet knew everything about Richie, including his long-term crush on her in their past life. And Richie knew everything important about Violet, except for her grisly dreams. She herself still doubted the significance of them and didn't feel ready to attempt to convince Richie of that supernatural curse upon her. He might suspect that a creature of madness had possessed her mind after she had to shoot her zombie-turned father. Then maybe he wouldn't have taken care of her the way he had for over a year now.

It was Richie who had nursed her back to a healthy state of mind, with time. He had sat by her side and given her a shoulder to cry on whenever the images from Gavin's boat or the alleyway rape surfaced in her mind. His arms were there to embrace her whenever she woke up screaming or gasping for air from the nightmares that consumed her from the inside. He would calm her down and run his fingers through her hair, caressing her tensions away, ridding her of distress. He was her sworn knight in shining armor who protected her from that day forth. Richie was no longer afraid of the infected, and neither was Violet. They were *the* surviving couple of this rising-dead Armageddon.

Violet set the can of green beans down and zipped up her red jacket after she felt the chilling intensity of the night's breeze. She blew some heat into her clenched fingers and then rubbed them under the jacket's sleeves. She turned to Richie who was just pulling his gray hood over his head. "Has anything ever happened to you in real life that you were absolutely, positively sure you saw happen in a dream?" Violet asked.

Richie shrugged and answered in a low register, "Um... does becoming your boyfriend count?"

"C'mon, Romeo," Violet teased. "You know I already love you. No need to dump that chick-flick romance crap on me. Answer the question properly this time. Dreams, like when you're asleep."

He sniggered and turned to look at her with a puzzled expression. His eyebrows were raised. He bit his lower lip and said, "I really don't know. Can't even remember what I dreamt of last time I had a dream. Honestly, I can't even remember *when* I last had a dream." A pause followed, and then Richie asked, "What brought up a strange question like that?"

Violet hesitated to speak the truth to the person whom she'd come to know not only as her best friend and protector but as her soul mate. Her predicament was complicated and paranormal, making it difficult to understand it even for her. If she were to present Richie with the truth, she must be surer than ever. There must be some evidence so she could believe it herself. *If* there was any reasonable evidence.

"Just something outside of the box, I thought of to start up a conversation. And since it has failed, now it's your turn. Go on now, intrigue me," Violet challenged.

"Don't really have anything... err... *intriguing* to say." He sounded tired still. "Not enough sleep," he yawned. "Any more of your... out-of-the-box questions? Maybe the next one'll get me more engaged."

Violet took a moment to think. "Nah, I got nothin'."

"Did your question about the dreams have anything to do with the nightmares you have so often?" Richie asked after actually processing her question. "Today in the car, when I woke you up, what did you dream about?"

She exhaled a mist of warm breath before she spoke. "Foggy ... can't remember a thing, but I can't help shake off this bad feeling since I woke up from it." *Do I tell him now? Would he believe me as much as I believe it?* "I don't know what to tell ya, Rich, but we need to be prepared in case something horrible happens." *I don't want him thinking his girlfriend's gone insane! But the least I can do is get him ready for the worst.* "We should have our most important stuff ready after our shift ends. You know—all in one place."

"All our important belongings *are* in one place," Richie said. "In that stuffy tent of ours, we call a bedroom. You're so worked up—all from a dream you had during a nap. C'mon, seriously, Vi? We're here to keep anything 'horrible' *from* happening, not to pack our stuff and run away from it."

I haven't even told him of the insane part about those dreams yet and he already suspects I'm crazy and a coward, too! I should change the subject. Talk about…

"You're right." She ended the conversation to start a new one. Only her head was filled with air that blew as hollow as the night's chilly gusts. An awkward silence followed for a moment, and then an echoing noise joined the conversation suddenly. Both were startled at the peace-disturbing sound from down below. It was either something falling down loudly or ramming against metal. Their ears couldn't quite discern between the two because of how quickly the noise stopped.

Richie twisted and turned the shinning cube of light from right to left, left to right, as far as the glow could stretch. The beam traveled along the sanctuary walls and far beyond the structure, revealing nothing but immobile vehicles and mildly overgrown shrubs.

"Do you see anything?" Violet asked, standing up, pistol ready, focusing on each item the shaft of light illuminated yet unsure, that her sight was sharp enough to detect movements in the dark.

"No," Richie said. "No one's out there. Not even zombies. Maybe just animals?" he speculated. "Or … h-hold on is that …" Richie paused when he spotted a shrub moving oddly. He concentrated the ray of light on the bush, and a shadowy outline appeared in the glow cast behind the bush. The shadow of the figure moved. It held something up. The beam of light highlighted a person dressed in black, wearing a pig's face for a mask, aiming a machine gun at the watchtower. "*Get down*!" Richie yelled. Gunshots thundered from the machine gun. The cue ball of light died. The glass that shielded the bulb inside exploded, pouring shards of glass down below. Richie veered away and forced Violet to duck down underneath him between the lawn chairs.

Bullets fired off in a frenzy, igniting wails of terror inside the arena walls. Richie and Violet stayed low as the rapid gunfire blew tiny bullet holes in the chairs' cloth. "*Violet, reach for your pistol, NOW!*" Richie ordered over the machine gun's clamor.

"*I already got it!*" Violet yelled back.

The machine gun stopped. "Start climbing down the post, and let's head to the tent!" Richie said. "I don't have many rounds. We're going to need our ammo."

Violet nodded and then crawled her way down the ladder, with

Richie immediately following her. Once they reached the stadium's top benches, they witnessed the chaos: masks of many colors and shapes covered the faces of the invaders with their guns defiling the peace and laying anarchy upon the innocent residents of Royce Pentagon Sanctuary.

23

THE HAPPENING

NIGHT 495

BANG! BLAM! BRATTA-TA-TA-TA!

Bullets exploded through the arena, cutting through the crowds running down the steps for their lives, heading for the inner stadium doors. It was an all-out war. Everywhere, people were dropping like flies. None were safe, neither the frantic residents of the sanctuary nor the masked invaders that kept pursuing the crowd.

Running, screaming, and pushing their way down into the new battlefield, some were attempting to escape while others were running towards the fight with their firearms, shooting back at the enemies invading their home. Some lost their footing or were shot and rolled down the steps to their doom. Some shielded themselves with their belongings, and others cowered inside their tents and under the seats.

Children were being carried in the arms of rescuing adults or, sometimes, shoved aside from a runner to be trampled over. Cries of fear and wails of agony became louder than the gunshots. The tents and arena grounds ran red from the blood of innocent survivors: men, women, and children. It made no difference to the ambushers—the famous Masked Rebels of Cliffroyce Bay everyone wanted to avoid when being out in town.

Tonight, a band of misfits and thieves, murderers and ex-convicts of all backgrounds, when law and order had played a role in keeping the likes of these evildoers off the streets, destroyed the sanctuary. The Masked Rebels formed only to loot, hunt, and kill other survivors they came across. And tonight, they had reached Cliffroyce Bay's largest populated sanctuary. In a world where law and order no longer existed, what was there to stop them other than the residents of the sanctuary themselves?

The arena had six entrance gates, along with a vast parking lot area. "The bandits could have breached through one, two, three, or all of the six gates, from the looks of it." Richie analyzed the situation on the way down the benches. The mystery of how the Masked Rebel band had infiltrated the arena despite the security perimeter and armed watchers below and above remained unsolved. No horns sounded the alarm. No flare guns shone over the black sky. None of the watchers had the chance to alert the residents of the approaching danger. The massacre continued as voices rang out excruciatingly as though cruel flames licked at them from all corners.

Richie and Violet were stepping through a graveyard after escaping the stadium benches without getting shot. On the arena grounds, they fired a couple of blind shots at the masked faces, watching their step to avoid stomping on the dead bodies of their former neighbors until they reached their tent. Richie disappeared into the tent, but Violet stopped to look at the neighboring tent to their left. In front of it sat a little boy on his knees, hands over his eyes, sobbing.

Violet knew him. Kenny rode on his bicycle all over the arena grounds most of the day. Only six years old, but he was kneeling in a puddle of blood that wasn't his. Kenny cried with tears pouring down his face and snot out his nose. His face was painted as red as the puddle of blood he knelt in. It came from the wounds in his father's no-longer-recognizable face. It was an image so awfully disturbing: a little boy whimpering over his father's gored corpse in the midst of mayhem. Alone, scared, and now fatherless.

Richie was still inside the tent fumbling in his and Violet's backpacks for ammo when he called, "Violet, where are you?" and then sticking his head out of the tent to find her on the ground embracing little Kenny next to the body of his father, shielding his eyes from the sight.

"Get our backpacks ready quick, Rich," Violet demanded. "Stuff whatever's outside in them, and let's get the hell—" Suddenly gunshots came so close that Violet ducked automatically, taking Kenny down with her. Richie went all the way down as well, but not before targeting their shooter: a woman wearing a panda mask. She held up a nine-millimeter revolver and aimed it at Richie, who had his shotgun nestled underneath him. No time to draw it out, he took aim and shot at her while being on his belly before she could shoot him, both missing.

Violet, however, was even faster on her belly. She drew her pistol out from underneath her and shot in a flash. At the same moment, the panda-masked girl pulled the trigger, but her aim was off while Violet's bullet went through her core. Panda face shot her revolver senselessly in their direction, no longer able to take a precise aim.

BANG! The bullet burnt a hole in their tent.

BANG! The second bullet came close to Violet and Kenny, but missed and hit the tent behind them.

BANG! The third and the last bullet she was able to shoot, as she fell down to one knee, met a living target. Kenny's little head sprayed blood onto Violet's face and jacket, staining the latter almost black.

After seeing what the third shot had done, Richie wasted no more time staying low. One blast of the shotgun and the panda-masked murderer was sent flying backward a couple of feet, landing on an even smaller tent than theirs. Violet did not hear the gun's blast. She did not hear the numerous shootings around her in the arena. She did not hear the peoples' cries anymore.

She stared traumatizingly into Kenny's soulless blue eyes. He was still in her arms. The top of his head still dripped blood from the deep bullet wound that had killed him in an instant. Violet did not cry or check for more masked shooters lurking nearby while holding the small innocent in her arms.

Once she managed to let go, Kenny's body slipped from her grasp, and only his skinny arm stayed on her lap. *Billy's lacerated arm!* Violet's heart raced, and her breathing became heavy. Her eardrums almost popped from the thunderous din of reality returning, but her eyes did not adjust yet. Her surroundings went black. *The dark place!* She was so lightheaded from the powerful reek of blood, and the shock, that it felt as though she were bobbing on a watery surface. *A red boat, there was.* Her eyes stared straight ahead at a swarm of silvery glittering objects flying at her way in the darkness. *The storm of bullets!*

Violet was blinded by the vivid red-filled memories from the blackest corners of her mind. *No, no, no! It's happening!* Richie sprang to the rescue just before the storm could take her. He yanked her towards him in front of their tent when a green troll face started shooting in their direction with his submachine gun. The deceased bodies of Kenny and his father got pierced by the storm when Violet was moved at the last second.

The shooter was covered with blood from the slaughter of his victims, and Violet was able to remember the last remaining piece in the puzzle that she *did not* want to believe fit in the gaps. *The red man!*

24

TROLL HUNTERS

NIGHT 495

The red man from her dream was a combination of two beings: the troll-mask-wearing rebel who currently unleashed a fury of bullets, and her father who'd tried to eat her alive on the red bow of his boat over a year ago.

The wave of bullets missed their target, but they did not stop coming. The green-and-red faced troll, with an unsettling grin emphasizing the rubber of the mask's yellow pointed fangs, did not take his finger off the trigger. He only shifted his aim towards the tent, firing a rain of bullets that punctured the blue cloth. They penetrated easily and hit the tent in front of it, trapping Richie and Violet in the middle.

The gunfire was drumming sharply, but the pain of a bullet grazing Richie's left shoulder and another one against his triceps was far sharper. Red stained his gray cotton hoodie, and Richie staggered from the stinging pain. He growled in frustration. Violet saw the blood and was infuriated. She raised her pistol above the tent and shot three times blindly. Whether any of the three shots hit the troll or not, Violet did not know.

When Richie realized that the submachine gun was no longer firing and heard the *click* of the barrel, he knew, he knew that the troll had run out of ammo.

Violet took cover again and turned to Richie. "Give me the shotgun! I missed and I'm all out." Richie did not comply. He would not risk her life if he was still able to stand and move his right arm to shoot the bulky shotgun. "No, Richie!" Violet said as Richie rose.

He saw the troll busy reloading the gun. Richie took quick, unsteady aim and pulled the trigger—and almost stumbled from the force of the blow missing the masked man by a long shot. The clumsy gun blast alerted the rebel to take cover behind a tent. Richie balanced himself and shot again, only to blow a hole through the roof of the tent. Richie cursed as the recoil of the second shot hit him harder than the first. It took him backward, towards the ground. The troll face reappeared and started shooting again as he walked forward, heading closer and closer, finger glued to the trigger.

The submachine gun's barrel rattled on. BRATTA-TA-TA-TA!

Violet had no time to go inside the tent to reload her pistol with ammo from her backpack. She crawled speedily towards Richie and the shotgun.

BRATTA-TA-TA-TA! The submachine gun was suddenly silenced.

BLAM! A shot took the Masked Rebel in the side of his head, bringing the sadistically grinning troll to the same fate he'd handed to so many before running into Violet and Richie. Although, it was neither Violet nor Richie who were able to bring him down.

Violet sat on her knees, shotgun pointed, finger nowhere near the trigger, when a tall scrawny figure came rushing in—a rifle with smoke still puffing from the muzzle in his hands. It was Elliot, the newly recruited hunter, who stopped closer to Violet. "Are you guys okay?" he asked, shifting his brown eyes rapidly between the blood-saturated Violet and a bleeding Richie.

"Richie got shot," Violet said anxiously.

"Not shot! Don't be so dramatic," Richie said through gritted teeth, trying to sound fine. "Just got scratched ... no big deal, I'll walk it off." He sat up slowly, feeling the stinging pain as he moved and then he felt some dizziness. Violet rolled up his sleeve quickly but gently. Richie hissed from the stabs that felt like tiny knives poking through the gashes.

"Let's get him inside the tent," Violet said to Elliot.

Inside, Violet ripped one of Richie's shirts in two and wrapped them firmly around the gashes.

"He needs to get stitched up. My dad has a medical kit in his car," Elliot said. "The inner stadium facilities aren't safe; rebels are already inside. It may not be practical to make it to the medic room with only Richie's bullet scratches to worry about—*if* we could even get there in one piece."

Violet looked as if she wasn't even listening, so caught up she was in packing Richie's and her backpacks in a hurry, even so, she heard.

"Nowhere is safe around here anymore, Elliot. Do you have the keys to your dad's car?"

"No, he does."

"Where is he then?"

"Where he always is ... the parking lot."

Violet handed Elliot her pistol and box of ammo. "Load it up," she told him. "We're running to the parking lot as fast as we can. You hold onto Richie, and I'll shoot the ones that get in our way." She clenched the barrel of Richie's shotgun to demonstrate her stance.

25

PARKING HAVOC

NIGHT 495

A horn blew amidst all the shootings and the screaming. It was meant to alert the residents of an emergency, but it was far too late. None were ready. None took precautions. Many died and others were still being shot dead in cold blood. And many still fled with their children and their belongings.

It was in the vast parking area that they found the lucky escapees who'd made it. This area had suffered minor shooting when the first bunch of invaders pried their way in through the gate, only to be put down by veteran marksman Gunter. Thanks to his military experience and an eagle eye, he had to pull the trigger only once for each masked infiltrator. Five out of six fell with bleeding head wounds. One was apprehended by other watchers and stabbed to death.

As of yet, not a single rebel had made it through the gate since the watchers had acted quickly and locked it again with steel chains. The watchers picked up their firearms to go aid the rest, but they didn't make it far before a torrent of fleeing survivors came pouring into the parking lot, pushing the backup back out.

Gunter looked through in his vicinity, checking for any masked faces among the panicking crowd that had just arrived. "Oh crap," he muttered. In addition to having to worry about more Masked Rebels breaching the sanctuary, residents were crowding inside the vehicles to drive out of the gate. A few law enforcers were trying to calm the hysteria because they were inside the stadium fighting off the rebels, if not dead.

"They're killing everyone inside!" a woman cried.

"My baby! Help me find my baby, *please!*" another woman bellowed.

"You don't understand, they're already everywhere inside! You have to open the gate. We have to leave, *now!*"

In mere minutes, the crowd had increased immensely, and none could prevent them from forcing themselves into cars, buses, and vans. Two of the three helicopters were soon airborne: one above the arena and the other outside, behind the parking gate. Both choppers opened fire on the attackers. Rebels shot back. Soon one helicopter's propellers began glittering with sparks that kindled a blaze, which sent the flyer twirling uncontrollably, away from the building and into the dark desolation of Cliffroyce Bay.

KABOOM! The explosion took the shape of an unearthly fireball that glowed at least two miles from the Royce Pentagon Sanctuary, discouraging the second chopper from pressing the attack. It chose the coward's way out, flying away, out of reach and out of sight.

Gunter caught three individuals treading in confusion from car to car—Violet and Richie with half his arm around Elliot's shoulder. Gunter lowered the rifle and trotted towards them. "Are you all right?" Gunter asked without directing the question to any of the three in particular.

"Richie's been shot, Dad. He's bleeding badly. We need to get him stitched up," Elliot said.

"Your car, Gunter," Violet cut in. "We need that medical kit in your car."

They were standing not far from the gate. The thumping on the gate had become more violent. Gunter lost his words over all the terrible noise, but he found them again the minute the shooting erupted louder than ever. "Here, start the car." Gunter handed Elliot the keys and then hefted the rifle up to aim at where the crowd came from and shot one bullet at the masks that covered the faces of two rebels which splattered blood as it went through their temples. "What are you waiting for? *Go!*" He yelled at the three as they stood amazed.

"What about you?" Elliot demanded.

"I'm right behind you. Now, *move, God damn it!*"

They ran. Gunter pulled the trigger silently once more, putting down a gorilla Masked Rebel that was veering their way. Then Gunter ran behind them to catch up.

Engines roared and tires screeched their way through the chain-sealed gate. The chains broke loose easily, allowing the gate to spread wide open. Behind the gate, the anxiously waiting mob of Masked Rebels were skirmishing against the third army, late to join the war—the army of the living dead.

Masked faces and walking carcasses went flying atop of car hoods. Meat and bones squashed and broke underneath the tires. Drivers were determined not to stop nor slow down. They broke out in fright and focused on getting as far as possible from the death sentence that had come upon their sanctuary. Inside one of the many cars that had raced out that gate, Elliot was at the wheel while Gunter stitched up Richie in the backseat.

Violet sat uncomfortably in the front seat, looking through her side mirror at the reflection of Royce Pentagon Sanctuary, her and Richie's home—no longer a sanctuary from anything. A plague far worse than the one that birthed the undead had come: the plague of corrupt men, the spawns of the demon of greed. But this home had not fallen to dust and ashes just yet. It only stood taken from them and all who had helped to make it a home.

26

STRANDED

DAY 501

The clouds dispersed. No longer did they provide shade from the glowing ball of heat smiling down upon earth that day. The sun cast its beams of light freely on the paths of destruction wending their way through the town. Wind, swept down the empty highway between two vacant patches of sandy landscapes that stretched endless miles north, heading towards the wilderness-like parts of town. The sun's beams struck the group of four survivors traveling by car: war veteran and his nineteen-year-old son in front, Violet and Richie in the back.

That is, they *had* been traveling by car. Now they pushed the fuel-empty vehicle along the road. Foreheads dripped sweat from the combination of exhaustive labor and the afternoon's warm sun overpowering the wind. Those wearing jackets had taken them off and either left them inside the car or wrapped them neatly around their waist, like Violet did, exposing her pink tank top, which made her feel a little bit insecure from the sweat stains forming in the back and front. But at least it was less hot and sweaty than wearing her smelly blood-drenched jacket.

FEAR IN FLESH

The fuel tank had run out of gas about six miles back. They had pushed with diminishing hope until they ran into a road sign that indicated only three more miles north for a gas station. Since then, they had quickened their pace. No more breaks to consume the last remaining ounces of canned food and water, hoping that once they reached the gas station there'd be a still-not-raided minimart or vending machine or anything at all. Just something for them to restock with and someplace safe for them to shelter in for the night. After all, they had seen their fair share of wildlife during these past miles—coyotes, vultures, snakes—and lord knew what else was out there with them. Better wild animals than having to worry about the dead lurking beside them in those long dry dunes of sand, all four agreed.

They'd had to endure almost a week in the heart of Cliffroyce's ruins, running into living corpses out seeking red lumps of flesh. Their days and nights were full of staying put and running scared, keeping their eyes on every bush, car, and corner they passed.

They were the prey. They were the breakfast, lunch, and dinner on wheels. Mostly they kept themselves locked inside Gunter's car that had almost a quarter tank of gas, which kept them going thanks to the half-full bottle of petrol he kept in the glove compartment. They only went out during the day when they *thought* the coast was clear for them to scavenge for more food, water, or shelter. Each time they ended up with the same outcome, although they managed to snag some food here and there. Always they had to retreat to the car whenever the ghastly howls sounded loud and close.

They were stranded now on an open road with no buildings or walls to block their view, nor any vehicles or even bushes to hide corpses sneaking up on them when they stopped to do their business on the flat sandy terrain with speckles of rocks and cactuses everywhere.

"We're almost there," Gunter assured them. "I think we've got less than a mile to keep pushing."

"Let's hope so. I'm so thirsty, I'm starting to drink up my own sweat," Richie said with utter exhaustion and disgust.

"At this rate, I might even settle for drinking my own pee if I had to. We oughta start training anyhow. We each probably have two days' worth of water left by now." Violet joked about facing even harsher circumstances to lighten the tone, even though it didn't make her feel any better. Nothing would do that: it was still too soon for all of them, Violet especially. She saw no use in continuing to grieve, but it almost felt wrong to feel good or be merry at such an early stage. *Staying like that won't keep us alive,* Violet thought. *It won't hurt to crack a smile now and then.* "Just pray that there will be an actual minimart out there—untouched."

"Don't forget about the gas," Elliot added.

"Yeah, that too," Violet said.

The car suddenly halted when Gunter pulled up the parking brake up without any warning. Elliot, Richie, and Violet bumped into the car, surprised by its sudden resistance. Curses flew along with the demands of why Gunter had stopped the car. He only drew out his rifle and aimed northward.

"What's the matter, Dad? Do you see corpses nearby?" Elliot scanned the same area through his own rifle's scope.

"Only two."

Elliot saw them himself. "We can take 'em out along the way."

Gunter lowered his rifle but continued gazing north. "We can't be too sure that there are only two till we get closer. Like I said, we got less than a mile to reach the gas station." He released the parking brake again, and they resumed pushing.

The image of the two wandering corpses limping awkwardly was much more easily spotted without the use of a rifle scope.

"I'm gonna stop the car now," Gunter announced this time before pulling up the parking brake. Elliot sat inside on the passenger seat to rest, and Richie and Violet leaned over the trunk to catch their breath and wipe off some of their sweat with their jackets. Gunter climbed atop the hood of the car to get a better view. Way beyond the two lost corpses, he was able to see the gas station and all that surrounded it. Full of the living dead.

"Do you see anything out there, Gunter?" Richie asked.

"Remember how you explained your theory one time after you came back from a scavenger hunt, Richie? About how the zombies could actually communicate with each other? Gunter asked while scouting through his rifle scope.

"Yeah, it's like … whenever we encounter a very small number of zombies in a large area, I expect a herd to be nearby, waiting for the pair that drifted away to run into prey and make them cause as much noise as possible. Then the rest of the herd hears and comes limping. That's why we mostly run into them gathered in larger groups these days because nowadays, wherever you go, there's usually quiet. They groan all the time, so once they hear each other, they stay and walk next to each other without tearing one another apart 'cause it's counterintuitive otherwise as their numbers ensure their strength as a group while the sounds help them move—gives them a sense of direction."

"*Yeah*, would've been more than enough of an answer. But you called it. You can see for yourself." Gunter offered Richie the rifle.

"Whaddaya think?"

Richie, mesmerized, couldn't find the right words—or any words at all—when his eye caught the giant colony of stirring carcasses. Once he lowered the rifle scope from his eye, he kept looking north and said, "Now, that is one ... big ass herd up there. I dunno how the hell we are gonna ... or *if* we can even get close to that station. It's fully swarmed!"

"We gotta think of something," Gunter responded. "You're the expert here. Can't you figure out a way to clear the path for us to quickly move in and scavenge the station?"

"That's the problem. It was hard enough to distract those walking rot-bags even when we were in teams of twenty or more hunters. This time we're up against an army with not enough soldiers or weaponry to back us up!"

"Well, we need to think fast," Elliot said, "because the two 'scouting' zombies might be sensing our presence. They're headed this way." He pointed.

"Keep talking in that register, and they'll start running this way," Violet said. "Now, let's go take care of them, Elliot. You take baldy, and I'll handle the topless damsel in distress."

Violet lunged to face the sickly corpses up close and personal. She drew out a lethal machete from a black leather sheath she had strapped around her right thigh and dodged the grab attempt of the bald zombie. She walked straight up to the nude female with her breasts sloughed off, baring her entire ribcage. Elliot was running right behind her with a hammer in his hand.

The bald corpse missed Violet and met the pointy end of the hammer, that's normally used for removing nails, with his skull, and it penetrated deep. Then came Violet's turn. With one swing of the machete, the female corpse's head went flying clean off her shoulders. It landed in the dirt, not far from the rest of its body, groaning, with still-clenched rotten teeth.

Violet then hammered the machete right into the middle of the head, attempting to slice it in half like a melon. The machete got wedged only halfway into the bone structure; nevertheless, the zombie's head groaned no more. Violet started tugging the jammed weapon, loose. Sounds of a liquidized substance mixed with the crunching of the bones accompanied the freeing of her machete.

The machete dripped a trail of extra dark blood on the sand, as Violet walked back to the car. "Well, we don't have to worry about those two messengers telling on us anymore," she announced. "Say, do you guys see a minimart over there?"

Gunter said, "Yep, but lots of zombies are already inside. And that's very bad since I can tell from *way* over here." He lowered the rifle, looked at Violet, and then back at Richie. "So, what's our plan now, scavengers? Do we fight? Or do we keep moving and ignore the possibility of gas, food, and water, and let nature take us out in the next week or so?"

Violet and Richie exchanged conflicted looks, not knowing what the answer should be even after Gunter had made it so perfectly clear to them. It was fear that clouded their decision. No. They couldn't back out now. They were the experts. They should think of something. It was now or never. But what if they risked their lives and found nothing at all for their efforts?

Still ... better nothing than regret and a lingering death, the two expert scavengers thought as if reading each other's minds.

"I think we don't really have a choice," Richie finally said after a few seconds' quiet thinking. "The wise decision would be to keep moving, but we will probably die of thirst if we do. The stupid decision is to fight that many zombies with only four people and very limited ammo, but unfortunately, it's also the right decision."

"So, we'll go with plan A: we fight," Violet concurred. "And if we're gonna fight, then we'll have to be extra clever when doing so. They might be slow and dumb, but one false move could be the end of it all."

And so, the plan was decided upon.

27

A PLAN IN MOTION

DAY 501

They were to push the car along the highway until the station was fully visible. Then, they would push the car onto the rocky terrain close by, but not so close that they risked the dead hearing them. Once the parking brake was up, the car parked yards away from the station, one group member moved out. Gunter stayed on top of the car's hood again, looking anxiously through his rifle scope with the barrel loaded and a finger resting on the trigger, waiting to see when his long-distance assistance was needed.

Richie was the first one to make a move, to kick-start only one of the many dangerous parts of their insane plan. His mission was to distract the herd and lure it away from the station, keeping it on him long enough for Violet and Elliot to scavenge the place clean. And a horde of zombies that size would need something loud to grab their attention, something very loud.

Richie raised the shotgun high and fired a shot that echoed, sounding like fireworks had erupted above the desert for every living creature to hear. Heads turned sluggishly, and legs started to limp away from the gas station, east. Sounds of sorrow and pain approached Richie. He stood his ground and strapped the shotgun to his back. Then, he picked up two hand-sized rocks from the ground and started striking them against one another. Clack! Clack! Clack! Clack! He hoped it would keep the corpses interested without wasting any ammo. As they got closer and closer, Richie started stepping backward, slowly, so he would stay within an audible range with their slow pace. He was leading them deeper into the eastern side of the desert and away from the station, continuously clapping the stones for the groans to spread, presumably leading on to the cluster at the back.

* * *

Now, it was time for the second most dangerous phase.

Gunter ordered Violet and Elliot to move towards the station once he was able to see that the rear of the herd was over forty yards away, pursuing Richie. Both of them were scrawny and light on their feet. They reached the station in less than twenty seconds, breathing hard from the sprint, but not tired, yet. Adrenaline had just started pumping. Even with the herd gone, they still carried weapons at the ready. "I'll go check the minimart; you go check for the gas," Violet ordered her less-experienced escort. Elliot nodded and she took off.

It didn't take Elliot long to realize that all the fuel tanks were empty. *Great, what now?* Elliot headed for the minimart, their last hope to redeem an otherwise pointless risk. *Let's see if Violet managed to find anything useful over there.*

* * *

Violet wasted no time infiltrating the minimart. She tapped the machete against the door a couple of times, causing noise to see if anything was still in there to respond. *No one!* The placed was cleared. Violet stepped in and looked around quickly. Aside from it being empty of groaning corpses, it seemed to be empty of all food and drinks as well. Shelves and cooling fridges were occupied by spider webs and trash.

Violet breathed a disappointed sigh. *Let's hope Elliot at least managed to find some gas.* She went over to the counter and saw nothing there either, only dried blood on and under the counter with hints of a splattering on the cash register. Violet looked up then and saw a door behind the counter. It was slightly open: a gap so narrow she could barely fit her fingers in. She peeked through it and saw stacks of shelves, an awkward room obviously used for storage. Violet noticed that a table had been blocking the door from the inside—barricading it, more likely.

She pushed the door open, her teeth gritted as the screeching noise of the table against the ceramic floor erupted. Violet pushed it halfway open, as far as it would go, and squeezed in. She saw snacks of all kinds: chips, biscuits, marshmallows, bags of gummy bears, and more sweets. She also noticed cans of soda, water bottles, and ... she couldn't tell what the rest of the inventory was. The ceramic floor came rushing up at her when something gripped her ankle and yanked at her.

The machete slipped from her hand when she fell, skidding out of reach. A dark-skinned hand with long blackened fingernails was gripping her right ankle. A zombie pulled itself out from under the table that had blocked the door. Violet tried reaching for her machete. No good. She wanted to go for her pistol but was too late. She needed both hands just to keep the zombie's snarling, saliva-dripping jaws away from her face. It pressed forward; she pressed back.

Her mistake was that she hadn't checked what was behind the door when it wouldn't open any further. One second, she was gazing at an unbelievable reward for the group's valor; and the next second, she was gazing into death's maw. *One false move could be the end of it all.* She'd said so herself before venturing here. This was the end for her, Violet thought. The corpse's rotting teeth were only two inches away from her face, and her strength was fading by the second as fear of death gripped her.

The struggle stopped. Suddenly, Violet didn't feel the corpse's head pushing against her anymore. She heard a stab and a crunch. Something rough cracked a hole in the zombie's skull and its long-gone brain, shutting it down instantly. It fell to the side with a hammer stuck to the back of its head. *Elliot!* Her savior just in time. He gave Violet a helping hand.

"Are you all right?"

Violet took it. "I'm fine. Thanks for saving me."

"Looks like this guy thought he'd be safe here with a stash that big, but a corpse ate up most of his arm so he turned into *them*. Poor guy."

"Gas?" Violet asked. Elliot shook his head in response. Violet glanced back at the stacked shelves and said, "Well, at least it wasn't all in vain, right?"

28

VETERAN EXPERIENCE

DAY 501

The groans of a hundred zombies were music to his ears, and the two stones he clanked repeatedly against one another were his leading instruments to direct the putrefying singers. Richie and the herd of zombies were at least fifty yards away from the gas station now. He wasn't too worried about losing them, for once they got close to the source of a sound, they tended to cling to it, sensing the movement of the noise maker. Up until this close, they didn't need noise to guide them to Richie unless he was able to get miles away.

Undead bodies were cold as death and had no thermal energy to create a heat wave signature. As the front column of groaners was closest to Richie, they were lured in by his body heat, not the tapping of stones.

Those stones were dropped when the undead closest to Richie picked up another heat signal that clashed with Richie's. A wild dog leaped out of a thorny bush and tackled him to the ground. Just like Violet a minute ago, Richie was fighting back a hungry fiend with sharp teeth snapping at *his* face. His hands and fingers dug deep into the animal's fur, distancing its deadly jaws from the skin of his neck.

The situation was about to become even direr as the limping horde of corpses approached the skirmish between man and beast. Gunter was witnessing the whole ordeal through his rifle scope, but, because Richie was struggling and moving around a lot, Gunter could not aim precisely at the wild animal. He hesitated to shoot, fearing he'd hit Richie.

Gunter exhaled deeply, and the rifle stopped shaking. His hands did not budge. The bull's-eye of the scope dotted the hound's head. His finger lingered on the trigger and pulled. A bullet burst out of the muzzle. One of the dog's hind legs slipped over Richie's waist. It stumbled slightly to the right, and the silently flying bullet creased his other hind leg. The canine yelped painfully and pulled away from Richie. Gunter reloaded but saw Richie raise a rock and smack it against the dog's slobbering mouth. The impact dropped the animal right into the hands of a zombie leaning over. One second later, ten decaying hands grabbed at the defenseless animal, ripping its fur to shreds. Then out came a strip of its intestines and other guts.

Gunter heard the dog offer its last dying yelps. Then he saw Richie rolling over on the sand, getting away from the corpses still pursuing him until he got to his feet. He ran back to the car with most of the herd still hightailing him, with his shotgun safely strapped to his back.

"That was close," the marksman said to Richie.

Richie gasped for air. "Tell me about it, I was there!" he huffed and looked back to see that the zombies were not far behind. "Now they'll never leave me alone!"

"We need gas. There's no chance we can outrun them this way. They know you're here, and soon enough they're gonna sense me too! What the hell's taking Violet and Elliot so damn long?"

"We're here!" Violet jogged up with two large plastic bags. "We found supplies, but no gas."

"Shit!"

"Well, at least not all in vain, right?" Richie said, still catching his breath, looking at Violet with an exhausted expression. She smiled at his remark, the same one that she'd made to Elliot when they'd found the new supplies. For a second, she thought of embracing him and asking him why he looked so dusty, but then she noticed what was heading their way.

"Everyone strap on your backpacks: I have a plan!" Gunter declared. "Elliot, take the bags of food from Violet and head back to the station now!" Gunter snatched the bags from Violet and gave them to Elliot, who now carried four plastic bags.

"Are you serious? The station's so close; we can't outrun them now that they know we're here! We have to think of something to lure them away from our tracks first!"

"And that's what I meant by 'having a plan.' *Now go!*" Gunter growled at his son. Elliot left. Then the war veteran turned to the other two. He pulled a lever under the front seat of the car, and the trunk flung open. "Richie, clear the bags of ammo and melee weapons. Violet, gather whatever's important in the car and stuff it into your backpacks."

Both had already started doing as they were told before Gunter gathered his stuff and advanced a few feet ahead of the car. He stopped. Violet was out of the car in a jiffy with a backpack in each hand. Her eyes met the horrible blank gaze of a half-eaten face of an elderly man advancing right at her with its gnarly gums showing. There was no escape. The old man's teeth snapped at her with a sickening red grin.

But, the bite fell on something surprisingly solid, not like tender skin or flesh at all. It was solid steel. Richie had hurled a lumber ax directly between its teeth before they snapped closed. The old man's corpse bit on the metal, and Richie drove it all the way through to the backside of its head, detaching the upper jaw with a perfect horizontal cut.

He pushed Violet back in the car and crawled inside with her, shutting the door close just before four, eight, fifteen, then twenty, corpses rammed against the hunk of metal, even swarming the other side. Violet and Richie were trapped. Gunter was out there, standing between the gas station and the car. *Help them.* That had been Gunter's intention all along, to use them as decoys. The marksman fired a silenced shot. It went cleanly through the car's windshield, cracking it completely.

Richie got the idea. "Cover your ears, Vi," he advised and then raised the shotgun towards the front windshield and ... BLAM!

The windshield fell into infinite twinkling pieces like very tiny diamonds shining under the sun. Richie and Violet reeled outside, through the now open space, on top of the car's bonnet, slicing off clawing fingers with their jagged melee weapons.

They ran and reached Gunter when he started running to them, which he shouldn't have done. He was heading back towards the car.

"*What the hell!*" Richie bellowed at the veteran. "Is this a part of the plan too?" But Richie didn't need an answer: they both saw what one of his left hand's fingers wore—a silver ring with a stretchy needle attached. In his right hand, he raised and hurled a green grenade, landing it in the car through the broken windshield. *This oughta make enough noise to lure them away,* the war veteran knew.

"*Run!*" Gunter howled. All three sprinted away. In a few seconds, they were closer to the station than the car. BOOM!

The grenade went off, and the car shot up at least five feet into the air. Sparks flew, black smoke billowed out, and a fireball smoldered. The inferno that used to be a vehicle plummeted downwards, landing thunderously on the gravelly earth. Hundreds of rotting faces turned their blemished eyes towards the flaming car. It was enough noise to be considered a theme park attraction for the undead, and one by one they walked so close to the blaze that they caught fire and cooked themselves to a cinder.

29

DAYDREAMING

DAY 505

The four survivors walked northwest to where there were able to see high-reaching hills all the way from the gas station, where they recently took shelter, fed their stomachs, rested their bodies, and regained their strengths to travel more miles, this time without a car. They were already headed towards the edge of a town on the main road that would take them outside Cliffroyce Bay's district; however, Gunter decided to lead his troops off the road, where the chances of running into armed survivors would be less of a concern, and they would still remain in town.

Why would they leave their temporary safe haven in the gas station? It was in the middle of nowhere. Not much life was around. They had food and water. Toilet facilities were available, even though they didn't work. Still, no one had to do their business outside on the dirt like a wild animal. They slept uncomfortably but safely inside the minimart, taking turns standing watch outside. It was the safest they'd been since the day Royce Pentagon Sanctuary went to hell. So why leave all that behind and march towards the unknown?

FEAR IN FLESH

The place was indeed isolated, which meant that they were far away from other resources once they ran out of food and water. The car was useless, so they had to rely on their own stamina with extra loads on their backs, carrying all sorts of necessary supplies, from ammo to Gunter's special weapons he was keeping for situations such as the recent attack.

Among other reasons for them to part ways with the gas station included one, fear of more hungry predators, especially ones that benefited from the dim light provided by the moon. Darkness would be their mortal enemy, but an ally for the predators of the night. Two, there wasn't much to use to barricade the station or set alarm systems to alert them in case of intruders. Three, the area around the station was caught in the stench of charred meat from the ample overcooked corpses. Four, other scavengers or bandits would surely check for gas and other supplies, and they'd have to deal with them. Just the day before, they had the experienced such a visit, when two individuals on a scooter showed up and demanded that they be welcomed, by pointing a gun at Elliot. They retreated quickly when they saw that they were outnumbered two to one. And that's when all four started thinking: What if *we're* outnumbered two to one the next time?

They hiked on hard sandy terrain to reach the hills because Gunter knew that beyond those hills lay a forest that he used to hunt in with some of his veteran friends. That meant food.

The three men were walking without looking back. The desert was empty, with only them and occasionally small rodents and lizards popping up near a rock or a shrub. Violet was falling behind. No one had noticed yet, but she was slowing down with each step, half asleep, eyes unfocused from the lack of sleep. There had been no restful nights for her since Royce Pentagon Sanctuary had been taken away from them. Two to three hours of power naps were all she could manage. Always fighting to stay awake, she was unwilling to go into a deep slumber, where her bad dreams would get the better of her, showing her more tragedies yet to strike.

Her eyes were half closed half open while twitching to keep the lids up. Her head felt as light as a feather. Bags sagged under her eyes. Still, Violet kept on walking reluctantly, trying hard to keep up with the men. But then came the hills. The more she advanced, the steeper the hills became, and she felt as though she were on a treadmill, not making real progress. She cocked her head sideways as she walked and saw Richie, Gunter, and Elliot looked sort of ant-sized from the distance that stretched between them and her as if they were walking a mile ahead of her. The only logical explanation was that either Violet was dreaming or she was just walking backward.

Violet was not walking backward. When she looked down at her feet, she saw them moving forward. It was the gritty surface beneath them that was moving her backward, dragging her along as if she were stuck in an endless walk on an escalator that was descending.

She was sure it was only her; the earth kept towing her back while she saw a gerbil scurry past her to disappear into a hole in the ground. Then she looked left and right, and nothing moved, not even dirt or pebbles or that long shadowy figure that stood just a few feet from her.

The very glimpse at that figure in the middle of the desert not far from her stilled her feet from walking. Violet rubbed her eyes with her fists. Then she even slapped herself sharply, reddening her right cheek. Just to be perfectly sure she'd tried everything to wake herself, Violet pinched the skin of her shoulder and then bit on her index finger.

She still saw it: the figure wouldn't go away. Whether a figment of her deluded, very exhausted imagination, the long shadowy figure with a raven black cloak completely covering it, still stood there. Two skinless hands were all that escaped the cloak. One long bony finger pointed in the direction from which Violet and the others had come, while a metallic sounding whisper was echoing ominously inside her mind and her ears telling her to *go back*.

"But why?" Violet demanded of the shadowy figure, not believing herself that she spoke to such a thing that made her flesh tingle by just looking at it.

"Did you say something, Vi?" Richie turned around, from where he and the rest stood, only ten feet away. Closer to her even than the Grim-Reaper-looking-thing ... where did it go?

She'd only glanced away for a second, but when she turned back, the cloaked figure was gone, disappeared into thin air like nothing more than a desert mirage. The hills were still steep but stationary, unlike a few minutes ago. Richie, Gunter, and Elliot were staring at her, waiting for her to speak. "I think this heat is making me see things," she finally managed to say. "I'm not feeling so good."

"What heat? It's been cloudy all day, and it looks like it's going to rain," Elliot said, pointing at the gray morning sky, growing dim with clouds.

"Oh." Violet stared dully. "Guys, I have a bad feeling about this. We should go back to the gas station and use the main road."

"We can't go back there just because you have a 'bad feeling' now, Violet," Gunter said. "Don't tell me you're afraid of a few drops of rain? Besides, we've made it this far; it's only an hour, max, till we reach that tall hill. Over there we can recuperate for a while."

"It's not the rain. It's just that ... I don't feel like we're making the right move leaving the station just yet."

"Are you kidding, Violet? Those two creeps on the scooter would've shot me yesterday if you guys hadn't shown up on time," Elliot reminded her. "We all voted on this. You said 'yes.' We're all tired, but we have to keep moving."

"B-but ... I ..." Violet stuttered, not knowing what to say or how to explain where her "bad feeling" was coming from. What was she supposed to tell them? *A ghost looking like the Grim Reaper appeared to me from thin air while I heard words echo in my mind and whispers coming from everywhere telling me to go back. So that's why we should go back. Yes, guys, I'm going nuts 'cause I haven't been getting enough sleep. I'm always worried that I'll have one of those rare dreams that predicts the future somehow, and something very bad will happen. And it's always death, death, suffering, anxiety, and death.* Some of that she had actually written in her diary when she found the time during a night's watch at the gas station.

Violet stood there, muttering to herself in her thoughts, until Richie came up to her and said, "You're just tired, Vi. Do you think I haven't been noticing you only sleeping a couple of hours a day? Sometimes you don't even reach an hour! Let me take this load off your back." He slid her backpack off and slung it over his one shoulder. "You don't need to be scared or worried. I'm here, and I won't let *anything* bad happen to you, okay?" he assured her sympathetically, yet unconvincingly.

Violet shrugged with a sigh. "This is hardly the time or place to start being mushy, Richie," she said with her usual snark. Richie smiled, leaned over with the tip of his index finger under her chin, and lifted her head up for a kiss.

For a moment, Violet blushed and felt a bit embarrassed, as if

Richie were kissing her in front of her parents before taking her out on their date. It was a quick kiss. She wanted to pull away at first to make it even shorter, out of respect for Gunter and Elliot waiting for them only a few feet away. But, how could she? It was moments like these that made her forget about everything she'd been through, comforting her with a bit of warmth and happiness because he was right there with her through the awfulness of the reality confronting her.

Richie pulled away, put an arm around her shoulders, and started walking again steadily, side by side with Violet, keeping pace with Gunter and Elliot—while the sky above began to flash with an occasional bolt of lightning.

30

INTO THE WILDERNESS

NIGHT 506

The downpour of rain was clamorous and seemed to be never-ending. In fact, there had been only brief pauses throughout the day, and it rained nonstop at night—the moon completely obscured by the clouds and lighting. The four survivors had treaded their way through the hills, taken a few hours' rests there, and then dived straight into the depths of the forest that Gunter had said would be there.

All four stumbled on, haggardly forcing their way through mazes of trees, ducking under branches, and kicking through piles of leaves blocking their path. All with the extra weight of the wet backpacks, plus the burden of walking in wet shoes on muddy ground that tried to swallow the foot with each step.

"Say, Dad." Elliot raised his voice over the heavy rain. "Do you think we've made the right call in leaving the hills so late at night, in this weather? I mean ... do you even know where we're heading?"

"A forest ranger cabin," his father answered.

"How far is it?"

"Just at the other end of this forest. All we need to look for now is a running stream. It should lead us right, to the cabin, where we can dry off and stay warm for the night. Just keep your eyes peeled open for any zombies—and *living* creatures out in the dark, too."

"Yes, sir," Elliot said, brushing his soggy hair back with his hand.

Violet kept trying to see in every direction, veering narrowly around every new turn, anxiously looking for someone or *something* that wasn't quite there, she was sure. Even if it *was* there, she wouldn't be able to see it, not until lighting struck and offered its flash of brightness to illuminate the cloak-wearing fiend in the dark. *One with the night, huh ... can't spot you anywhere, but you're clearly watching us under that faceless hood of yours, somewhere.* Violet shook herself. *Shut up, you big baby! You were in a state of exhaustion, on the border of consciousness and unconsciousness. It wasn't real, so quit worrying about it, and watch where you step.*

Even her own words of encouragement didn't make her stop shifting her gaze with every marshy step she took, and she couldn't get rid of the familiar feeling that something bad was bound to happen. No dream to warn her this time. Only voices in the back of her mind that said *go back*. She shook off a shiver, not quite sure if it was from her thoughts or the chilly rain.

Richie noticed Violet's odd movements just in front of him since he was traveling at the back of the line. "Looking for something, Vi?" he asked her.

She didn't answer right away, too busy probing the area. A few seconds later, she said, "Just making sure there aren't any zombies nearby. It's hard to hear their groans over the rain."

"I'm more worried about the leaves we're stepping upon. It would suck to accidentally walk upon poison ivy. Getting a rash when it's raining, fighting the urge to scratch your skin off … whew, you'd wish a zombie would just bite that area right off." Richie paused, awaiting Violet's snarky remarks or her sardonic laugh, which he hadn't heard for a while now.

Violet said nothing. She sank back into the silence, as did Gunter and Elliot, who'd been having their own conversation. Richie, too, joined in the hush when a strange sound could be heard over a clap of thunder.

A growl!

So audible, so unmistakable, so close that they could hear the splat of heavy footsteps over the muddy ground. The groaning grew in volume as the footsteps closed in. The cluster of bushes on the survivors' left writhed, and an enormous beast leaped out right in front of them. They all jumped back a few feet, weapons aimed at the massive shadow, only slightly darker than the night. Until a bolt of lightning cast a revealing glow on the black bear with what looked like scratches and bite marks all over its flesh.

The bear fled into the bushes on the opposite side, leaving a trail of gigantic paw prints pressed into the mud along with a trail of blood in its path. It growled weakly as it left them.

"That bear … it looked badly hurt!" Elliot was the first one to comment on the most unexpected encounter. "You don't think it's from—"

"Zombies? Yeah, maybe," Gunter said. "Or could be another pack of hungry predators out here that we haven't run into yet. A pack of wolves or … whatever. To hell with them, let's just stay focused on finding the stream and keeping absolutely quiet."

"Guys, I think I hear something coming from there." Violet pointed in the direction of the waterlogged bushes on their right, where the injured bear had darted out from. She cautiously approached the area.

Richie followed her for a couple of steps. "Violet, wait. What if—" Violet raised one hand swiftly, gesturing for him to keep quiet. She stood as if frozen. So, did Richie, Gunter, and Elliot. They all stood with their feet rooted in the slimy mud, for what came out of those bushes was just what Elliot had feared: *zombies*.

31

DOMINO EFFECT

NIGHT 506

Only a couple emerged from the bushes and limped by Violet, bypassing her without noticing her presence. Unable to see her, they couldn't sense her either because she hadn't made any sudden movements after they'd hobbled out, and she was as quiet as a mouse. The rest of the group followed Violet's lead in silence and stillness in order to say camouflaged from the six undead marauders.

It seemed to be working. They stood like four dominos, each a few feet from the next. If one of them happened to be knocked over, the other wouldn't fall instantaneously. They would, however, receive the same fate if one of them did eventually fall, get knocked aside, or simply forced to move away from a limping figure.

A couple of corpses made it halfway through the domino gaps, still in pursuit of the fleeing bear. But things were about to get harder. More zombies hobbled out of the bushes in pairs and groups of three. Groans were now louder than the sound of the downpour and thunder. Fear started to overwhelm the four, but all remained where they stood, unyielding. They could not risk running. There was nothing for it but to wait and remain calm.

Violet hadn't even moved her left hand since raising it, her fingers vibrating slightly as she clutched her machete hilt in the right. *GO BACK I get it now! We should've gone back while we still had the chance. Thanks from the heads-up, Mr. Cloak-man, but you could've at least warned the others too so they'd believe me. Now look what happened!*

Richie grasped his axe in two solidly clenched fists. He kept his gaze locked on Violet and any walking corpse that neared her, prepared in case she was the first to be spotted. *It's only a matter of time for any one of us.*

Gunter was the calmest of the four even though his rifle was still strapped to his back. His hand was paused just an inch away from his knife secured by his belt. The other hand was on Elliot's shoulder, trying to steady his shaky son. *We're all in this together. Don't blow it now, son*!

Elliot wasn't as calm as the rest. Fear burst out of him in a series of nervous shakes, clenching the muscles of his scrawny body. He gulped a few times, feeling as though his mouth was completely drained of saliva. He fought the urge to move his hair from his eyes again, though it bothered him like an itch he could not reach. Despite his father's reassuring presence, he couldn't help but pray to God like the Christian his late mother had taught him to be. *Though I walk through the valley of the shadow of death, I will*— and the soundless prayer was cut short by a clumsy limping corpse that bumped into Elliot. *Shoulda prayed faster!*

The corpse turned on Elliot with gleaming white eyes. Elliot shuddered more violently than ever. No point staying still now. With a trembling hand, Elliot swept his hair from his eyes. Finally, the bothersome itch had been scratched, but there was no relief as the corpse opened its repulsive oral captivity and let out a screechy hiss in Elliot's face.

32

HUNT PARTY

NIGHT 506

Thunder crashed and rain pounded. A flash of lightning illuminated the decayed open crater screeching in Elliot's face. Weakened from fear, Elliot smacked the zombie with his hammer only enough to push it aside without inflicting any serious damage to its skull. The blow pushed the zombie closer to Gunter, however, and the war veteran wasted not a second in drawing his knife. A severe graze appeared on the noisy corpse's temple, and blood dripped from the edge of Gunter's weapon.

Such great speed for a man closing in on sixty, and he would need all that speed for yet another struggle against the hoard of the living dead. In the middle of a dark forest during an earth-shaking storm, they had to fight in order to survive. For the corpse was not about to let a four-course meal just standing there be passed by unnoticed and wasted. Soon after the screech ended, the hunting party turned their visionless eyes toward their new prey.

Father and son would have to stand and fight off their hunters: Violet and Rich knew that all too well, but the undead *still* didn't know they stood there in the gloom as well. Staying rooted there was not such a practical strategy, though, because zombies were moving in from all sides, tracking Gunter and Elliot. Violet was in the way of three approaching limpers. She was the traffic cone blocking their lane. Odds were, at least one would come into contact with her and blow her cover. Or she could blow her own cover by getting out of the way, drawing their attention from Gunter and Elliot with her body heat and movement, serving as bait.

Decisions, decisions, and only mere seconds away from the collision course. Violet was going to have to act fast. *I'll be in trouble either way. Might as well start it before trouble finds me,* Violet thought as she prepared her machete for battle.

A burst of energy collided with the nearest zombies just as she'd made her decision. It was Richie springing into action with all the power of a gifted football player. He rammed into one zombie, shoulder to chest, and the limping corpse went flying. If zombies could still feel pain from a broken ribcage, then its groan as it flew onto a second limping corpse would have been a cry of absolute anguish.

Richie then raised his axe high at the same moment lightning flashed. He stood over the two sludge-plastered zombies he'd just tackled down and dropped the axe down on their heads; chopping their skulls open repeatedly like a lumberjack splitting hard wood.

Before a third zombie could realize what was happening to its partners, Violet joined the fight. She swung the machete through the creature's temple, spilling its blackened brains over the chopped remnants of its twice-dead allies.

Richie raised his gore-covered axe from the slaughterhouse of a mess he'd made. He and Violet stood backpack to backpack, wielding jagged weapons that screamed *slaughter* as the battle raged on, and the living dead were now as interested in Violet and Richie as they had been in Gunter and Elliot Waters. From all sides they circled, trapping the couple in a great circle and closing in on them.

"You have my back, I have yours." Richie shouted over the thunder and groans.

"Looks like it!" Violet's reply was also loud and clear since silence would no longer help them out of their perilous position.

※ ※ ※

Gunter was as self-sufficient as always, hitting every mark—this time without the use of his trusty rifle. Instead, he was relying completely on speed and melee tactics against the ambushing corpses. Their sluggishness and lack of coordinated planning was to Gunter's advantage. In his younger days on the field, he had survived more than one ambush that involved flash grenades, explosions, and bullets flying everywhere. He and his troop brothers fought back valiantly against the enemy's coordinated attacks till the bitter end, and won.

His new ambushers may be on top of the food chain in this ruined world, but they were no highly trained soldiers and therefore nowhere near as fast as Gunter was with his bowie knife, which he thrust into the tender side of the closest groaner's head. Its spoiled brain was pierced, shutting down its movement completely. Its body gave in and was about to crumble, but the veteran held it up to use as a shield.

When another zombie closed in on him, he'd push his recently deceased attacker onto his new attacker, forcing it to the ground under the sudden weight that its clumsiness could not support. He used the same tactic with four more zombies and piled them all on top of each other in a heap of furious groans, which ended when Gunter easily took them out one by one with the knife.

Gunter swiftly sent six living corpses to their final rest using this tactic, and now there were four more coming in on him from behind. Without catching his breath, Gunter sprang quickly and kicked the nearest corpse its shin. The corpse toppled and landed with an open mouth right onto Gunter's blade, which he pressed up till the tip of the knife poked through the back of the zombie's head. The war veteran then grabbed the second zombie by its hair and brought it down, forehead first, right onto the tip of the blade poking out the back of its first victim's head.

The two zombies' heads collided, and Gunter would require some time to heave his knife out of the stack of heads. Gunter cursed under his breath as he pulled on the hilt, barely budging the blade. The third corpse extended its grimy hands toward Gunter. The veteran grabbed hold of both wrists, rotted skin sloughing off. The corpse snapped its teeth closer to Gunter's face, while he backed up initially and then, with full force, brought the top of his head crashing into the teeth-snapper's nose. Its nose crunched and body fell to the muddy soil, stock-still. The fourth and last zombie of the group was armless but was upon Gunter before he could notice its missing arms. Jaws would have closed on Gunter's face if he had not delivered a swift uppercut with his right that snapped the armless corpse's lower jaw upward. Then came a solid crack as the skin-eater fell and hit the ground.

When lightning shed some brightness on the woods, Gunter could see both zombies were trying to recover near a mud-encrusted boulder half sunken in the ground. So Gunter knelt down and grabbed the heads of the last two corpses he'd broke but not yet destroyed. He started pummeling their faces into the boulder again and again, until their faces hideously decorated the sides of the boulder with teeth, pieces of flesh, skin, and an eye ball or two.

Meanwhile, Elliot was too busy trying to prevent the number of the undead on the field from increasing to pay attention to what his adrenaline-fueled father was doing. With the absence of light, Elliot found it difficult to spot zombies' heads through his rifle. Nonetheless, as he fired, the flash of light from the gun helped him take stock of the corpses. He strategically aimed at the ones emerging from the bushes. He squeezed the trigger, firing shot after shot, until the ammo was spent. Still, Elliot had not gotten all of the zombies. He'd eliminated even more than his father, but he'd done so by causing too much noise, drawing unwanted attention to himself.

One of the cannibal fiends he missed got to him, a fairly chubby corpse with grubby hands. It grabbed hold of his rifle. Elliot, still gripping the rifle, pushed back against the corpse. The moist soil was to Elliot's advantage. The zombie slipped and, hands persistently clenched around the gun, pulled Elliot down with it. Luckily, Elliot landed only an inch from its mouth, for he had time to reach for his hammer and drive it down on the head of his rifle-nabber.

Elliot was trying to lug the hammer out from the corpse's skull, gawking nervously at the shadows moving in the obscurity toward him. Not many options were left for Elliot but to pick up his rifle and swing it like a club. The first two hits were well swung. The third one barely even put his stalker to the ground, for Elliot's energy was running out. His scrawny figure did not give him much power. He improvised the best he could after running out of bullets, but panic was overwhelming him once more.

Lightning lit a scene of hopelessness and death, as Elliot weakened after every swing. Death crept ever nearer until a figure of salvation and hope shimmered beneath the lightning as it twirled in midair. Gunter put his knife right between the lifeless eyes of the zombie threatening his son.

"Are you all right?"

Elliot gasped for air and exhaled haggardly before he could answer. "Yes."

"You have ammo?"

"In my backpack,"

"Then *don't* think about reloading here," Gunter warned. "Pull my bowie knife out of that bastard's head and cover me!" Then Gunter pulled his own rifle from his back and aimed it directly at the great circle that Violet and Richie were caught in. He released a few soundless shots, taking down a few zombies to aid his troops in battle and seize their awareness. The marksman called their names out and pointed to the trail of the bear's blood. *"Over there, I cleared a path! Let's meet on the other side of those bushes!"* Gunter then grabbed his son's hand. "C'mon!" And the Waters disappeared in a rustle of leaves.

33

CIRCLE OF DEATH

NIGHT 506

The feral night was not completely obscure, but relying on eyesight was a big handicap for the survivors, while the dead were blessed with other senses and were unhindered in their accustomed darkness. Lighting provided some assistance every now and then, and, overall, it was not all that difficult to distinguish the living from the living dead, especially when up close. Violet and Richie stood back to back inside a shrinking circle formed by the undead, with rain pouring down on them like a thousand painless needles.

Richie charged at the zombies with the axe gripped in both hands. There was no time to draw out his firearm now; too many hands stretched out to get him. He roared and, with a typhoon-like power, spun with the axe, striking high and low, hacking off limbs that he could not even make out in the gloom. Living corpses ought to fear him, if they could even experience fear, for any that attacked the ruthless axe-wielder ended up bathing in in its own blood and guts.

Violet wielded the machete as if she were a knight wielding a sword, sworn to protect her king from invading enemies. She clasped the wooden handle and thrust the cutting metal at the heads of the disgusting creatures with all the might her body could muster. She slashed at temples and dodged teeth, stabbed faces gruesomely and kicked their feet. Her enemies fell to the mud one by one, and the machete swept down once more, scattering their blackened brains all over the ground.

Both fighters retreated to the center to catch their breath. They stood back to back in the midst of a now smaller circle, the numbers of the undead having decreased drastically. A few still stood, waiting to join their fallen comrades. Violet had only two coming at her, whereas Richie had three stalking him.

Violet raised the machete high when one corpse got too close and plunged it down so hard that it slid deep into the scalp, stubbornly remaining sheathed inside its skull as the zombie's body crumbled. Violet, refusing to let go of the machete's hilt, was also dragged down, with little help from the slippery surface. The second corpse was not far behind. She could see it, so well that her eyes were able to seize the tiny hole that came out with a puss of blood from between its whitely shaded eyes, dropping it dead face first into the mud.

Richie swirled the axe just to warm up his swing as two of the three zombies advanced. *That's close enough,* he thought, and flung the axe to take down two heads with one shot. But a woodcutter's axe is not as good as a machete for hacking flesh, and it made it partially through only one zombie's neck. The gurgling groaner dropped with the axe in its larynx, not at all what Richie'd had in mind. And worse, two limpers were still out to get him. When Richie looked at the lingering zombie, as if Richie's eyes shot bullets, blood suddenly found its way out of the zombie's head and dripped down with the rain. He quickly shifted his eyes to the other still limping corpse, and the same thing happened.

Both fighters heard their names called out. "Richie! Violet!" They turned to see the cause of the zombies' swift, silent death. *"Over there, I cleared a path! Let's meet on the other side of those bushes!"* they heard Gunter yell.

They didn't reply, as Gunter and Elliot had already dashed into the bushes, and they needed to catch up to them. The second Richie had pulled the axe out the gargling zombie's throat, they bolted. Violet drifted a little further ahead but then to felt a sense of foreboding. She could only hear two pairs of feet running over the grounds, not Richie's. She looked back at the circle to see the Richie remained there.

He had not made it out of the circle when they'd bolted. Richie had tripped immediately because the corpse with his axe in its throat grabbed his ankle. Richie could not scream; his breath was cut short by the fall. His mouth was full of dirt, and his hands were holding the crooked jaws of the zombie shut as it climbed over him instantly. The axe hadn't cut far enough to detach the head from the shoulders. Arteries spilled blood while its head hung crookedly. Richie only wished now he'd finished it off before trying to escape.

"*Richie!*" Violet screamed, turning and running back to the circle with a pistol in hand.

"Violet, go! I got this!" Richie spat out the words with flecks of dirt and rain water. He was wrong. For there were still more living corpses looking to him for a feast, which was why Violet used her pistol to shoot them down. That gave Richie the time and focus he needed to take care of his crooked assailant.

The zombie's hands grabbed Richie's hoodie but were no threat. Its bacteria-infested teeth were what worried Richie most, so he pushed with one palm against the corpse's chin while the other hand was wrapped around the corpse's tattered braid. Pressing against the chin upward and pulling the braid downward, Richie was able to contort the corpse's neck still further. When the skin tore on the right side, arteries burst. The damage was nearly complete, and the corpse's head hung loosely against its own spine, staring blindly at the world upside down. Richie shoved the carcass off, took his axe, and ran with Violet into the bushes.

Sopping-wet leaves rustled, hitting the runners' faces and bodies as if warding off unwanted visitors. Violet and Richie pushed forward and made it out to the other side triumphant, with the reward of finding their friends. A man true to his word, Gunter was waiting for them on the other side. Only he was on the ground, bloody, still alive but screaming.

34

FROM PERILOUS TO DIRE

NIGHT 506

After Gunter and his son fought their way out from the storm-whipped plant life walling off their escape path, they made it out onto a small field. When lightning had illuminated the area, they'd caught only a glimpse of what lay beyond the bushes, so Gunter and Elliot could not be more astonished to find the running stream awaiting them only a few yards away. It was what Gunter had set out for since insisting on dragging them into the godforsaken forest. He had hopes they could now find the cabin he'd claimed was located on the east side of the stream.

All they had to do was get east of the river, but not until after Violet and Richie joined them. Sight was much clearer here on the field than it had been in the thickness of tall trees and grass. Trees and grass were sparser on this side, obscuring the view less. The lightning show had nearly ceased, but they could still see what else was on the field besides themselves and the stream. They didn't pay much attention to thick puddles and trails of blood painted across the land being washed into the stream by rainwater. They were mostly concerned about whom this mess belonged to.

Impossible, they thought. The fleeing bear should have bled out and died from the multiple wounds it had endured. Yet another bolt of lightning revealed the darkness of its coat, spattered with blood. The black bear stood between them and the running stream, nostrils steaming, jaws stretched in a snarl with jagged teeth glinting and saliva dripping.

The bear had several hollow spots, with missing chunks of flesh and fur. The explanation for how it still stood was obvious, yet shocking. The zombie infection had brought the dead animal back to life, to rise once more and walk among the clan of the living dead. Their living *beast!*

Judging from how bright the bear's starlit eyes gleamed at them the second they sprawled out of the bushes, the virus had taken it over completely. Gunter and Elliot shuddered at the sight of the slowly approaching bear. For over a year they had survived contaminated humans turned into remorseless cannibals who had taken over the planet, but until now none of them had considered that the virus might take over animals. They had been in a sanctuary in the middle of a city, where wildlife was scarce, aside from birds and the occasional stray cat.

Now they were on the wildlife's turf—a kingdom ruled by man's second in terms of the food chain. They'd wandered from the hills, retreating from the howls of wolves and growls of mountain lions, into the woods, where they had become prey in the blind eyes of two different species with the same illness.

The dead bear finally broke into a lazy run. The beast speedily covered the few yards between it and its prey. Neither Elliot nor Gunter were prepared for this unexpected attack; Elliot's ammo was still in his backpack, and Gunter didn't know how many shots he had left, let alone whether they were enough to put down the animal kingdom's version of a tank.

FEAR IN FLESH

Astonishment shifted to panic; marksman Gunter took an amateur's unsteady aim. He fired two shots, each missing its mark. One took out the bear's left ear, and the other only dented its flaring nostrils, failing to stop the force sprinting clumsily toward them on all fours. Gunter had but one chance left, only a second away from getting shredded by the ferocious, fur-coated tank. Either he could risk pulling the trigger one more time with a fifty-fifty chance of hitting the bear right between the eyes, or he could get out of the way.

Wise and quick enough, the veteran pushed himself and Elliot out of the way, so the bear rammed into nothing but air as it pulled on the brakes, stopping between them, undecided which to attack first. Gunter thought about running back into the bushes to lead the bear astray and come out again, but what of Richie and Violet? What if he lead the bear to them as they made their way through? *They'll be dead for sure,* he thought.

As he sat on the ground collecting his thoughts, the bear made a decision and turned its rabid features on Elliot, also on the ground, clutching the bowie knife his father had given him earlier. Gunter fixed his aim on one of the bear's hind legs and squeezed the trigger, but only to have the gun click so softly that even the dead bear didn't hear it. That left Gunter with nothing else to use but his bare hands. He grabbed the bear's small tail to get its attention. The bear responded and left Elliot be, but, to Gunter's misfortune, the bear spun unexpectedly swiftly. A massive paw with razor-sharp claws raised and gauged Gunter's chest, ripping through his blue vest, white shirt, and skin. Four claw marks left stains of red flowing down the war veteran's chest as he lay next to his empty rifle.

Gunter lost hope when the bear stood tall on two legs, towering over the world around him. The beast would soon drop down with its teeth and claws to devour him, fitting his limbs nicely inside that enormous coffin of a stomach. Gunter covered his wounds with his arms and breathed what he thought was his last breath. However, his son was not such a coward as to sit and watch a zombie bear fill its belly with portions of the man who'd raised and protected him his entire life.

The infection, of course, prevented the bear from reacting to pain, but still it could feel physical contact and movement. The bear certainly noticed when a jab of steel poked into its back. Elliot thrust the bowie knife into the bear to distract the rabid animal as his father had done to save him. The blade got caught, and Elliot knew there was not much time, so he let go of the hilt and backed away just before the bear swung its massive paws around again. Disappointed, the bear struck air and landed on all fours, pursuing Elliot as the boy walked backward, defenseless and terrified.

"It ain't ... over yet, you fat ... son of a bitch," Gunter spat between breaths as he hefted himself up with the heavy backpack still intact. Adrenalin fueled him, more concerned for his son than his own wounds. The war veteran leapt forward, abandoning his empty rifle and mounting the undead beast. Gunter sat on the bear's back, clasping the hilt of the trapped blade with one hand and, with the other, grabbing onto the dark sodden fur to keep balanced like a cowboy riding a bull. The knife was in deep, but Gunter could feel it slipping out slowly.

The bear twisted its neck as far back as it could bend, unable to reach Gunter's feet with its jaws. It shook itself and spun around in circles, trying relentlessly to throw its rider until it lost its footing while attempting to rise on its hind legs. Growling, it tumbled to one side, landing on one of Gunter's legs with 600 pounds of slowly rotting flesh.

Worst yet, one hand of Gunter's still gripped the bear's back where he fell.

Gunter kept tugging on the hilt, compelling the bloodied metal out inch by inch. It was a job for both hands, he figured, but he was unable to bring his other hand up. He felt a stab of pain in his left leg from the weight atop it, but sharper pain bloomed in his other arm, like numerous spikes jabbing both sides of the forearm. Gunter was unsuccessful in holding back his screams; he wailed, and the pain still did not fade. The arm was ensnared between the upper and lower jaws of the rising bear, lifting itself and half of Gunter's body up with it, allowing the blade to finally slip out in its prey's tight grip.

"*Dad!*" Elliot bellowed and rushed to aid his fallen father the best he could by punching and yanking on the bear's fur from behind, to no avail. While the arm-grinding fiend latched on, Gunter unleashed blows, one after another with the bowie knife, to the side of his biter's neck, trying desperately to reach the head. Each stab followed with a curse and a scream from frustration at not killing the thing, for the bear's hide was still thick.

It was not until Gunter managed to stab the bear behind its ear that it loosened its grip on his arm, dropping him to the ground. Gunter fell, breathless and semi-conscious, while the bear resumed growling. Its movements seemed dull and awkward, as if the animal was struggling to keep steady, and the growls had softened into milder purrs caught in its throat.

The bear turned its unstable attention to the bushes when loud sounds called to it: the sounds of gunfire coming from Violet's pistol and Richie's shotgun, blasting through the side where the bowie knife had stabbed. The beast finally fell to its definitive demise, half its face frozen in a terrible snarl and the other featureless from having lost so much skin and muscle that it could not snarl on that side too.

All three rushed to their fallen leader, who was far beyond rescuing now, knowing very well what would become of him in hours, or maybe only minutes. Gunter waited wearily on the front steps of the afterlife, waiting for the door to open and welcome him—then lead him back to live once more, a life any decent human being would dread.

As Elliot and Richie gently helped Gunter to his feet, Violet retrieved his fallen weapons, and at that moment she saw them striding toward her through the cluster of bushes: the pack of unfinished zombies they had left back there. The persistent abominations had followed them, diving straight after them and getting lost in the jumble of weeds. Once shots were fired, though, the pursuers had pinpointed their prey's location.

"Zombies coming in from the bushes!" Violet alerted the men. "Do we fight?"

"No, we already wasted enough ammo on that goddamn bear!" Gunter said. The war veteran was injured beyond healing, but he still gave orders—a force of habit that would follow this bold soldier to his grave. "Into the stream ... *Move!*" he shouted, offering one last order.

35

A VETERAN'S RETIRMENT

NIGHT 506

The stream's black waters were cold with a fierce current thanks to the massive storm. Richie and Elliot had Gunter embraced between them, crossing the raging waters away from the living dead.

Violet hung onto Richie's backpack with a tight grip on a strap, so they would all make it to the other shore despite the violent torrents. The water level was already up to their waists and crept higher as their feet moved in slow motioned.

Side by side they fought their way over and made it to shore without any of them getting dragged under, unlike the crooked walking corpses, who did not make it even halfway before the undercurrent overpowered them, sending them downriver into obscure parts of the woods.

On shore they settled beneath a large cluster of trees with writhing branches and leaves that dripped rainwater. They sat Gunter on a log so that the barely conscious veteran could have his last moments of peace before the infection conquered his failing body. Peace and serenity were the last two things he could think of, though. Unlike the wounds on his chewed up arm, his head was unscathed, yet he felt it constantly pulsing in throbs turning from bad to worse with each passing minute. The claw marks on his his chest stung in harmony with the pounding of his head.

His left arm was a ruin from elbow and down, his skin and flesh mangled and the blood loss significant. The bones were obviously shattered, given how the hand was bent and dangled sickeningly from the wrist. As Gunter leaned back on the log, the chewed arm rested in the mud next to him like an attachment, for he had no control over the muscles in that arm anymore. He gritted his teeth, holding back a cry that was cut short anyway from coughing that went on seemingly forever.

"Oh my God, Gunter." There was a hint of emotion in Violet's tone after she took a good long look at the man for the first time since they'd escaped. She realized that Gunter was standing in his grave, with no hope of surviving. Even so, she couldn't stop herself from trying. "We have to do something, or he'll bleed to death." Violet looked to Richie for guidance.

"We need to cover up his wounds with something," Richie agreed. *We could still save someone from bleeding out.* He wanted to make himself believe it. But not Gunter, not with these severe wounds inflected upon him and a nasty disease running through his bloodstream, slowing down every breath he took, prolonging his suffering. It was too late and Richie knew it, but didn't want to admit it. "Check for any dry clothes or pieces of cloth in your backpacks. We can still—"

A cackle burst out from Gunter, cutting Richie off. It was the first they had ever heard him laugh so: it sounded like he was choking on his laughter. "I appreciate your concern, troops." Gunter spoke weekly. "It's not bleeding to death that worries me. Hell, I just keep praying that in a couple of seconds I'll be drained out so this damn pain will go away." Gunter closed his eyes and gritted his teeth against the pain he was talking about.

"You're gonna drain out of nothing, Gunter," Richie said. "I'll make sure of that. Don't you give up on us now." Richie and Violet were searching their backpacks while Elliot stood like a log and did nothing. "If it were one of us, you'd be saying the same."

"Aah! But it's too late for me now, son," Gunter said despairingly. "And *how* exactly will you do something about it, Richie? Covering it won't do; it's already festering. You can cut my arm off, sure, but how will you stitch that all up, eh? Will you have enough clean, dry clothes to cover this up too?" Gunter pulled down on his clothes to expose the claw marks in his chest. "Face it, son ... we all know what's coming after I die. I'm sure as hell not looking forward to that, but I have to accept it. It's coming and I can feel it spreading inside me. It's like—" And before Gunter could finish, he started another round of coughing that sounded more violent than the first.

"Gunter, you saying that you've been bitten ... by a zombie." Violet did not believe the words as they came out of her mouth. She looked at Elliot, a shadow standing still, his face a mask of sorrow framed by wet strands of dark hair. He closed his eyes and nodded to her in a wordless reply. "But the hand was the bear's doing!" Violet said.

The coughs halted when Gunter spat out red-colored phlegm and then cleared his throat. "The only way you can help me is if ... you put a bullet in my head." Gunter spoke with effort, in a voice that didn't sound like his. "Ahh!" he cried, fingering both sides of his temple with his good hand. "Feels like ants are munching on the inside of my head. It's only a matter of time till my brain goes black like theirs ... and my eyes white ... Then I'll try to bite chunks outta you guys ... so you oughta hurry up with your good-byes."

"When were you bit, and how bad?" Richie asked, wanting to determine how much time Gunter had left, though it was pretty obvious that he hadn't much. The more severe or numerous the bites were, the less likely a victim would stay alive for longer than few minutes of anguish.

"Are you blind like those damn zombies, Richie? Or just being deliberately stupid?" Gunter replied, with a sharply drawn grin. Then he stared down, disgusted by his damaged arm. He pointed at it.

"That's the bear's doing, like Violet said. There weren't any zombies in sight till after we shot it dead," Richie told him.

"The bear *was* the zombie! Didn't you take a good look at its eyes when you shot it? They were *white* ... zombie white!" He breathed heavily, exhausted from talking.

Both Richie and Violet seemed baffled at the notion of a bear being infected by the same illness that turned people into remorseless flesh-eating ghouls. "Animals can turn too?" Richie asked, dumbfounded. Looking toward Violet, he said, "All the scavenger hunt trips we made over a year, and we never encountered animals becoming zombies too! We never even thought of it! After all this time, this damn sickness still has ways of making our lives *worse*?"

After Richie's outburst, Gunter again fell into painful coughing. Elliot finally stepped out of the shadows and spoke. "Birds were the most common animals we saw during our time in the sanctuary. They're hard to catch, even for us with guns. So I'm guessing we're the living dead's favorite meal because of our availability and slowness compared to some animals with wings and four legs."

"The bear came at us so quickly," Elliot went on. "We weren't ready for another attack. Ammo was scarce. And it all just happened so fast! The bear wasn't as slow as human zombies are, no. It almost got me on the first attack. Dad distracted it and got clawed. Then I did the same to save him, hoping that you two would show up before the whole thing escalated any further. But ... my dad jumped in again, and I didn't do enough to grab its attention the next time around, which lead to him getting—"

"Shut the hell up, boy!" Gunter found his rasping voice again. "No one's pointing the finger at you! You're not at fault in any of this; none of you are! I dragged us down here in the first place and got us all tangled up in this mess. So I'm glad it was me the bear got to roughhouse. I shoulda listened to you, Violet, when you had a bad feeling before ..." Wet coughs disabled his speech once more, but the marksman quickly recovered. "Besides, how many men my age could say that they rode a black bear and thrust a knife in its skull before it could finish tearing their arm off, eh?" Gunter guffawed derisively. The others attempted pained smiles to support the old man's humor and endurance, but only for an instant.

Elliot knelt beside his tormented father and cupped Gunter's good hand in both of his. Jolts of pain spread throughout Gunter's body with each cough. Muscles spasmed, and Gunter gripped Elliot's hand with a squeezing force.

Blood leaked from Gunter's mouth and wormed down his chin after the coughs had stopped. And still the man claiming to be *old* had fight left in him, though the paleness of his face grew monstrous with dark veins popping out from his neck. He broke his hand free from Elliot's grasp and placed it on his boy's right cheek firmly, staring at him with his fading eyes. "You're not a boy anymore," he said, breathing heavily. "You're a man, son. You've been a man for a long time ... and a brave man at that, no matter how scared you get sometimes. You still face your fears. You thought you lacked courage, but it always comes out in moments of desperation, and you ... you overcome. Not because you choose to, but because you're meant to ... all three of you." Gunter paused to stubbornly fight back an oncoming cough.

"I'm sorry, Dad. I just—"

"Shush ... almost outta time, so let me finish," Gunter demanded. "I taught you everything I could about survival, and I wish I could still be around to teach you more. You're a good learner, Elliot, and I'm proud of you, and I know that your mother and grandmother would also be proud of you if they were still ... here with us." Tears welled in Gunter's fading eyes.

Elliot's eyes turned sorrowfully watery at the memory of his mother and grandmother. They were early victims of the infection before anyone knew how the sickness worked, and Gunter had no choice but to put them both down, feeling more intense fear and loathing than ever before in his life, including on the battlefield.

Gunter coughed so thunderously that if zombies happened to be nearby, they'd be rushing in for a meal. "Get outta here before you run across another herd," he advised them. "Follow the stream to the east and find the ranger cabin. By then you shouldn't be far from the countryside. You guys didn't survive this long to die so young. Don't let it all be in vain." Exhausted and feverish, his arm felt scalding hot on Elliot's cheek as his body temperature rocketed, losing the battle against the infection. Gunter drew back his hand quickly to cover his mouth from the burst of nonstop coughing that came with more blood this time, spouting out from between his fingers.

"Dad!"

FEAR IN FLESH

The war veteran had lost a lot of blood, and still he remained conscious and alive—barely. He said, with a voice draining away faster than his life, "Always stick together and never separate from one another. Loyalty ... and trust ... will keep you strong." He paused for a cough, but resumed, determined to finish. "The strong will survive, so you have to be stronger than those trying to take your life. Never be afraid to take someone's life ... if they're threatening to take yours ... either from the already dead ... or the still living. Your enemies ... are every ... where." And the coughing took him once more.

Like exploding fire crackers had been lit in his chest, glutinous chunks spewed out that could only have come from his lungs: grotesque fragments that ended the torment of the veteran marksman. His head hung low and throbbed no more. His eyes shut and did not flicker back open. His good hand was dark red, palm up, stock-still. His heart went silent.

36

FROM AN UNDEAD VIEWPOINT

DAWN 506

Though Gunter's demise was indeed horrid for them to witness, it was the aftermath of his passing that consumed them. None had yet lifted a finger to give Gunter the mercy of an ultimate death, a painless end before his corpse rose again.

Elliot took his leave after saying his good-byes to his deceased father and walked back into the shadows of the trees. With a face soaked from tears and rain, it was difficult to make out the difference. The monster his father was about to become was no sight for him to see. Violet averted her eyes from the hurled out lungs and blood, looking up at the sobbing sky and joining its misery.

Richie was as angry as the storm. Due to just a few moments of separation, they had lost their most powerful ally, and such a good friend and leader who gave them courage in every situation they'd encountered. During his final breaths, he'd still given them his words of encouragement to keep them going. Though grief reigned supreme, Richie did not utter a cry nor shed a tear like the other two did. Time was of the essence; the illness worked its wonders fast. Someone had to put something through Gunter's brain before it corrupted his former humanity for good. Something must be done, and *fast*.

"Violet, hand me the bowie knife, now," Richie commanded. Violet wiped away the tears on her face before she turned and walked to Richie. She did as commanded without a word. "Violet, you need to go take Elliot away from here," Richie told her, taking the knife from her wet hand. "Not too far away; keep in sight."

Violet nodded and briskly walked away from the scene with Elliot by her side. They stood near the stream with their backs to Richie, who eyed the blade in admiration, looking as though he were examining the watery depths of each droplet of rain on the steel, unable to bring himself to thrust it in the temple of the dead marksman. *C'mon, you can do it,* Richie encouraged himself. *Gunter wants you to do it!* He took a deep breath, firmed his grip on the hilt, and turned the jagged point to face the milky white eyes of Gunter's corpse. Richie's gaze shifted from the knife to the paleness staring right back at him, as cold shivers ran down his spine. *You failed him.*

※ ※ ※

When Gunter woke, or rather his corpse woke, his old conscience and soul had left the body for a new host to seek control, wrapping itself around Gunter's neural system and engulfing his brain with black corruption. The murkiness of white fog descended around his dark brown pupil as if rain clouds hovered over the sun till it became hardly visible. The whole world was dark static to his new eyes.

Figureless shadows appeared in the static vision with a glow of radiating heat within them whenever something lurked nearby. For now, it was only the softening drops of rain through leaves that were causing sounds in the static world, and they kindled no interest in Gunter. Still not fully aware of himself, Gunter's corpse did not move to stand or even flinch. It sat up the same way it had before Gunter coughed his last breath.

A stretchy slender shadow moved before his gaze, and slowly the glow of the heat signature spread to paint a dismantled portrait within the static. The glow showed a human body that was not whole. And just like sharks sniffing spilled blood in water, the living corpse of Gunter could almost smell the stench of raw meat beneath toppings of muscle tissue and fresh layers of skin.

Part of the glow crept closer to his right. Before the corpse could do anything, its enhanced hearing detected another signal ... a stronger one, a wild dinning that rocked the inner blackness in his brain. It was coming from the glow itself, only a muttering of words that were alien to Gunter the corpse. "Sorry for being late, Gunter; it's just too hard," the glowing shadow in the dark said. "It's been an honor surviving with you, sir." All that just made Gunter angry from the deafening sounds that trumpeted against his sensitive ears, making him want to scream and then feed on the living flesh beneath that noisy glow.

His scream came out as a low groan that none could hear but the glowing shadow that was Richie, and with a THUCK from a sharp object, the corpse quieted. It went through the side of his temple, poking into the core of the corruption. The blackened brain shut down, and quickly the glowing shadow faded, along with the surrounding static.

His consciousness lapsed once again into the limitless mouth of darkness. But this time it would be a plummet that could last an eternity. Then Richie woke ...

37

A NEW DAMN, A NEW DAY

DAY 506

Violet woke to the diminishing sounds of Richie's mutterings. "I failed him ... I failed ... him ... I'm ... I'm sorry, Gunter," he murmured in his sleep. They shared the same mattress and sheets, which were meant for a single person, and Richie's broad chest was her pillow. A few feet away, Elliot lay on a brown couch, cradling his father's rifle tightly in his arms like a child embracing his favorite stuffed toy, helping him to fall asleep.

Her bladder was heavy. When she sat up, the covers slipped down to her lap, revealing the pink tank top she's worn as an undergarment for so long now that she thought it stank. Daylight shone through the curtained window, filling Violet with a sense of blissfulness and relief for a second till her bladder kicked in again. She patted Richie on the shoulder and called his name repeatedly till the heavy sleeper woke up, escaping his horrific nightmare of hours past. The memory made him shiver; however, he concealed it from Violet once he realized she was the one who'd awakened him. "What's going on?" he asked her in a low whisper.

"Sorry to wake you up, but I need to pee, and you said not to go outside alone," Violet said, equally quietly. "So ..."

He turned to Violet, head still planted on the pillow, looking at her for a second with vision blurred from sleep. Then he rubbed his eyes callously till the whiteness around his pupil darkened red. "All right, let's go." He slid the covers off as he sat up. He also wore a sleeveless shirt, once white but now bearing several yellow spots from sweat stains.

"Should I wake Elliot up too and tell him where we're going?"

Richie looked at Elliot sound asleep on the couch. "Nah," he answered. "Leave the poor kid to sleep for as long as he wants. God knows he needs it. We shouldn't be worrying about leaving this place anytime soon."

They marched across the hardwood floor with their firearms, passing Elliot. A circular window above the couch let in the morning's beams, which struck the wall on their left that held a mounted map of the forest. Beneath it stood a low, broken mini-fridge that smelled of rotten apples and alcohol. Next to it was a tall wooden closet with two doors that had been empty before they placed their backpacks in it. Back on the right side, nearing the oak door there was a coat hanger, which held their soaked hoodies, and a wooden office desk. Another round window let in light from near the door. Dust danced in the light over the desk that was without a chair but was stockpiled with paper, pencils, and pens scattered all over. There were a number of other office supplies that were useless to most people these days, except for Violet. She had restocked some of her writing supplies before going to sleep.

A great number of pages in Violet's diary were consumed recording what they had undergone these past hours in the woods, which they learned was called Laveaux's Forest Hunting Grounds from the map in the cabin.

FEAR IN FLESH

The two left the cabin. The sun rose high, casting glistening gold upon the greens of the woods. The wind whistled softly as light clouds gathered away from the sun, sending calming breezes through the tree leaves, rustling them gently in nature's symphony. The chirping songs of many unseen birds provided the melody.

They walked yards away from the cabin to the high undergrowth between the closest trees, not venturing deeper into the mouth of the forest again. Violet went behind a tree while Richie waited for her on the other side, keeping a watchful eye for any zombies lingering in the area.

After Violet had finished, they headed back to the cabin quietly, both eager to slide back under the cozy covers and resume their slumber as if they had not a care in the world. Weary as they were, though, their eyes still narrowed in on the stranger looming closer to the cabin than they were, heading toward it. They stopped.

The stranger moved in a human fashion, quietly and without staggering. No limping, no groaning, so they had to rule out zombie. They made it halfway through the open area between the forest and cabin, and from that distance they could tell it was a male—too squat to be Elliot, hair hidden beneath a cap.

"Just a scavenger perhaps?" Violet whispered.

"Maybe," Richie said. "But even so, scavengers are often armed and could be dangerous. Scavenger or not, I gotta get to him before he reaches the cabin. I can't tell if he has a weapon on him from here." Richie started forward, and Violet was on his tail. He waved her to halt. "You stay here," he said. "I'll try talking to him peacefully, and I need you to keep a sharp lookout in case anybody else is nearby. Keep your gun ready in case *he* pulls something out on me, got it?"

Violet nodded and did as she was bid, thinking for a moment that

Richie sounded just like Gunter, with the same determination and confidence—and tendency to give commands in dangerous situations—leader materials. The torch had been passed, and Richie was holding it cautiously as he made his way to confront the stout man.

38

KEEPING A WATCHFUL EYE

DAY 506

"Hey, you!" Richie called, as he walked steadily to catch up with the cabin's visitor. He kept his shotgun clutched in both hands, where the man could see what he'd be up against if he tried anything hostile. "Where do you think you're going?" Richie asked him gruffly.

"The … cabin," the man said, sounding unsure of his answer. Aside from the red-and-black cap, he wore a green shirt with the face of Lady Liberty printed on the front and beige shorts that reached his knees. His boots were covered in mud. "I'm sorry," the man apologized, "is this cabin yours? I wasn't meaning to barge in or steal anything. I'm n-not looking for any trouble, buddy. I'm only lost out here and trying to find a place to rest for a while." He sounded convincing, but something about him raised suspicion in Richie's heart.

How odd was it that a *lost* survivor walking around empty-handed, with nothing to protect himself with, could make it here? *Unless he didn't come from here*, Richie thought. With doubt pounding his thoughts, Richie tried to keep himself from doing or saying something irrational. *Peacefully,* he reminded himself. "There's nothing here for you. Go back the way you came from," Richie demanded, shotgun waiting to be unleashed.

"Not a problem, man. It's like I said, I'm not looking for any trouble. Just another survivor like you, trying to ... you know ... survive." The man's voice sounded oddly younger now, Richie noted. He had both arms halfway up, as though to show he had no weapons, when he explained himself. His armpits were clearly damp, and the weather was nowhere near hot yet. Beads of sweat also dripped from his cheeks, uniting at the edge of his chin to fall.

Could be nervous, Richie reflected, *or he could've been walking for hours.*

Richie was calm and unnerving, while his squat opponent was tense and sweating. "I'll be leaving now," the man announced and made a preparatory step toward the forest.

Richie moved and intercepted him immediately. "You came from that way." He redirected the sweating man with a point of the shotgun's muzzle toward the opposite side, which led to a safer-looking path—west, beyond the cabin.

"And I'll be going this way now to wash up at the stream." He took a side step to get past Richie's intercepting stance.

Faster this time, Richie moved and stepped closer to the man, whose face was shaded by his cap, hiding his anxious eyes. "You say you're lost, but you know where the stream is, ha?" Richie grew more suspicious than ever and was beginning to run out of patience.

"Well, you see ... I'm ..." the man took a few seconds to find a logical answer. "I've been lost here for days and trying to memorize my way around so that—"

FEAR IN FLESH

"Stop blabbing lies," Richie said sharply. "You're feeding me bull that reeks nastier than your armpits! You're telling me that this is some kind of magical cabin that wasn't here when you made your way across from the forest to the other side? Did it only appear just now when you were on your way back to the same forest you wandered out of? Alone, without any protection? You must have guts. Would be a shame if zombies were to rip 'em out, since you have nothing to defend yourself with against them!" Richie mocked. "How did you even make it this far?" Expecting no truthful answers from this man's mouth, he glared at him, and so did his shotgun.

"Simple." The man's voice turned soothing, and his chapped lips curled into a malicious grin. "With your help, I've managed to grab your attention long enough for my friend Jerry to move quietly and grab the girl you're with. That's how I made it this far!" Not willing to believe the words from a liar's mouth, Richie was doubtful but could not resist turning back to Violet.

Apprehended she was, by a fellow not much taller than she was. One long purple sleeve was coiled around her chest, clamping her arms down without her pistol in either hand. A small knife was held to her throat, as she and her captive walked slowly toward where Richie stood.

"Watch out!" Violet shouted.

In that scant second, Richie could feel a tug on the shotgun in his hands. In a heartbeat, Richie wheeled around and swung the firearm, smashing it into the stout man's nose. The cap flew off his head, uncovering a tangled mop of black hair, as he hit the dust.

"Now, now, let's play nice here, or else your lady friend gets a hickey from this knife so red, it'll spill actual blood," the purple-sleeved man warned from a few feet away. His fallen comrade had blood running out his nose, seeping through his fingers. Violet's captor, Jerry, looked fairly young and slender; his plump freckled face suggested he was not a day older than nineteen. His shaggy blond mohawk seemed to confirm his youth. Richie kept shifting his gun from one attacker to the other, panicking and trying his best not to show it. "Kermit, you all right, dude?" Jerry asked of his bleeding friend.

"Aughhh!" Kermit moaned as he sat up, red-stained fingers tentatively touching his nose. "I think he broke my nose!" His voice sounded weepy.

"That one's on you, man," Jerry said. "You were supposed to hit him over the head once he had his back turned to you and *then* reach for the gun!"

Richie realized now that, without his cap on, the stout guy looked even younger than the blond one. Oh, how easy it would have been for Richie to take them both down if Violet's life were not in jeopardy. Concerned for her safety, he must find a subtler way to handle the matter. "What do you two clowns want?" Richie sounded furious.

"*Our* cabin," Jerry replied instantly. "And ... your guns, too, 'cause you see, we lost our own firearms somewhere in the forest yesterday during the storm. We can't seem to find them, but we found you two instead. Which reminds me, Kermit, drag your fat ass down to the trees. The girl dropped her pistol down there when I snuck up on her. You can claim her pistol while I negotiate a trade with our cranky client over here."

Kermit worked his way back to his feet. The twin barrels descended closer to his eyes. "Stay down, Kermit." Richie's voice was a whip. And Kermit obeyed, for the threat staring at him was a far worse consequence than just a broken nose. His eyes, brow, nose, mouth—all facial features—would cease to exist if that muzzle erupted, blowing his face to smithereens.

"Lower your gun, man," Jerry told Richie. "We mean you guys no harm if you'll cooperate. Focus here, on me." Richie's eyes remained on Kermit while Jerry went on ranting. "I'm the one holding a knife to her throat, and I will slice it open if you don't let Kermit get up! It's just a simple request. He'll go fetch her gun while I wait for yours. That is all we need, plus the two of you away from here." Richie silently considered that for a moment as Jerry waited for his acceptance. "So, if you still want the girl back, you'll have to put your gun away first," Jerry added.

Richard Morey did not require further convincing; after all, it was Violet's life at stake here. Though now, the shotgun aimed at the solidified mud as he turned to face her blond captive again, his eyes blazed with fury. His strong grip on the firearm was still unyielding. "Unharmed," he demanded abruptly.

"As long as you give us what we want, we'll make sure to return the favor," Jerry assured him.

"You don't have to do this," Richie counseled. "We can work together. Help each other out instead of this. No need for threats or anyone getting hurt."

"You're the one who's hurting people!" Jerry objected like a child. "After what you did to Kermit, I don't want that to happen again. I'm good with talking things out, and if you are too, then you should prove it by laying down your gun! That way I'll know for sure that we're on the same page."

And how can I be sure that you won't turn to a different page once you have the gun? Richie was thinking. "You can have the gun once you free her," Richie declared stubbornly.

"I can only let her go when I have something else to hold on to, like that shotgun you're refusing to let go of."

"Which is exactly why you should let go of her first—so that your hands are free to take the shotgun from me." Richie kept the argument going, delaying the inevitable.

"Take the shotgun *from you?* I might be blond, but I'm not dumb, man!"

"*Found it!*" Kermit had to shout over the distance.

"Well, looks like Kermit will be the one you hand that shotgun to," Jerry said with amusement. "And if you obey, then I *might* just hand this sweet-looking vanilla cupcake back to you." He sniffed at Violet's tussled hair. The word "might" caused Richie's face to darken with rage: such a fear-inducing word.

Violet, on the other hand, was thinking, *I wish I had a cupcake to shove down your throat, choking you to death! I'm not some kinda trophy for you to 'hand' to anyone, you little prick!* However, Violet kept her emotions discreetly hidden, disgusted as she was. Maintaining a brave face was the only thing she could do for now. The chill of the sharp blade biting at her neck was scary enough as it was, but Richie's face grew ever scarier, overwhelmed with rage as she had never seen him before. *When the other goon gets here, this could definitely end in blood if I don't calm Richie down.*

If Jerry didn't hold to his end of the bargain, than this quarrel would surely ignite gunfire, and Violet would perish with a slit of her throat no matter who was the bullets' targets. Either Richie yielded to their demands or the odds must shift for them to win this. And then she finally saw a change in their odds: staring at them wide-eyed through the cabin's front round window.

"Richie," her voice called, as mellow as a gentle breeze. "Do as he says ... please." Then, two very rapid blinks from her told Richie that she was up to something. He hoped for her sake it was a sure thing because he was running out of options himself while anger was consuming him. He agreed with a single nod and then crouched down to leave the shotgun at his feet.

Too quick for the eye, it cut the air with no sound and bit the ground in front of Kermit's feet. He froze, only a few feet from Jerry and Violet when specks of dust flew over his boots from the bullet's strike, but no one had heard a shot being fired. The bullet got the attention of everyone present, who all stared at the small clouds of dust at Kermit's feet.

"What the—" Kermit was about to swear, but the words ended when Richie made his move. He saw the opening and immediately knew it was Elliot. Richie seized the moment of distraction, a mere second to reach out and close his fingers around the sharp edge of the blade that had threatened the warm skin of Violet's neck for too long. His grip tightened on the piercing metal; his other hand still carried the shotgun from the trigger joint. Violet swiftly clamped her teeth on Jerry's knife-wielding hand before he could attempt to wrench it from Richie's grip. Jerry squealed while Kermit panicked and struggled to take aim with Violet's pistol.

The scuffle took only two seconds before Jerry's endurance ended, giving up his hold on the knife and on Violet. When Violet took her first step away from Jerry, another silent bullet shot through the shattered glass of the cabin's window, piercing the purple shirt that Jerry wore through the right shoulder blade. He promptly fell with a high-pitched squeal. Blood coursed down from his shoulder, creating a darker shade of red on the purple cloth.

The pistol was aimed in Kermit's shaky hands before Jerry even took his fall. Now, his friend would not get in the way. Kermit pulled the trigger over and over and over. The gun only clicked and clicked and clicked with each finger squeeze. But not Richie's shotgun: its clip did not click. Richie threw the knife away, freeing his red fingers to hold the shotgun with both hands, and fired at Kermit. BAM!

Twin shots burst from the muzzles, making particles of mud and broken leaves to explode right under Kermit's feet and ballooning belly. Kermit tumbled to the ground in shock, screaming and begging for mercy—the mercy already given to him when Richie had purposely missed the boy.

Thus the confrontation had come to an end, with blood, as Violet had suspected. Now, they were left with one assailant wounded by a clean shot through his shoulder blade and the other one wet around his short's crotch area, liquid dripping down his hairy knees. Elliot came running, his late father's rifle strapped on, bouncing up and down on his back. He wanted to be present if needed, but had not a clue of what should be done with the two.

"What's wrong?" Richie addressed Kermit. "You were so sneaky and cunning back when it was just the two of us. What happened now?"

Kermit was on urine-covered knees with his hands behind his head, looking like a hostage. "I-I d-don't like it when … when I-I get shot at!"

Violet walked up to them, and said, "Well, then you shouldn't have tried to fire at us; now, should you?" She leaned down and retrieved the pistol. "Lucky for you Richie wanted to miss. And lucky for *us* I had my gun on safety mode still. Guess 'cunning' isn't your strong suit after all! Didn't even bother to check the gun before heading back. How stupid!" Though she knew the one to blame was Jerry. Her tears were shimmering on the edge of her lower lashes, threating to run down her cheeks. Her fear had been great and had grown with each passing moment that knife was pressed at her throat. Now, she could be on the other side, holding the knife to Jerry's throat and even slit it open without as much as a warning. But for what purpose? He was crying and bleeding. A minute ago he was terrifying and dangerous; now he was no more harmful than a zombie with no arms, legs, or teeth. Violet was not the type of person to take pleasure in someone else's torment. "What should we do with them now, Richie?" she asked, not really looking forward to the answer.

"Guess we're about to find out." Puzzled, she followed his gaze and saw an orange truck pulling up to the cabin. Two large men exited the vehicle with AK-47s slung over their shoulders.

39

THE STANDOFF

DAY 506

The tension was high *before* the orange truck pulled up to the cabin. With two additional men to double the intensity of the situation, one could use a knife to cut the tension.

Both men were dark-skinned and wore black boots with dark jeans that were even more battered than their footwear. One was taller than the other, with massive arms and upper body and tattoos from his wrists all the way to the base of his neck. A dense beard hid his chin and much of his neck from view, stretching his cruel face longer.

The other man had only an inch on Richie. His robust body, though not as gigantic as his companion's, was dressed in an unbuttoned gray shirt over a bold green t-shirt. He also had a thick bushy beard and matted hair, which hung round his face.

They walked toward the friends and former assailants huddled in the open field and stopped no more than ten feet from them. "That's close enough," Richie said from where he stood between Violet, who was holding her pistol over Jerry, and Elliot, on his left, with the rifle poking the back of Kermit's head. "You two gentlemen *lost* too?"

"Funny you should ask us that," the taller gentleman answered. "We's 'bout to ask you punks the same." His deep voice was threating, and so was the AK-47 that no longer hung from his tattooed shoulder; instead, it was pointed in their general direction. "Now, which one of y'all is the leader?"

"You're speaking to him." Richie deepened his voice to sound bolder rather than anxious. "Can I help you with anything?"

"Yeah?" the man answered. "You can start by saving yourself some trouble and back up!"

"I'm sorry, are those two yours?"

"Don't play dumb with me, boy. You'll lose big time if you keep on playin'!"

Richie lifted the shotgun. "*Playing dumb* is not my area of expertise. So I think my chances of winning would be low in *that* game. But then again, so are the chances for those two to live longer. Are you willing to risk it with that attitude of yours?" Richie spoke with daring ridicule and a face as hard as stone.

All it did was infuriate the murderous looking man. "That's enough!" he barked. "This is your last warning. Back the hell up or I won't care who dies, long as I blow off that smart mouth o' yours!"

"Easy there, Lamar. Jerry needs help." The other man intervened. "Let's not forget that you're not the only one here calling the shots on who lives and dies. You had your chance to speak; you're startin' to lose it, so now's my turn."

"Dwayne," Jerry called out, "they shot me! Just ... out of the blue, they shot me ... for no reason!" He pressed one hand against the bullet hole to keep pressure on the wound, though blood clearly still leaked into the cloth. "You can't let them—"

"Shut up!" she scolded. "You don't get to play the innocent here, you prick!" Violet scowled at the man called Dwayne. "Your boy here snuck up on me and put a knife to my throat, demanding our guns 'cause they can't find theirs!"

"I see." Dwayne grimaced. "Is this true?" All the answer he got from the two was a moan of pain from Jerry and a nervous nod from Kermit.

Dwayne cursed at the notion of Jerry and Kermit's rebellious stunt. "We did bring those two to look for the guns they lost yesterday during the storm. They should've known better than to try stealing from our *own kind*." His voice seemed to be boiling for a moment, but Dwayne reigned in his temper. "Dumb as they may be, they thought they could take on a lone girl. You proved them wrong. And from the looks of it, they've learned their lesson. But right now one of them will bleed out or get an infection if we don't fix him up soon. We need to get him back to our place for now."

"No," Richie responded with a nonchalance that grabbed both men's attention. "We can't risk you guys leaving, then coming back after us with more men. We're outnumbered as it is." *Stupid, Richie! You just revealed to the enemy that there's no more of you out here. That there's no backup! How could you be so reckless?* he scolded himself. *What would Gunter think if he saw this, you idiot?*

Lamar looked as if he were running out of patience—as if he had any to begin with—while his older brother sighed. "You're looking at all the men right here," he admitted to Richie. "We have two women with us who don't fight. You three probably came from the hunting grounds, right? So you saw how dangerous it was in there. I don't know how you guys made it, or how many you lost back there. But we lost plenty of our people back there once, and we do *not* intend to lose any more. We can work together. Help each other out."

"That's what I tried telling your boy Jerry here," Richie said immediately. "But he just wouldn't listen."

"We've wasted enough time with these fools, Dwayne." Lamar voiced his contempt. "We can take 'em out."

"Don't be stupid, Lamar. Even if we could, either Kermit or Jerry will be dead before we finish. Then what do we get, hmm? Fewer people to help improve our chances for survival, that's what we'll end up with!" Lamar fell silent, showing his contempt with a stone-cold expression. Dwayne turned back to the captors and hostages, but especially Richie. "Please listen to me, kid. You're being cautious: I don't blame you for that. But I can make you a deal."

"I'm listening."

Dwayne pointed to where the truck was parked. "Three and a half miles from here, there's a fence. Crossing that will lead you to a small ranch. That's where we sleep and grow our food; that's where we've been living for more than a year now. You could come with us, and we'll give you some food, ammunition if you want, and even clean clothes. Also the cabin—you can have the cabin. We only use it to keep watch when some of us go into the forest to get water from the stream. It's all yours, and all I want in return are the two boys. What do you say?"

Richie glanced thoughtfully between Violet and Elliot before making a decision. "I have some conditions first."

"Name them."

"All three of us will be coming along with you, plus Jerry," he began. "Big man will hand over the gun to you and stay here with Kermit till we get back."

"*Hell no!*" Lamar objected. "You're demanding *way* too much, boy!"

"Richie, are you sure about this?" Violet asked doubtfully. "They could still have more people with guns waiting for us there. It could be a trap."

As if Richie didn't hear Lamar's complaint or Violet's counsel, he went on. "Once we have what you've promised to give us, we'll drive back here. You'll pick up the two you left behind and be on your way, never to use this cabin again."

"Deal," Dwayne agreed.

"*What?* C'mon, dawg, he's playin' you fo' a fool," Lamar protested. "Don't be buyin' into his bull—"

"Lamar! Just hand it over and wait till we get back," he said irritably.

In the car, Richie sat in the passenger seat, shotgun in hand, while Dwayne handled the driving. Violet, Elliot, and Jerry bounced and rocked in the exposed pickup bed, with constant moans and swearing coming from Jerry.

"What's your name, kid?" Dwayne asked, as the vehicle passed through some clusters of tree.

"Richie."

Extending his hand, he said, "Dwayne."

Richie took the hand and said, "I know."

"I really like your style, Richie—very cautious, calm and decisive—unlike my guys. See, that's how I came to lead this group and not my little brother, Lamar."

"There's nothing little about him." Richie sniggered.

Dwayne gave a snort of laughter. "Touché. But he's really handy when it comes to surviving against the dead. Saved my ass plenty of times. Bet you're very good at surviving too with that small crew of yours. You don't seem like bad folk from what happened back there. You were pretty understanding, all things considered."

"Don't take me for naïve because of that, Dwayne. I still doubt we'll *only* find two women on that ranch of yours. And if we were to find a lot of backup, we'll both be kissing the deal good-bye, and one of us will come to regret running into the other today."

"Like I said, Richie," Dwayne mumbled. "Good folk, the kind that will be very useful to have on your team."

"What're you talking about?"

"Richie, we've lost a lot of people. We living folk ought to stay together. And to do that, you need supplies of food, water, and weapons. We've got plenty of that back on the ranch and more. Let's get there so you can see all of it for yourself, and maybe afterward we can discuss another deal that will benefit *both* our groups."

40

HOME FOR NOW

DAY 546

The small ranch had a security perimeter that consisted of stumps with taut cables stretched between them, forming a six-sided ring. Remnants of tin cans were hung from the cables to create an alarm if anyone attempted to climb over or squeeze through the perimeter, whether the undead, looters, or scavengers.

Within those perimeters it was clear that the survivors had given a lot of thought to protecting their small fortress in the midst of a jungle of the living dead and hungry wildlife. Their fields of growing vegetation had to be kept undisturbed so their cabbage, lettuce, tomatoes, potatoes, and corn would reach full size. However, the vegetables were not the only thing that kept them fed; they regularly ventured onto the hunting grounds to catch deer, rabbit, and fish from the stream that had a lifelong supply of tuna, mostly. And on unlucky meatless days, the survivors would come back to the ranch with freshly picked fruit from the forest to eat it or squeeze into juices.

Of course, duties had to be divided among the surviving members to make all this work. While some would go out to fetch food, others would clean and skin the kills, divide them into equal portions, and cook the meat. Those duties took place every single day. There were no days off for the survivors if they wanted to keep surviving.

Richie, Violet, and Elliot saw that Dwayne had told the truth about their numbers, and they noticed the fields of different vegetables and the water pump that not only pumped water from the soil, but also from a giant plastic barrel they occasionally filled up at the stream. The barrel was located between the small tool shed full of hay and tools, and a one-story house that had a working toilet, shower, and kitchen sink, all thanks to the pump and barrel.

After seeing the ranch, they realized that they would not survive long on their own if they were to turn down Dwayne's generous offer of joining forces. With all those provisions just for the price of helping out around the ranch, it seemed the best offer a zombie-apocalypse survivor could have. All three agreed to take the offer and sleep in the ranger cabin for a time till they got used to the company and moved to their new home. Then they would spend their nights in the tool shed just to be safer behind the security walls of the ranch, even though the cabin offered more comfort.

It was best for them to keep some distance from their new hosts, though. There remained a glimmer of heat between them and the boy thugs, Jerry and Kermit. Both parties would be bitter for a while.

A month passed by, and in that time, Violet, Richie, and Elliot had shown their worth to be greater than Jerry's and Kermit's over the course of a year. That made the boys sour, but they dared not say or do anything about except work harder to prove their worth. To do so, they had to work with people they did not like.

One day, Dwayne requested that Lamar take two escorts with him to the stream to collect the trap they set to catch fish and to pick some plums. Lamar dragged Kermit and Elliot along to help out. Kermit would pick plums, and Elliot would keep a sharp lookout with his rifle, which he always carried with him these day, while the big man would hoist the net and its catch.

Back at the ranch, Jerry, still mending from his wound, used that as an excuse on a regular basis to get out of doing any heavy lifting. He skipped the forest mission today and stayed behind to water the vegetable fields and help the olive-skinned beauty Angie pick cabbage. She was often charged with looking after the vegetables and cooking the meals. Angie was of Latin descent. Her skin, hair, eyes, and speech said it all. Like the others, she wore tall boots for practicality, but she also wore cut-off shorts and a neat button-down shirt that she tied above her slim belly, showing off her figure, which was full and curvy. Any man would want to work alongside Angie, picking cabbages.

Beyond the security perimeter, Dwayne had taken Richie with him to assist in constructing a seven-foot wall a couple of yards out from the cable border. It was a security upgrade they'd been working on since before the arrival of the three new survivors. The hope was that a seven-foot wall of thick wood would be harder to breach for zombies, animals, and man. They crafted the walls from lumber collected from the forest, using saws, hammers, nails, and shovels to plant the posts firmly in the ground. Only a quarter of the ranch was enclosed by them as of yet.

Meanwhile, Violet was tending to her own duties, she worked in the cornfield, holding a basket in one arm and an umbrella over the head of a slightly hunched-over old woman, whom she was following around to keep her shaded from the sun. The slow ancient hands unerringly picked the best yellow corn for the basket. "I know it's a task meant for one person," said the old woman, leaning on a cane to keep stable, "but when it comes to picking corn and tomatoes, I can tell the sweet ones from the unripe with a single touch."

"Why don't you use that talent of yours in cooking us a sweet meal for today then?" Violet asked.

The old woman sighed. "I'm afraid my cooking days are no more," she admitted. "Too slow in picking means even slower in cooking. All of us want to have at least two meals a day to keep our strength up. With my old hands handling the cooking instead of Angie, you might have to wait till supper to eat your first meal of the day."

Violet giggled at the old woman's remark. "Can't help but think that you're an awesome cook from all the advice you keep giving Angie in the kitchen."

"You thought right, child. I *was* an 'awesome cook' back before all this. So awesome, I was the head chef in a Chinese restaurant that me and my husband owned for forty-five years. It was in Cliffroyce midtown, famous for its pure Chinese dishes and delicious fortune cookies."

"I remember that place. My dad took me and my little brother there once for dinner. I was in my senior year in high school, and Billy was in kindergarten. I don't remember what I ordered from the menu exactly, but those fortune cookies I never forgot. They were sure tasty."

"I doubt anyone would remember the menu. My husband and I kept changing it every few months to keep customers interested. You would find the most authentic Chinese dishes of all time, including ones you hadn't known existed." The old woman listed a number of exotic dishes she used to cook. "But it was the cookies that no one forgets. Many customers even said that the fortunes they received actually came true!"

The old woman sounded amazed, herself.

"Cooking meals and granting wishes," Violet said. "That must've been a hell of a career for you, Miss Edna. Doing what you love for forty-five years, and you've survived the apocalypse to tell about it." *Wish I had that many years in my wrestling career,* Violet thought to herself, realizing in dismay that she would never have a wrestling career now.

"It was in the fortieth year I stopped cooking for the restaurant at all, when my age started affecting my performance." Edna was somewhere in her mid-eighties. "And five years later, the sickness broke out. It was a good thing that I'd kept myself busy practicing my grandmother's old Chinese medicinal recipes in that time." It was those herbal medicines that had made Edna their doctor at the ranch.

When Jerry was brought back to the ranch after the altercation between the two groups, Edna had put her herbs to use in cleaning the bullet wound and nursed him back to health from the fever that stayed with him for days after. She still removed his bandage periodically to rub some basil ointment on the wound, concocted from her grandmother's old recipe book.

"If it weren't for my medicines, I'd be just a slow old woman who annoys the group with her stories and cooking advice," Edna said, frowning at the corn.

"Let's not forget about sweet corn picking, chopping veggies, cleaning fish guts, and plucking feathers."

Then came a rustling sound, and out came Angie through the tall grass. "Hola, ladies. How's corn picking?" she asked, her voice thickly accented.

"Just fine, child, we're almost done here," Edna replied.

"I'm gonna start boiling the water then. When you're done, you come help me divide up portions and chop chop chop cabbage, okay?"

"Will do," Edna said. "I only need to make a final run near the scarecrow, and we'll be done picking corn for the rest of the week."

Angie left with a smile on her face, vanishing into the tall weeds. Violet followed Edna to the heart of the cornfield with the idea of a fortune cookie coming true still lingering in her mind. *Wish I could remember what my fortune cookie said. Maybe it came true without me knowing it.* The thought of things coming true reminded her of her dreams, the warning nightmares. She hadn't had any since Royce Pentagon Sanctuary, but she feared that they had taken a turn for the worse when she had daydream of the Grim Reaper. *Go back*, she heard the eerie voice say, and then the figure had disappeared as if it were no more than vapor.

That shadowy figure stood before her now, but it was a less scary version. Knots of straw gathered together on a long stick to resemble a human figure formed a scarecrow. Only this scarecrow didn't dress in ranch clothing like the traditional ones. Instead, all they'd been able to spare was a long tattered black cloak with a hood to cover the straw almost entirely. They'd added a skull mask for a face since they happened to have one, and what else was anyone going to do with it? And just for the sake of completing this ironic masterpiece, they'd placed a scythe at his side as the rightful weapon of the Grim Reaper.

With only a second's glimpse at the grim scarecrow perched on its stick, Violet felt a shiver run up her spine, making the hairs on the back of her neck stand up.

41

LUMBER WORK

DAY 546

"Marlin and Paul were the ones who came up with the idea of having some kind of security perimeter around the ranch," Dwayne was saying to Richie, as they hammered nails into the wood. "The ranch was just an open buffet back then, months after the virus broke out. Luckily, the two of 'em acted fast and put up those stumps with cable wires, but it just wasn't enough. One zombie was able to slip through without anyone noticing and bit three people. We had to increase our night watchers after that incident until another man came up with an extra security measure. His name was Damian Fletcher, a furniture craftsman back before the zombies took over. He suggested chopping wood from the forest so we could build walls."

Dwayne stopped his hammering and chattering to have a gulp of water from his canteen, quenching his thirst as droplets fell from between his lips and the canteen's head, dampening his green shirt. "So we went out in a big group each day," he continued, "and Damian would keep on crafting, till one day we ran into this pack of zombie men and hogs. They caught us by surprise. Me and Lamar were able to make it back to the ranch in one piece. Can't say the same about the rest of the crew and that included Marlin and Paul, who'd basically been in charge. We're all that's left—or were before you three came along."

"And what about the craftsman? Was he a victim of the slaughter too?"

"Not exactly." Dwayne sighed. "He was working at the ranch, but his son was a part of the forest crew. We told him that he didn't make it … still, that didn't stop Damian from running out to the forest with his gun. I tried reasoning with him, but it was no use. He came back hours later with what limbs were left of his son in his arms. He buried them a couple of yards outside the walls and wanted to be left alone for a while. A while later, we heard a gunshot … we rushed out and found that our brilliant craftsman had taken his own life."

"That's messed up," Richie said, aghast.

"We've all had our share of messed-up moments in this dying world of ours, Richie. Anything can easily kill a man nowadays if he's not strong enough—sickness, grief, fear, madness … people killing each other for power and resources." Dwayne shook his head disappointedly. "Damn human race. If people would just fight alongside each other instead of against one another, maybe we'd have a chance of winning the war against the dead, our *real* enemies. Instead, we got those no-good bastards running around, calling themselves the Masked Rebels, killing more living than they do the living dead. That's why these walls must go up. There aren't many decent folks like us out there no more."

"Well, it looks like Damian crafted enough walls to surround the whole ranch, but I don't think we have enough nails to stack 'em all up,"

Richie said, cautious of the resources. It looked like they were down to their last ten nails.

"There are more in the tool shed," Dwayne assured him.

"On it." Richie left his hammer next to the scattered nails and heaved himself up, brushing the sawdust off his baggy green trousers. He strolled around the wooden walls till he made it halfway across the ranch. At the south of the ranch, which was the front if someone was making their way from Laveaux's Forest, there was a small wooden gate, closed at the moment. Behind it, the perimeter cable had been detached to allow exit and entry to the ranch.

Richie strode back onto the ranch with speed but slowed once he was inside the tool shed. It was a jungle of hay and boxes. Blue barrels containing an arsenal of ammunition, translucent jugs of petrol, and spare tires were stacked on top of each other. It took Richie a while to look through this chaotic warehouse of goods without finding a single box of nails.

He pulled out and examined various tools in-search of the nails, but his mind was elsewhere. The stories of past group members' deaths filled his head with grim memories. *"We've all had our share of messed-up moments in this dying world of ours,"* he remembered Dwayne's wise voice saying.

The memories took Richie back to the day he was reunited with Violet on her father's boat in Lake Valley. The image of the slaughter of her kin on the red bow was enough to make him feel woozy for a moment. Marvin Conley, Richie's best friend. The memory of his round-figured friend and that jolly four-eyed face of his—Richie could weep for that face that was buried beneath the rubble of what was left of their Daily Comics shop. Then there was Gunter, who'd fought valiantly to save the rest and had given his life. They lost Gunter Waters the night before meeting their new allies, and ever since then, nothing had happened to ruin the peace.

However, those messed-up memories would haunt Richie for as long as he lived, forcing him to remember the gore and stench on the boat—and worst of all was the look of fear in Violet's eyes. The creature of guilt would never cease gnawing at his conscience at the memory of forsaking his friend Marvin, nor would the anguish of knowing that even the bravest and the greatest of soldiers could die in an instant when faced with their walking dead enemies.

Four deadly weapons could kill a man if he wasn't strong enough or willful enough to survive in this new cruel world, Dwayne had said. One of them was sickness, which would drain a man's strength and convert it into weakness, eventually leading to death and conversion to the side of the living dead. That was the physical sickness. There was also the sickness of the mind, a sickness that could tug on the cords of one's emotions and play with the keys of one's mind. Grief, fear, and madness could take down a survivor in moments of weakness, but not Richie Morey. No. He prevented sickness from latching onto his strength. He overcame grief because the sun would rise the next day. He controlled the madness for the sake of his sanity. He fought fear to defeat the terrors that stalked them for the kill. He needed to be this way in order to keep himself safe and those around him he cared for, even safer.

Richie realized how long it was taking him once he was down to the last toolbox, cursing and shoving random tools without a nail box in sight. He went to exit the shed, kicking through piles of hay till his sneakers found solid ground again. There, Angie bypassed him with a friendly smile. As he closed in on the ranch's exit, on his left he caught

Jerry in the cabbage field scowling at him. Richie paid no heed to the bitter teenager, walking on by as though he were not even there.

Richie returned to where Dwayne was waiting with the hammer and pieces of walls. "Dwayne," he called out. "I looked through all the boxes, and not a single nail was in there."

"Well, damn," Dwayne said. "I should've known. Took me some time this morning to find the boxes we already used up. And it seems they were the last of 'em."

"We have enough nails to put those last two pieces up, and then we'll have the south and the east completely zombie-proofed," Richie pointed out. "And that will leave us with the north and the west still with one level of security. So we have the pieces to stack up but not the nails that'll hold them together."

"Looks like Christmas shopping will start early this year," Dwayne announced merrily.

"Christmas shopping in September? Well, we'd sure miss the crowds. Not many early Christmas shoppers out there anymore."

"Oh, Richie, it's not the crowds of people we should be worried about. It's the crowds of the dead, doing their Thanksgiving turkey shopping. And we're the turkeys on sale, homie."

42

NIGHT IN THE SHED

NIGHT 546

Before the sun slanted down the horizon and the blackness of night was upon them, Big Lamar returned in the orange truck, along with Kermit and Elliot. They made it just in time for dinner. Richie and Dwayne had opened up the wooden gate to let them drive in soon after they were done setting up the last two walls on the east side.

The mission was more than a success. None had come back empty-handed: Lamar had the fishnet over one shoulder with a good catch of tuna and some trout. Kermit carried a basket full of freshly picked plums, and Elliot, most surprisingly, held two fuzzy tails in one hand, presenting the squirrels for a stew they'd be having that week. "Brought them down with one silent shell at a time," Elliot had bragged when Richie asked how he'd caught them. "They never saw it coming."

He'd been earning the nickname "Elliot the Hunter." Before the squirrels, he had caught wild rabbits roaming about the ranch, shot down pigeons and ducks, and, once, he'd snuck up stealthily on an elk.

Wielding his father's silenced rifle, he shot a bullet right into the great herbivore's heart. The elk had ululated his final call as the blood seeped down his neck and it fell to a quick death. Elliot felt bad watching all those innocent creatures die under the command of his finger, but it made no difference. Elliot and his companions had to eat; that was how the circle of life worked, after all.

They all went inside the house for dinner. Angie greeted all of them aloud and rushed to shower Lamar with kisses and a hug. Once all were seated and digging into their plates of fried vegetables, Dwayne mentioned the nail issue. Lamar suggested visiting the closest residential area, which was about thirty minutes' driving distance over the hills to the north. Whilst eating Dwayne announced who would be accompanying him on the mission the next morning to Hill-Ville County.

After approving the morning's mission, all went to bed. The one bedroom inside the house had belonged to Lamar and Angie, while the pullout sofa in the living room belonged to Edna. Dwayne and Jerry slept on the floor beside Edna, using sleeping bags to keep themselves cozy. Kermit was on night watch duty and so was Elliot, one posted on the west side, and the other to the north.

In the cold shed, they had blankets and cushions to protect them from the chilly and scratchy straw. It was one of the few nights that Violet and Richie would have the shed all to themselves while Elliot was on duty with someone other than them. Richie was one of the two chosen to accompany Dwayne the next day. "I can't believe you got picked to go without me," Violet protested. "And instead of choosing someone who's as experienced as you, Dwayne had to go with Blondie." Violet was referring to Jerry.

"Mmmm ... yeah," Richie moaned lazily. He was on his back

across the blankets, resting his head and neck in Violet's lap while she rubbed the sides of his temple.

One hand quit rubbing and smacked Richie lightly on the cheek to catch his attention. "Are you even listening, Sleeping Beauty?"

"Yeah, yeah," he responded. "Something about you not being chosen ... something ... experience, then something about a blond chick."

"Uh-huh." Violet grimaced. "A blond chick that goes by the name Jerry?"

"Oh, then ... a blond dude, I guess," Richie corrected. Violet tugged on a curl close to his scalp. "Ow!" he cried out. "I asked for a massage, not a haircut." His reaction made Violet guffaw.

"Speaking of haircuts," Violet said, "you need one. Your hair is getting to be past your shoulders." She began digging her fingers deep into the mop of his black curls. The feeling was sensational to Richie; his head felt lighter from the slithering movements of Violet's fingers in his hair. He didn't want it to stop.

"I actually like my hair this long," he protested. As it grew longer, the curls had softened into waves.

"Me too," Violet agreed and leaned over a bit to plant a kiss on his forehead, while her fingers kept digging and twisting in his hair. "But seriously, Jerry over me? The guy's *still* complaining about his shoulder. It's been over a month now. And Dwayne says that's why he wants him to come along, that he's not doing enough to contribute around the ranch."

"Maybe it's for the best," Richie said. "Maybe it'll help make a man out of him, and besides, we don't want to be leaving Elliot alone with those two punks. They still hold a grudge against us—Elliot most of all.

There's no telling what they might get away with while Lamar's in charge. He's not as responsible as his big brother is, but he'll at least have you and Elliot around to help with the heavy lifting."

"Yeah, but ..." Violet realized something. "You and I ... we've never been apart since before Royce Pentagon. We've fought zombies side by side every single time. We used to go in large groups. We used to go out there with a strategy. And now ..."

"Vi, I don't think we'll have to worry about zombies much on tomorrow's mission, all right?" Richie tried to ease her nerves. "I know Lamar called it 'Dead-Ville,' but Dwayne assured us that we won't actually be driving up the hill, where all the abandoned stores and the *dead* reside. We'll just stop by the big department store facing the hill from below. We'll check their warehouse for nails and be back within an hour or so—depending on the traffic of course," he said with a grin.

Surprisingly, Violet giggled—unlike the usual snarky chuckle, full of sarcasm, she usually rewarded him with when he cracked a joke. Her mean girl act was one of the qualities Richie loved the most about her. It was the quality that kept Violet more comic than dark, more lively than gloomy throughout all this misery and death that plagued them. Richie loved that about Violet and never wanted her to change. Even if it meant that he couldn't be the funny one.

However, this night he won an honest, adorable giggle from the woman he loved because tomorrow, he would be as far as he'd been from her since finding her on that boat. Only half an hour away by car, but still far for two people who had avoided being separated from each other in the world of the dead—always fighting and surviving side by side, as she'd said.

Violet ceased giggling only when her lips brushed against Richie's warm forehead again for a longer kiss this time. Her fingers had stopped wriggling in his hair and slid down to his cheeks, with their scraggly facial hair that he was still trying to grow out. Though touching her bare palms to his hairy cheeks felt thorny and ticklish, the touch of her warm lips to his felt soft and luscious. She stayed there for a long while.

When she pulled up, Richie's eyes remained shut as the tip of his tongue licked the remaining sweetness on his lips. "Kisses *and* giggles?" he asked in a tone of slight astonishment. "Does this mean I'm in for a lucky night in the shed?"

Violet giggled again with a wide smile and brought her forehead down gently to rest on Richie's forehead. "It might," she said, temptingly. She pinched both his cheeks fondly. "Only if you promise me that you *will* come back to me tomorrow after your little hike, with every single hair still intact. Remember, Richie, I won't be there flying to your rescue when you fall on your ass, screaming like a damsel in distress."

Richie snorted as he sat up, forcing Violet to sit up straight to face him. "You sure that *I'm* more likely to be the damsel in distress?" Violet's eyebrows shot up, and her mouth twisted into a smirk. Richie went on. "Correct me if I'm wrong, but isn't Prince Charming the one who flies on his steed to rescue this fair princess trapped in a castle, with a fire-breathing dragon to fight off?"

"Not if the princess can ride a steed and Prince Charming cannot." Violet turned the tables.

"Hmm … that could shift the odds in the dragon's favor," Richie admitted, for the fact was that Violet truly could ride a horse and he could not.

"But the princess still needs Prince Charming to be around the castle," Violet said. "That's the only way she'll be able to keep that distressing dragon away."

"Who's the dragon in this scenario anyway?" Richie asked, scratching his head.

Violet took a moment to think, tapping her chin with two fingers rhythmically. "Lamar, maybe," she answered, unsure. "He's a decent guy if you stay on his cool side, but he still has the temper of a hot-headed dragon when he's pissed."

Richie chuckled in agreement. "And he's big too. I wouldn't imagine him turning into a zombie. Whew, don't think he'd be as easy to put down as the rest of 'em in close combat. Never have I run into a corpse that size before." *Except for the bear that killed Gunter.* Richie remembered the sickening undead beast clamping his jaws on Gunter's arm, but decided not to mention it.

"What if you encounter Lamar-sized zombies on tomorrow's mission?" Violet asked hesitantly.

"I'll either blow or hack their heads off," Richie answered with confidence as if he'd been anticipating that question. Violet nodded, her face a mask hiding what Richie could tell was, concern. He embraced her, holding her to his broad chest, and then he kissed her on the top of her head, breathing in the scent of her hair. "I will be back tomorrow, I promise, way before the sun can set. I've told you time and time again: we're in this together. I will always be with you and would never leave your side unless I knew you'd be safe. And it'll be just for a little while. Dwayne will be with me, and he's already been there twice before. And both times the place was zombie-free, he said. So you're worrying about nothing."

"Fine," Violet said, pulling away from his chest to look into his eyes. "But you better come back with a souvenir."

"Tampons, noted." Richie winked.

"Best souvenir ever!" Violet giggled again, leaning back into his chest. His arms snuggled her tight as he chuckled with her. Then his fuzzy chin rested on top of her head, staying that way for some time.

She felt all warm and safe in Richie's arms until he began mumbling again about tomorrow's mission. "If we do find enough nails in that warehouse, the walls could go up in a week, covering the entire ranch! We would be hidden away safely again, with an endless supply of food and water and better hopes for our future together, maybe even for ... *tinier* versions of us in the future, running around the ranch, living the farm life."

Violet pulled away at that point, scowling at Richie. "What do you mean by 'tinier versions of us' in the future?" She didn't wait for him to answer. "Having kids during ... all of this is not something we should even be considering, Richie, let alone discussing."

Her reaction to the subject took him by surprise, and Richie struggled to find a safe answer. "I just thought maybe if we were safe at all times inside ... and ... and Angie was a nurse, she would know how to handle ..."

"Nothing," Violet finished. "Angie would know nothing of handling this type of situation because it will *never* happen! We thought Royce Pentagon was safe and look what happened!" Then there was a second of silence. "Richie, I love you, literally more than anything in the world right now, but you have to be insane to think that we can bring children into this world." Violet's brutal facts were hard to refute. "If it were our previous world, I would not even think twice about starting a family with you. But right now, here ... that's just wrong. It would be cruel to raise a child under these circumstances, growing up inside without exploring what the rest of the world looks like beyond those walls. No matter how safe we can make this place, even if you build it into a fortress, death will still rule outside those walls, trying to get in. And we can only hold the fortress for so long. We can't live forever, Richie. I'm sorry."

Richie was taken aback. The scolding was not something that he had anticipated, but it was good to know how Violet truly felt about that matter. Though that upset him more than the actual scolding and ruined the moment of romance they'd been sharing. "I shouldn't have brought it up," he said regretfully, "not now, at least. Maybe we should talk about this when the walls *do* go up and circumstances change for the better."

"We can never talk about this again." Violet's voice was irritably insistent.

It had escalated so quickly. Richie was tired and couldn't think straight. He sighed. "Look, Vi, I'm really tired now, and I have to wake up early tomorrow. So I think I might just hit the hay. Good night." He gave her quick smooch on the cheek and slipped under the covers.

Violet remained sitting cross-legged, not feeling sleepy. In a while, Richie started snoring a choir of whistles that bounced off the shed's aluminum walls. But all Violet heard was the sound of a child's joyful laughter in her head. Oddly enough, it resembled the laugh of her brother Billy when he used to run around the backyard with glee in his deep blue eyes on a warm summer's day.

43

A DUEL FOR SUPREMACY

DAY 547

As the sun rose, so did the residents of the ranch. They resumed the preparations for the day's mission recruits, bidding them farewell and good luck after they'd relished on plums dipped in honey and spiced boiled potatoes with water to wash it all down.

It was time for the two young watchers of the night to be relieved of their task and get some rest. Kermit said his good-byes to Jerry and Dwayne before entering the house, and Elliot saluted all three before escaping to his straw bed in the shed.

Violet's goodbye to Richie was an awkward kiss with a brief hug and a "Be careful. I still need you here." Then the three men were off in the orange truck, exiting via the only gate to the ranch.

The lot that remained on the ranch went ahead with their daily routines. Violet had hardly gotten any sleep the previous night and did less than an hour of gardening work before heading back to the shed for a nap. It was Edna who told her to go get some rest after seeing her doze off as she stood shoveling in the tomato field. "I will send Angie to wake you up in a couple of hours. But if the crew returns before then, I'll let Richie handle that task," Edna said, with all wrinkly smiles. So, Violet thanked the old woman and went, crawling under the covers where she and Richie had slept the night before, all cuddly at first and all high tension later on. *It would be a sin worse than all the seven if we brought a child into this world,* she thought as she lay back onto the cushions. *It was stupid of him to even think about it. And now, I can't stop thinking about it!*

She wanted to get her diary and write down some of her emotions and thoughts, but her backpack was far from reach, and Elliot was asleep. She was too comfy on her cushions already, and her eyes were becoming heavy, answering sleep's call. The light slipping into the shed kept her awake a few minutes, but sleep was a far more powerful opponent. It does not battle light: it swallows it into the black abyss of one's unconscious mind.

Within the abyss, light could be found in the darkness, and they clashed for hours inside the slumbering mind, where in reality, the clash would last no more than a few measly seconds. And to the victor go the spoils ... light, if the sleeper wakes, and darkness, if the sleeper never wakes. Life for light and death for darkness.

Violet's eyes shut, and her inner battle was about to begin ...

When her leafy green eyes shot open and she saw the contents of the shed, she didn't know how long the nap had lasted. *Not too long, it looks like.* Angie hadn't come to wake her up, and Elliot was still snuggled up in his sheets on the opposite side of the shed. She yawned, pushed herself up, and went to the door, squinting her eyes in anticipation of the sun blinding her. Violet wished she could go back to sleep, but there was a lot of farm work ahead of her today, waiting in the sun.

She pushed the door open, and the brightness of the sun *did not* blind her as she'd expected. The heat didn't warm her exposed skin, and no shadow stretched out beneath her feet. All because the sun was overtaken by a gloomy mass of gray clouds. On the ground, Violet could not even see as far as her ankle because of the dense fog that swallowed the entire ranch, making the place horrifically eerie.

A chill ran through her as if a ghost had just walked past. Violet, for some reason, was still barefooted when she exited the shed and had only her boxer shorts and an oversized jersey on, which made her get goosebumps when the mists touched her. She was just about to call out names when she caught a glimpse of two figures roaming in the fog. Violet immediately thought them to be Lamar and Angie since one was far bigger than the other. As she got closer, though, she realized that they were neither Angie nor Lamar. They were creatures dragged up from the blackness of hell itself, or so it seemed. One was wrought in jet black, and both had somber red holes for eyes, drilled into the center of their ghostly faces.

Soon there were more than four stalking red eyes. Dozens appeared behind them as more black shapes took form in the fog. Violet had no words to utter; she had no voice to speak or scream. Silence prevailed.

Suddenly, the silence was broken by a high-pitched screeching that would have made Violet's eardrums burst if she had not covered them with her palms so quickly. Out of the misty grounds came skinless, sharp-clawed hands stretching out towards her—too many to count. She immediately spun around, both hands still covering her ears, and ran the opposite way for her dear life, without even turning back to see if she was being chased. But she knew she was. She had to know. The screeching was as relentless as the hands.

Violet ran for the tool shed, where her weapons were ... where Elliot was. "Elliot!" she cried. She pelted through the shed's open door, but where there should have been hay beneath her feet, there was fog. Her body should have rammed into a wall since her legs did not stop running, but no aluminum walls were there to barricade her path. The shed seemed infinite. The mists stretched endlessly forward, till her eyes could see desolate houses with overgrown shrubbery, cars devoured by rust, and buildings collapsed in ruin as she loped on with exhausted breaths. She was not on the ranch anymore, she knew for certain.

A town or a village perhaps—Violet did not know. All she knew was that she couldn't stop running or the skinless clawed hands would impale her. The misty road led nowhere but forward, so she sprinted in that direction as the deafening screeches maintained pursuit and the pallid fog shaded black to swallow all that surrounded her. The unseen surface that Violet's bare feet ran upon was gone. She was falling. Hands and legs were flailing frantically. Her long silky hair flapped madly, as did the baseball jersey her slender body had borne. The screeching died out as Violet's screams took over during her endless plummet down the black pit. A pit that was nothing but pitch darkness until they appeared again at the bottom—the skinless hands like moving spikes, by the hundreds, awaiting their screaming victim.

A spark of pure white light slashed through the spiky claws. A figure encased in gleaming white armor that pushed the malicious blackness away had halted Violet's decent, carrying her gently down to the surface. Slowly, the surrounding darkness faded into bleach white from the presence of this mysterious savior. *A knight in shining armor!*

It was just as the fairytales had promised her. During a princess's worst hours of distress, a knight in shining armor would fly to seek her and gain her heart for a happily ever after. But who? Who was this gallant knight in white? Violet's true knight in shining armor had gone to explore the realm of the living dead and left her here, wherever "here" was. Could it be Richie underneath that splendid white armor touched with silver on the chest, gauntlets, and helm? Would it be his handsome face she'd see if she lifted off that helm with silvery angelic wings on the sides?

Well, there was only one way to find out. The knight was still as stone, standing before Violet. Her breathing grew shallow when her hands moved hesitantly to his helm. "Who are you?" she asked in a whisper, as her fingers brushed against the helm's wings but did not latch on. Her eyes were focused on where his eyes should be, behind the fine silvery work that reflected her face and more ...

Behind her, she saw the reflection of black corruption scouring the bone-white surroundings. It was those black fog creatures with red eyes eating at the knight's light. Darkness had once again found a way to swallow the light, trapping Violet and her knight in the very narrow space of his armor's light.

Out of the blackness stepped forward an ebony-armored behemoth. His rough armor showed only when the light licked at him. The crimson of his eyes was the only other color, like his followers; enormous horns erupted from his helm's sides, though his giant's stature would have distinguished him from the rest without a helm.

The white knight stood his ground, though. He refused to be intimidated even by the double-edged longaxe or the devilishly sharp gauntlets. The knight brought an armored arm in front of Violet to shield her and drew his silvery sword out from its white scabbard to answer the demon's challenge.

The duel between light and darkness began as the surrounding creatures screeched in a cacophony. The double-edged ax twirled, and the glistening sword flashed, as both challengers advanced to meet the other, hungry for supremacy. The white knight's sword swung up with ferocity, aiming to take off the black demon's head at first thrust, but the ax had blocked the advance, while the red eyes looked down upon the shining white helm. The din of steel biting on steel echoed throughout the void, drowning out the garish screeches and making Violet's ears ring.

Exhaustion was beginning to work its way through Violet's arms since she'd kept the palms pressed tightly over her ears for quite a while, as steel clashed against steel in an exchange of unyielding blows and the screeching increased. She had no choice but to watch and endure the overwhelming noise. There was nowhere to run: the glow of her knight's armor was all the light there ever was, and a light was what she needed to stay alive.

The light that kept the darkness at bay was slowly fading. Darkness was closing in. The white knight's valor was impressive, but his might could not match the demon's brutishness. No matter how precise the thrust of his gleaming sword was, an edge of the ax always blocked and frustrated the knight's next move. The longaxe would twirl like a cyclone, supported by its massive spiked gauntlets, and dent the silver sword with every strike. Sparks flew each time the blades met until there was only one weapon left on the narrow field, the one with double edges crafted from black steel and kissed by hellfire.

The skinless hands had come out to play, grabbing away the knight's sword, leaving him weaponless and without defense. More clawed hands extended from the darkness to grab hold of every inch of the white knight. His magnificent armor was scratched and dented, parts of it cracked, and one of his helm's wings had broken off. Soon the other wing was torn apart when spiked gauntlets came hammering upon the helm with repeated jabs, shattering the helm's faceguard to reveal the knight's features.

He was not Richie at all, as she'd suspected earlier, but a homely man even before his face had swollen from the beating. Just a gallant man who held back the darkness for a while but could not defeat it. The last of his light was dying out with him when the pummeling ceased and the claws began to impale his armor, tearing him apart limb from limb.

"*Noooooooooooo!*" Violet shrieked in horror.

The murderous fiend never even turned to her as the light faded. His back was to her, and soon he was camouflaged by the growing blackness. Only red eyes broke the monotony of the murkiness around her. And if those eyes were glaring at Violet, they would see tears of fear and a grimace of hatred on her face, because darkness had won this battle.

Violet knew she was entombed for eternity, to wander this infinite black universe among the screeching red-eyed shadows. Nothing of the white knight's shimmering armor was left behind to light her torch of hope. Only a spec …

A spec that remained afloat her tear-stained face. It came down to poke her between the eyes, forcing them to close.

Once her leafy greens flickered back open, something was still poking at her forehead. Violet seized the fingers that were stroking her sweaty forehead, gripping and twisting them. "Ow-ow-ow! It's me, Vi!" blurted the owner of the two twisted fingers before she could break them.

"*Vi*" That was Richie's pet name for her because she had refused to let him call her "babe." Only, this was not his voice. It sounded thin and brittle like Elliot's. Violet released her hold on his fingers and sat up warily. "What are you doing?" she asked.

Elliot rubbed his two sore fingers. "You woke me up when you screamed in your sleep. I-I came over, saw you sweating ... sooo ... I wanted to check you for a fever. Just in case, you know ... standard procedures like they taught us in the Pentagon."

Violet wiped the sweat from her forehead with a palm and felt no alarming temperature rise. "Sorry," she apologized for waking Elliot. "I was just having a weird—"

"*Aaieeeeee!*" A scream three times as alarming as Violet's erupted from outside. Elliot quickly ran back to his sheets to grab his rifle and dashed to the door, while Violet pulled on her farm boots without putting on pants. She got up in her oversized jersey and boxer shorts. She took both bare weapons, the machete without its sheath and the pistol without its hip holster and then bolted to the door after Elliot.

44

WAREHOUSE INFILTRATION

DAY 547

The orange truck pulled over next to a department store in an empty parking lot. The gray surface was cracked, and the white parking lines had faded with time. The greens of flourishing weeds added a bit more color to the dreary-looking place; however, not even the morning sun could add any cheer to the dead atmosphere. The four living corpses wobbling about and groaning certainly added an air of death and gloom to the place.

Richie had noticed none of it when Dwayne brought the truck to a stop and took the keys out of the ignition to quieten the engine. All three were crammed in front of the truck: Jerry was in the middle since he was the thinnest.

"So we go out there and put an end to them, quickly and quietly …" Dwayne was saying.

I've never seen her snap before, Richie was thinking. *Not at me. She's a fierce chick an' all, but loving and warm too. Is the idea of having kids really that sensitive of a subject to her?*

"Which means we'll only use our melee weapons ..." Dwayne went on.

She's got a point. With the handful of dead kids, we've seen over time and living dead kids and ... Billy. I can see where she's coming from. It was stupid to think that, Richie. You can be such an idiot sometimes! Not only did you ruin a night that was about to get perfect, but you made her upset. Which made him upset, but Richie was not thinking about himself at the moment. Violet's unforeseen closeminded reaction had caught him off guard. Then again, it was an honest reaction to a question that had never been asked but had always needed an answer. *Never,* was certainly the right blunt answer.

"No firearms, we clear?" Dwayne said.

When we're all done here and back on the ranch, I should apologize to her. Not that I've done anything wrong, but ... it's the right thing to do. She didn't seem any more upset than I was this morning, though, Richie realized. *But I did strike a nerve last night, and the whole thing was dumb and uncalled for. I should just say I'm sorry so we can both forget about it and move on. The princess needs her Prince Charming as much as he needs her. And in a few days, we can have another night to ourselves in the shed to make up for the one we lost.*

"Rich!" Dwayne snapped his fingers at Richie multiple times to catch his attention. When Richie finally responded with a stumped look, Dwayne asked again, "Are we clear?"

Richie was dumbfounded, not knowing what the question was, let alone how to answer it. He glanced out the wide front window and found a clue. "Yeah, we kill the zombies out there."

"And which one will you be killing?" Dwayne asked.

"Not one, two," Richie retorted. "The ones limping over there in the middle of the parking lot."

"I admire your courage, Rich." Dwayne smiled. "But how about you let me handle those two? You can take out the one hangin' next to the store's entrance. And Jerry, you take out the crawling one over there with the missing leg." Lamar pointed to the east of the parking lot, no farther than forty yards away. "Think you can handle that?"

Jerry's cheeks flushed red at the question. "Maybe we should let Richie take care of the crawler. I can take out the one near the entrance just fine," Jerry said, aggravated.

"Nah, I'm good," Richie retaliated. "I could actually take out both of them myself if I had to. You can stay in the truck and rest your shoulder for a while." Jerry's face turned red in humiliation at Richie's needling remark. Face frozen in an expression of anger, he turned to him and saw that Richie was fixated on the window, studying the movements of the zombies outside.

"Ladies, ladies," Dwayne said, trying to thaw the tension. "Let's just' stick with the zombies I gave you and go bash their brains out, okay? C'mon now, get outta the truck, move."

So Richie exited and Jerry was right behind him. Each went their separate ways; Jerry made his way for the crawling corpse with a long stick in his hand that had a blade attached to one end. Jerry drove the blade right into the mushy back of the crawler's head from a good distance, from as far as the stick could extend. He jabbed it with repeated thrusts till it crawled no more. Richie, on the other hand, went face-to-face with his zombie, bringing him down with a big boot to the chest. The groaning limper went down hard on its back, and then came the ax, hacking the head in two.

As for the two remaining groaners in the center, Dwayne saw to them with his curved sickle. He marched at them head-on without attempting any stealthy maneuvers, grabbing one by the fragments of its clothing and pushing it against the other. Dwayne had gotten them close to each other so he could wrap the sickle around both their necks at once, looping them within the sickle's sharp inner curve, twisting and turning the blade into the rotten flesh and tearing through the skin and tissue of both necks. He sawed till their heads abandoned their bodies and bounced on the tarmac.

All three regrouped near the truck after taking out the skulking threats. "All right, it'll go just as we'd planned it yesterday," Dwayne said. "Richie and I will go in for the search, and Jerry will stay out here as the lookout. You got your walkie-talkie: radio us if anything goes down, and I'll do the same if we need help, got it?" Jerry nodded. "Let's go." Dwayne and Richie went into the department store with their melee weapons, firearms, and flashlights.

Inside was a raiders crime scene, though, it certainly wasn't *cleanly* raided. The floors were speckled with dried blood and rotted guts of long-dead bodies left to stink up the place with the odor of decay. There was no juice left in the bodies to attract the zombie appetite; all the splattered organs and brains had gone green and failed to appeal to the tastes of the undead. Only colonies of flies found pleasure in the deceased cuisine.

Humans had found few resources venturing into this department store. For one, the smell was unbearable; also, all that remained of food and drink was broken shards of glass sharing shelves with spider webs. Whatever nutrition was once in those jars had long ago bled across the shelves, seeped to the floors, and dried out. Everything else, however, was raided clean.

They made it to the back of the building and found a door that led them to a stairway going down. Before descending, Richie stopped to retch what plums and potatoes he'd had for breakfast. "You could've warned me about the smell," Richie wheezed.

"I thought after all this time, the smell of the dead would seem as natural as air to you," Dwayne stated.

"Yeah ... but it still wouldn't hurt to wrap some cloth around my mouth and nose to avoid it." Richie spat and then followed Dwayne down the flight of steps. At the bottom, they found the indoor warehouse packed full of pallets of cardboard boxes of many sizes. The warehouse was not colossal: only twelve one-meter-long racks stood tall on the right-hand side and a heap of pallets occupied the left side, labeled *Picking Zones*. Dwayne half jogged through the dim aisles between racks, flashing light on box labels from bottom to top. It was the top stacks that he found hard to read, but thankfully there weren't many stacked up there.

Richie had to squeeze through very narrow spaces between the ground stacks to look for nails, as he went from one chaotic picking zone to the other. After finding nothing, he heard Dwayne call for him. "Richie, come over here. I need your help." So Richie went, flashlight guiding his way to the blue-and-orange steel racks. When he reached Dwayne, it was as if he were standing on top of a chaotic terrain higher than the ground level Richie was standing on.

"Whoa ..." exhaled Richie. "What the hell happened here?" He moved his flashlight around to uncover what havoc had befallen those last couple of aisles. It seemed a rack near the back had collapsed and toppled over the last two racks like gigantic dominos of twisted steel.

Broken pallets and destroyed boxes were buried beneath the dunes of rubble. A dust-consumed forklift peered out of the rubble, and Dwayne was standing on its roof. Most likely the expired vehicle was the cause of this mayhem, but none knew now what had happened. And so Richie's question never found an answer.

"You done looking through your side of the warehouse?" Dwayne asked from up there.

"Yeah. All I found was useless junk, no nails." *Not even tampons for Violet.*

"Then come up here and help me look through this mess. I found the item checklist in one of the aisles earlier. It said that the home improvement merchandise will be somewhere in the last two aisles, which, as you can see, is now one big pile."

From the bottom and the top of the wreckage, they rummaged for a while in the stuffy warehouse, with sweat dripping down their scalps and clothes. Disappointed at the demolished boxes and what they found inside them, they feared that a box of nails may have easily been scattered deep within the rubble. It did not stop them from digging deeper for any inanimate survivors that might be buried down there. And so they found them: two average-sized boxes that were somewhat flattened. The labels on the boxes stated that there were over twenty cartons of five-inch nails in each; the stock-keeping unit number on the label alleged that there were four more boxes available, but did not mention their whereabouts.

They were determined to search for the remaining ones; however, a static noise alerted them that someone was trying to make contact with Dwayne's walkie-talkie. "D-D ... Dwayne ..." More static interruptions made it difficult to hear Jerry. "Dwayne, ca-can yo ... ou hear ... me?

Ov ... er."

Dwayne picked up the walkie-talkie and pressed the button to respond. "Yes, Jerry, I hear you. What is it? Over."

"You gotta come quick. Survivors showed up out of nowhere." That came through clearer. "They're here in the park ... ing ... lot. I shot one by accide ... nt! I didn't ... know he was—hey, what ... are you ... s-stop!" BAM! BAM!

Both Dwayne and Richie heard the gunshots loud and clear through the walkie-talkie. "Jerry, what's happening?" Dwayne's voice was panicky. But the signal wasn't transmitting. "God damn it! C'mon, Richie, let's go!" They hastened over the mountain of rubble to make it down to the ground. The word "survivors" was like a curse word to their ears. Living strangers could be far more dangerous than the living dead. And the gunshots from Jerry's end of the radio transmission had certainly proved that point true so far.

The rubble hill's terrain was uneven, with many gaps that could trip a man or suck him further under. Dwayne's foot was caught in one as he ran carelessly. He tripped and dropped the box of nails in front of him. It was still within reaching distance, but his leg was stuck. Richie came to his aid, putting down his box next to Dwayne's. Richie tugged Dwayne's arm, but the more the tugging persisted, the further Dwayne's foot sank—knee high, now. *"Aaarrgh!"* Dwayne growled. "Something's pulling at my leg, Richie!"

"Hold on!" Richie jumped to the other side and started digging his leg out of the rubble. *Maybe this will work better.* Richie had stopped with the useless pulling because there was some force pulling back, and that opposing force belonged to two beaten hands all dusty and covered in cuts beneath the rubble. *Survivors!*

Yes, survivors from the warehouse collision accident, who groaned audibly. Living survivors of the *living dead*, that is. Their damaged hands were not desperately reaching for rescue, but to satiate their cannibalistic hunger. Richie instantly drew out the ax from his waist to hack at the hands. The only problem was, that the ax's blade couldn't chop all the way through the rubble surrounding the zombies' hands. So, he sheathed his ax and drew out the shotgun from the strap slung around his back. Its lengthy twin muzzles were thin enough to mouse through the rubble and locate the hands without barriers standing between them.

It was a risky position with the shotgun: too close to hands that clasped Dwayne's ankle and foot. A single shot could definitely blow the hands apart, but there was the risk of piercing Dwayne's leg in the process. With a quick thought, Richie flicked the flashlight open to illuminate the trap hole and saw the wrists beneath the gun's barrels. He shifted his aim and squeezed the trigger ... BAM!

Bone joints erupted as dark blood and spoiled flesh mixed with the rubble, and the air from the hole stank of the ripe smell of gunpowder with a hint of decay. Dwayne was thus able to pull his foot back out with the zombies' hands and fingers still latched on without life or strength to them.

As they reached the entrance of the department store, they were running so fast, that they did not even notice the reek of death that had made Richie vomit just a little earlier. They threw the nail boxes down, outside, when they got to the parking lot and held up their firearms instead, ready to join the shooting. But all was silent. Jerry stood near the truck, shaking, with his gun in his hand. The corpse count in the parking lot had changed from four to six, as there were two fresh ones lying in a pool of their own streaming blood. Unlike the four corpses they had put to rest, these didn't have skin rot issues yet.

"What the hell happened here, Jerry?" Dwayne demanded.

Jerry gulped and, with a quivering finger, pointed at a man's corpse that had an ashen beard dyed red with blood at the edges. "I was taking a p-piss when I saw that guy walking over to me with a limp. I thought he was a zombie, so I shot him right between the eyes." Jerry's voice was shaking. "Then that woman came screaming, running to his corpse ... crying. He freaked me out; I didn't know he was alive!" Jerry diverted his quivering finger to point at the woman's corpse next to his first kill. Her clothing was ragged and torn. Two bullet holes were engraved in her chest. "She pulled a gun on me from the guy's pants! So I shot her before she could get me! I-It was self-defense this time, honest!" Jerry's voice had turned to plead.

"It's okay, Jerry," Dwayne said. "You never knew what their intentions were."

"You think there're more of them around?" Richie asked with suspicion.

"Big chance," Dwayne replied. "Go grab the nail boxes. They'll be enough for the remaining walls ... hopefully. We need to leave."

Within two minutes, the nail boxes were in the trunk, and all three men were in the vehicle, heading back to the ranch to start putting up the walls on the remaining sides. Prince Charming was on his way back to his princess in their soon-to-be fully fortified castle, safe in each other's arms.

45

WE'VE GOT VISITORS

DAY 547

Old Edna's voice had always sounded so fragile, and any words that came out of her mouth were full of wisdom. "*Aaiieeee!*" That scream—she sounded petrified as if the Grim Reaper himself were attacking her with his soul-reaping scythe. For a woman of her age, the sheer intensity of her scream should have made her lungs burst. Over eight decades of living, including surviving the zombie apocalypse, had never had Edna felt so mortified, shrieking the way she had a second ago till Lamar and Angie reached her in the tomato field.

The screams had drawn Elliot from the toolshed in his day-old clothing of stained black jeans and a plain orange shirt, followed by Violet in her slouchy sleepwear. Both were armed and anxious. Without knowing anything of what was happening, they jumped right into the turmoil. They saw Angie and Lamar carry a feeble Edna to the house. On the porch, Angie saw them and yelled, "Perimeter's breached!" before the door closed behind them.

"That's insane," Elliot said with a strange calmness. "How can a zombie get through the perimeter without anyone hearing?" It was bizarre. The cable with the tin cans was there not only so that the zombies couldn't get in, but also to warn them that something was *trying* to get in so they could put a stop to it.

"Oh my God. Edna," Violet said and sprinted towards the house. Coming her way was a gray-furred rabbit hopping clumsily. Violet's feet planted themselves when she saw the fuzzy animal. The door to the house was opened again, and Lamar stepped out into the porch.

"Get to higher ground, *now!*" the big man roared. Violet looked at Lamar for just a second; when she turned back, the rabbit was a lot closer, leaping at her. Its beady black eyes had shifted to milky white, Violet realized. At the last second, she lifted her foot so that the large farm boot hit the rabbit and so, it fell back down. It turned itself over clumsily but fast, with its hind legs pushing themselves up for another leap. A far sharper object than a boot came down this time. Violet's machete hand reacted quicker than the pistol and split the rabbit in two as it leaped. Violet stumbled backward with a squeal and fell on her backside. The cruel machete had completely disemboweled the creature; its entrails spilled to the ground, as did its hind and front body halves.

The hind legs and the fuzzball tail quivered as the creature's blood and organs oozed out in a messy stream. The smaller front legs were still trying to move, beady white eyes gazing at Violet, and pointed ears twitching as the rodent's big frontal teeth gnashed repeatedly for a taste of her flesh. The front part of the rabbit was still alive no matter how empty of entrails it was. It pulled itself towards Violet, who was frozen in horror on the ground.

A big boot came down on the rabbit's skull and crushed it as a boulder would crush a glass bottle, leaving a broken skull under the flattened skin. Violet's heart was racing as she stared at Lamar and the rabbit he'd finished off. He offered Violet a hand, hauled her up, and then slung her on his shoulder like his AK-47 and ran. "Get up on the water barrel," he yelled at Elliot.

The barrel was wide enough to hold all three of them. "Are there more of them?" Violet asked, mortified as she checked her pistol for shells and turned the safety off.

"This was the second bastard I've killed," Lamar said.

"Yesterday, Kermit and I saw a zombie gnawing at what looked like a rabbit's head in the woods," Elliot said. "You don't think—"

Lamar slapped Elliot on the shoulder with a rough palm, quieting him. "How 'bout you scope the rest of 'em out, boy, 'cause Angie said she saw five, breach, and I already killed two. Put that rifle of yours to use and find those damn things."

The big man was not that much of a talker—Elliot and Violet knew that much. In the sudden peril, Lamar considered himself to be in charge in the absence of his older brother. Elliot began scoping, and Violet turned to Lamar. "Edna, Lamar ... is Edna ..." She could not bring herself to finish her shaky question.

"She got bit," Lamar answered. "The bite wasn't that deep, though, and Angie is workin' on suckin' the infected blood out with a tube. Now we need to focus on killing the rest of 'em, you hear? So stop worrying 'bout the old woman and *focus*," he snapped. "That's why we wanted walls up all along. The smaller the goddamned zombies get, the easier they slip in without no one noticin'. Other people on the ranch with us almost shit themselves when Dwayne confronted 'em with the possibilities." The big man's face twisted in a grin. "Rats, squirrels, anything small might sneak in under the wires for more than just our vegetable fields. But the past leaders just laughed it off so no one would panic. They said those rodents were too fast to get caught and infected. And here they are!"

"I've spotted all three," Elliot announced, still looking through the scope. "There's one in the potato field and two hopping around the cabbages."

The big man climbed down the water barrel with a single step. "C'mon, let's go." Lamar gestured to Violet. "You're taking on the one in the potato field, but first things first: you need to drive it out before wastin' it. We don't wanna be spoilin' our potato supply with their infected blood. Use that pistol first, then the machete. Target's head is too small to be sure you can hit it with a pistol—aim for the body and then finish it off.

Violet jumped down the barrel and landed on her feet with a thud. "What about you?"

"Whaddya think?" Lamar said. "I'm gonna take out the two hoppers in the cabbage field." He raised his AK-47 high. "I'll drive 'em out with this and shoot them the hell up afterward. Drive out, then kill, got it?" Violet responded with a curt nod. "Boy," he said to Elliot, "you keep a close eye through that scope on the both of us, you hear? You see an opening, you take the shot, and you keep a sharp eye in case there's more of them."

"Right," Elliot said. "Be careful, Vi."

With a nervous smile, Violet turned and strode off to the potato field. The loaded pistol was in her left hand and the lethal machete in her right gripped tightly. As she stood in front of the field, it was easy to spot the sand brown rabbit corpse sluggishly hopping around half-grown potatoes. Her breathing was as shaky as her hands, at the thought of purposely drawing the rabbit out.

One of them bit Edna. How can they know that they've sucked all the infected blood out? It spreads so quickly. Violet took a deep breath and exhaled steadily to quieten her shaking. She raised her left arm up to point the pistol skyward and pulled the trigger. The din drew the zombie rodent right out of the potato field.

Elliot saw it hopping towards Violet through his scope. He, too, inhaled and stilled his finger over the trigger of his silenced rifle, waiting for the opening to shoot if needed. He saw Violet swing clumsily with the machete and slice the tips of its long ears off. The corpse rabbit twisted its body with such speed that Violet lost sight of its decaying fur for a moment. It went between her legs and nibbled at the foot of her right boot. That was not the opening Elliot was hoping for, so he waited. Violet twisted her entire body around violently when she saw where the rabbit was, taking herself to the ground. Her right foot left the ground in a kick that sent the nibbling runt on a midair joyride. Elliot's rifle followed the flying rabbit to where it landed less than ten yards away, and he finally exhaled when the silent shot blew the whiskers off the rabid corpse.

Violet stood and examined her boots, making sure that the right one had not been nibbled all the way through. She looked back up and exchanged a thumbs-up with Elliot to reassure him that she was fine.

BRA-TA-TA-TA-TA!

Lamar's AK-47 unloaded on the two cabbage-raiding rabbits when they hopped out of the field. The assault rifle had pierced the mutated rodents from head to tail, leaving them dead again in the open field, bathed in dark blood that made it difficult to tell what color their fur had been. He turned to Violet on one side and Elliot on the other, each still lingering where they were assigned. "Shot the hell outta them bastards!" Lamar boasted loudly.

Wild rabbits, however, are remarkably light on their feet. Not only can they run fast, but they can also travel very quietly and remain unspotted. One black-and-white rabbit would have reached its target unseen if it hadn't been for its lopsided movement that drew Lamar's eye to the weeds of the cabbage field. Lamar moved, but not as swiftly as the rabbit's leap.

When the four-legged herbivore-now-carnivore found its way to the loud boaster, it caught him off guard. Fortunately for Lamar, his height, combined with his tall boots, made it hard for even the highest-leaping rodent to reach unprotected flesh. The attacker just barely managed to grab the top edge of the leather with its frontal choppers. Lamar dropped his assault rifle at the sudden ambush and had to tug on its long ears to slow its gnawing. He tried to yank it off, but the rabbit's stubborn grip was shockingly strong, and Lamar only managed to tear the ears off instead, along with the top fuzz and skin that was spotted with post-death greenish-black mold.

Despite the brutal skinning, the fleshy monstrosity that remained of the rabbit continued gnawing; its teeth had reached the rough slacks behind the leather. Lamar didn't go for his rifle just yet—shooting it close range could endanger his leg as well. There was nothing but his massive hands to use. This time Lamar grabbed hold of its neck, circling the puny naked body with his hand like a python squeezing the life out of its prey. Crushing the corpse rabbit's tiny throat might not be enough to kill, Lamar was focused solely on snatching the damned rodent off of him. His arm muscles bulged, and the tattoos scarring him from shoulder to wrist seemed to enlarge and glisten with sweat.

The pasty-eyed rabbit gave a garish squeal when the overpowering strength of its giant prey wrenched it from his boot and hurled it in the air. Airborne, it continued to squeal till the mutilated carcass landed nastily in front of Violet, who was jogging over to aid Lamar—only to have the foe delivered right to her in a sickening state of evisceration, glistening with moisture from the exposed innards and ripe with the odor of decay.

Its faded eyes still suggested life after it hit the ground. In its blindness, though, it did not notice the sharp blade descending. Violet brought down the machete in a forceful blow that put an end to the ranch's unwanted visitors.

46

THERE AND BACK AGAIN

DAY 547

I ran out of the toolshed and helped kill a bunch of dead rabbits that invaded the ranch today while having this feeling that I'd forgotten something important. There was a lot going on in my mind at that time. There was Edna on my mind when I walked into the house to check on her after she was bitten. I was thinking about Richie too when I walked out. He hasn't returned to me yet. It's been over an hour now since he went with Dwayne and Jerry.

I went back to the toolshed, and everything was going through my head, but still, there was something I could not remember. It's like my brain is experiencing memory lapses. I read something about this online once, back before the zombies, when the world still had power and Internet. It's moments like these when you walk from one room to another and forget why you did it in the first place. That there was a purpose to it, but it escaped your mind, and you can't get it to come back.

Such an annoying struggle—it's driving me nuts. Today, day 547, everything is going wrong, and I have a feeling that it's about to get even worse ...

Violet paused from her writing to scrub the tears away from her eyes:

I don't want Edna to die. She's too good of a woman to die like this. And I want Richie to come back to me. Then I'll never leave his side again. He'll want the same after he sees what happened around here when he wasn't here. Then he'll never leave the ranch without his princess again. This has been survivor Violet Turner on Day 547 ...

FEAR IN FLESH

still alive and surviving on The Ranch.

Just when she'd closed her diary and placed it back inside her backpack, Elliot's voice came from outside. *"They're back!"* Violet immediately grabbed her gear again. Only the blood-stained machete made the cut this time; the pistol would just be extra weight against the pesky dead rabbits. She heard honking when she trotted out. "Truck's at the gate," Elliot said.

The small gate was slid open and the orange truck drove in. All three men climbed out looking confident and unscathed by their brush with the outside world of the undead. Their moment of triumph was brief, though, as Elliot greeted them at the gate to catch them up on what had gone amiss. Their expressions went from joy to dismay in a second. Dwayne darted towards the house with Jerry tailing him. Elliot and Richie followed the same path, noticing the abysmal odor coming from the pile of rabbit carcasses that had been collected from the fields.

All went inside the house except Richie, who stopped in front of the steps when he saw Violet coming out of the shed. They rushed to one another and wrapped their arms around each other for a warm embrace and a kiss. After they broke away from their reunion, Richie cupped Violet's face with both hands. "Did any of them hurt you?" He looked at her freckly face for any signs of harm and moved on to inspect her arms and hands.

She pulled away gently as Richie found no sign of any sort of injury. "I'm fine," she said. "They were freaky fast, but I ... *we* managed. Elliot and Lamar had my back."

Richie pulled her back in for a tighter embrace. Kissing her forehead, he said, "I'm sorry I wasn't here to have your back." He sounded dismayed. "Dwayne told me about the possibility of something like this happening; that's why they put the walls up in the first place. But I just never really imagined it would happen since it never *has* before! Rabbits turning into flesh-eating carnivores and crawling through the perimeter?"

"It's okay. You were right: I was in safe hands. When push came to shove, Lamar took the lead, and no one got hurt after the breach. Except for—"

"—Edna," Richie finished. "I wanna go see how she's holding up." Elliot had already filled them in at the gate, so Richie knew of poor Edna's predicament and her possible fate, though he still had to see her and say his goodbyes. It was not the first time he'd had to go through such a hard farewell. But the sight of her was not as horrendous as that of Gunter. Both were fated to suffer from the living dead wildlife that roamed the woods around them. Now they would have to take extra precautions to hold their land against their foes of many species.

Death was slowly taking over the elderly herbalist as she sat up on her sofa bed, a fluffy pillow behind her neck and a colorful blanket draped over her legs. The fever was starting to show by the sweat beading on her forehead, but her face did not give any indication of pain. Edna was smiling her usual smile, though she looked tired. Angie was placing a wet towel over Edna's head in an attempt to tame the fever. "I tried sucking all the bad blood out," she said to all who stood around the sofa bed. "But she started to feel really dizzy, so I don't know how much good *or* bad I got out."

"It's fine, dear," Edna said feebly. "It's not your fault this sickness isn't curable." Her wrinkly smile deepened. "I am too old to survive this apocalypse any longer. My time was up far before the rabbits died and came back."

Violet, Richie, and Elliot were reminded of Gunter by this brave act of humor as the victim faded slowly. However, Edna's case was not as severe. *She's not coughing yet*, Violet noted.

"Don't say that yet, Edna," Dwayne said. "There's gotta be something in your medicine boxes we could use to save you. You always talked about some … strange recipes that you might be able to cook up for cleaning the infected blood."

"Ah, yes," the dying woman replied. "When I first started my career with healing medicine, there was this one patient that was brought to me, dying. Poor boy had suffered a terrible bite from the jaws of a vile Komodo dragon. Their saliva is known to be full of bacteria, and once it's injected into the skin, it will quickly spread and corrupt the victim's blood cells. The boy was lucky enough to escape, but his soul was slowly departing as his blood cells went black. I had this old recipe that required my box of rare herbs. I used them on the boy to burn out all the corruption in the bloodstream, saving him without having to saw off his bitten leg."

"Yes," Angie blurted out, "sawing off a leg won't work. Just like snake poison—when people in my old village get bitten by a snake, we don't cut them. We suck the poison out like I tried doing. But this …" She couldn't find a word for it. "This zombie poison spreads a lot faster! Ay, Edna, I'm so sorry." Angie cupped Edna's warm wrinkled hand in both of hers and held it to her forehead, sobbing.

Richie whispered to Violet, "Where was Edna bitten?"

"Left leg," she replied just as quietly

"Where's the box of rare herbs?" Dwayne asked. "Maybe you can give Angie instructions so she can cook up the medicine for you. There's still time. It worked for a Komodo dragon's bite; it could work for the zombies too."

"It might," said Edna with a broken smile. "Though unfortunately, it was among the boxes I forgot during the evacuation. The policemen were trying to get us on the buses so quick; I couldn't grab everything in such a short time."

"If you knew this medicine might work on a zombie bite, why didn't you tell us about it before?" Lamar was astonished.

"Because I didn't want anyone risking their lives to go visit a place that *you* call Dead-Ville, just to retrieve some old plants that might not even work," Edna answered sternly.

"But this could've been the cure all along, Edna," Richie said. "We have to try." He turned to Dwayne, who nodded.

"He's right," Dwayne agreed. "This could be life-changing. It's gonna be messy, but we have to try."

"I'm with ya," Lamar said.

"Ay, no!" Angie protested. "Papi, you can't go there. No way will *all* of you come back from Dead-Ville. I love Edna, but ... it's ... it's a ... crazy idea!"

"It's a foolish idea is what Angie means to say," Edna remarked. "A very foolish one. Suicidal, it is. With the time needed for you to make it there and back here again, I will be long gone. It's useless to risk your lives saving my old dying bones."

"Stop saying that, Edna." Dwayne put one hand on her forehead to check her temperature. She was burning up, but Dwayne still had hope for her. The bite was not that deep, after all. "You still have time. We can make this work."

"Even if you make it back here before I've changed, didn't you consider the preparation of the recipe itself may take time? If that can't persuade you out of going, I don't know what will."

Dwayne looked right into Edna's eyes and said, "Nothing will." He kissed her on the head and then began laying his orders on the line. "Angie, you stay inside with Edna. Jerry, Kermit, I want you two to close the gate behind us and grab your guns to keep watch over the ranch, understand me?"

"That means no falling asleep when dead bunny rabbits come to visit, got it, Kermit?" Lamar said in a scolding tone.

"Y-Yes, got it."

"Violet," Dwayne said, "I'll need you to stay here. Help Angie if she needs it and keep those two in line. You're the big gun in case somethin' goes wrong."

Violet seemed displeased with the order. "Why do I have to stay? Elliot will be here to help out. I can come with you guys."

"Elliot's comin' with us," Dwayne told her. "Elliot, get ammo for your rifle." Elliot, without the slightest hesitation, left the house to do as he was told. "Lamar, gas," the big man exited the house. "Edna, I promise we will all come back and fix you up."

"Dwayne, don't—" Edna tried one last time to talk Dwayne out of his ludicrous plan when a cough interrupted her speech. "Please ... don't."

"Stay strong, Edna." He turned to Richie. "Come with me," he said as he walked to the door. Richie only walked out of the house only when Violet went to the door, following Dwayne outside.

47

PRE-DEPARTURE

DAY 547

"Dwayne, wait," Violet said when she was on the porch and Dwayne had made his way down the four wooden steps. Dwayne stopped and turned. "You can't leave me here; I'll be much more useful if I come along with you guys."

"We can't do that, Violet." Dwayne's reply was husky. "I need enough people to stay and look after the ranch while half of us are gone. There might still be more of 'em out there. If they get in, you'll know what to do better than either Kermit or Jerry."

"If you're looking for an expert zombie bunny exterminator, then you should hire your brother, Lamar, for the job. He did most of the killing himself after the breach. And besides, we already looked, checked the perimeters and beyond, and there was no sign of any more rabbits. We caught 'em all. So just let Jerry stand guard on one side of the perimeters and Kermit on the other."

Dwayne pinched the bridge of his nose and sighed. "Violet, it's Kermit and Jerry standing guard over the ranch *alone* while we're gone that's the problem. There has to be someone more … experienced here if somethin' goes wrong. It's not necessarily gonna be the rabbits again, but you need to stay here; you're the ranch's big gun while we're out."

"Screw your big gun!" Violet growled. "I don't 'need' to stay anywhere; I wanna go where Richie goes. You want big guns; how about handing the biggest guns you own to Jerry and Kermit and have them stand on buckets. That should make them big enough with guns."

"It's too damn dangerous out there. I need everyone focused, and I can't afford Richie losing his focus, trying to protect you!"

"Protect me?" Violet's tone turned dangerous. "Clearly you've never seen me and Richie team up to fight zombies before. We do it better side by side than separated."

"He fought perfectly fine with me earlier at the Hill-Mart."

"There were zombies over there?" Violet turned to Richie, standing at her side during the whole of the squabble. Richie had nothing to say to that. "Whatever. However many you fought over there will be nothing compared to the place you call 'Dead-Ville'. So you'll need as many fighters as you can get. And I'm stepping up."

"For what? I'm not asking for any volunteers. I assigned the fighters, and you didn't make the cut, girl."

The word "girl," the way Dwayne spat it at her, sounded like an insult, but Violet decided to let it slide. "I'm gonna change my clothes, grab my gear, and be in the truck within a minute." Violet descended the steps, walking past Dwayne.

Frustrated, Dwayne's desire to argue faded. "I'm not wasting any more time on this shit," he said to Richie. "She wants to come, let her come. But I will not be held responsible for whatever happens to her out there, you got me?"

With a single silent nod, Richie sealed Dwayne's agreement. As he climbed down the steps to follow her to the toolshed, the four wooden steps creaked loudly when his boots trod on them.

Inside the confines of the shed, they were once again alone, preparing for what was to come. Violet had taken off her baseball jersey and put on a long-sleeved shirt the shade of chestnuts, replaced her boxers for slim black jeans. Meanwhile, Richie kept on his camouflage slacks and changed to a new plain black shirt that showed more of his athletic physique. With his high boots, he looked like an actual member of the army minus the full military gear. Violet took notice.

The young soldier sorted out ammo for his shotgun and Violet's pistol, as his tough princess finished donning her mission attire. They had but a few precious moments together in the shed before their departure to battle the dead. "You sure about doing this, Vi?" asked Richie somberly. "I mean, the guys will be there, and all of us will have each other's backs. There's no need to put yourself at risk."

"You didn't use to say that back when we went scavenger hunting outside the Pentagon," Violet said sternly without looking at him directly.

"It was different back at the Pentagon. Like you said last night, we used to head out in larger groups. It was less dangerous."

"So, the more of us to head to Hill-Ville, the better our chances of survival." Violet turned to Richie as she strapped on her gun holster about her hip. "You honestly think you'll be better fighting a horde of zombies out there with them instead of me?"

"It's not like that. It's just that ... it's safer *here*."

"Really?" Violet asked. "*If* it happens that I was wrong and more zombie bunnies do show up, don't expect Kermit and Jerry will have my back like the rest will have yours out there. They'll probably run back to the house, pretending to keep Edna and Angie safe, while I'll be left outside to feed the rabbits bits of my ass. They're not so easily taken out, Rich. And never forget what Gunter told us—before he died."

"Always stick together and never separate from one another," Richie repeated the words out loud and then sighed, knowing that there was nothing to say that would change her mind. "Fine, then you'll need these." He handed her a box half full of pistol rounds.

He knew from the start of this useless conversation that there was no talking me out of this. "Thanks." Violet took the box and stepped closer to Richie, looking him right in the eyes. "We made a promise to each other that we'd always keep the other safe. It doesn't only have to come from your end, Rich. I have to live up to that promise, too. I wanna be by your side, in safety or in danger, always."

Richie gave up as their lips met for a swift kiss. Only then he remembered why he'd truly started the conversation in the first place. It was to apologize for the dialogue he had opened up last night in the shed that had ruined their rare night together. He was trying to work his way up to an apology, though Violet seemed less upset now anyways as if she'd forgotten about it. "Look, Vi," Richie started, "I'm so—" The truck's horn beeped, calling them out of the shed.

Their few precious moments alone were up. "C'mon, we have to go," Violet urged. She collected the remainder of her weapons and headed for the door. But Richie grasped her hand before she could exit.

"Vi," he said softly, "I just want you to know that last night ... I didn't mean to ..."

"It's okay, Richie." She put an open palm against one of his fuzzy cheeks. "Let's just forget about it for now and go find this cure." And they left together just as another impatient honk summoned them.

They drove off the ranch with high hopes of finding the ingredients for a cure to the plague, saving Edna's life before the rabbit's bite reached her head and took hold of her senses.

48

WELCOME TO DEAD-VILLE COUNTY

DAY 547

The clouds were slow-dancing across the gray sky as a brisk breeze swept through the county of the dead. The sun peeked through the hovering white wisps to shed some of its light on the earth below, as the orange truck climbed the hill's narrow zigzagging roads to the peak. They came across a green sign that had once read, *Welcome to Hill-Ville County*. However, the word *Hill* had long been covered with splatters of dried blood and over it—using the same substance—someone had written *Dead* instead.

So it read, *Welcome to Dead-Ville County*.

Big Lamar was steady at the wheel. Dwayne sat in the passenger seat with a sickle and assault rifle on his lap. The other three soldiers were seated in the flatbed, where the wind beat against their clothing and their hair, both of which flapped madly as the truck soared onwards.

Here and there along the pathway, they encountered a small number of the undead, limping about their business until the truck swept by with its revving engine that practically screamed, *follow me!* And to no one's surprise, the living dead did one of the few things they did best and followed the noise with their restless, famished groans.

Richie knocked on the truck's sliding glass window that could only be opened from the inside, where the driver and the passenger, sat. Dwayne turned and slid it open. "Dwayne," Richie shouted over the engine and the wind. "You sure there isn't another way we can get through? You know, with less noise maybe. 'Cause the closer we get, the more their numbers grow."

"We head straight on," Dwayne declared. "No chance for stealth. And more importantly, we ain't got much time." Dwayne slid the window shut again. Richie, Violet, and Elliot weren't used to this—heading straight on to fight the dead without a plan. Sure there'd been times when they'd had to improvise and adapt to the sudden occurrence of perilous events but never had they *purposely* taken on a challenge knowing the odds were gravely against them. *Putting our lives at risk to save someone who's been bitten,* Richie thought. *A chance to find a cure.* He found that notion to be absurd and hard to believe. *We never should've come—it's a suicide mission.*

The warning signs of the dead increasing in numbers as they drove proved accurate. The last time he'd come, the dead had mostly roamed the edges of the road, but as the road took them higher to where the small village stood, the mission seemed dire.

Houses, shops, apartments, and office buildings stood silent and strong on top of the hill. Just like an ant hill, the zombies crawled everywhere in search of food, groaning and salivating for the tender plumpness that rode in the orange truck. A dozen of them intercepted the truck's path from a distance. Lamar cursed when he had to hit the brakes.

The sudden screeching of rubber, followed by a rough stop, sent the three passengers in the back to their hands and knees. The back window was slid open again by Dwayne. "Everyone, okay?" he checked.

"Yeah," Elliot replied, "a little warning next time would be appreciated."

"What's the problem?" Richie had to ask. "Why did we stop?"

"Look over the hood," Dwayne told him so he could see the answer for himself.

All three knelt up and peaked over the roof of the pickup truck. Woe and terror wrapped around their hearts in a knot. Silence reigned at the sight of what loomed behind the herd of milky-eyed limpers: a mass of death fifty feet high, stalking the engine noises, the king of the living dead.

"No way." Elliot tried denying what his eyes beheld. "Is that—?"

"A cluster." Violet and Richie finished in unison.

49

THE CLUSTER KING

DAY 547

It came lumbering towards the truck on its lumpy feet, pushing through and crushing its own species of smaller beings beneath its mass of fleshy decay without seeming to know it did so. The creature, the king of all the living dead, dubbed as a *Cluster* was a far worse abomination born of the outbreak and forged by the dead's everlasting gluttony. For once a zombie over consumed its prey, whether it be human meat or animal, it became something far more monstrous than nature had ever intended.

Consumed by its own blind hunger, it ceased not when dining on its prey's entrails and limbs—even after the prey had almost awoken as a zombie itself. Usually, once the turn occurred, the living dead no longer craved the new zombie's flesh, rotting away. However, in rare cases, a zombie kept feasting even after the turn. Thus they had the victim's blackening brain in their bellies before it went completely corrupt.

Inside the belly of the feaster, the brain, the blood, and the body parts morphed to create disfigured embodiments of the previous prey: misshaped body features, including flawed faces appearing from the inside out, taking a place where a face should not. Incomplete arms and legs would tear their way out as well with moldy flesh and dripping gore instead of skin and muscle over the bones. And the more the monster consumed, the more it gave birth to new tumors of hungry groaning mouths with grabby hands and quivering feet. That is how the Cluster came to exist.

"What do we do now?" Elliot asked anxiously.

Richie hunched down to speak through the sliding window. "Why are we stopping?"

"We can't decide whether to turn back or keep going," answered Lamar, his voice betraying his nerves. Richie could see the big man's face and neck beading with sweat. Still, Lamar managed to keep firm hands on the wheel and a callous tone. "Well, Dwayne? What's it gonna be, man?"

His brother didn't reply. His stare was fixed upon the many-faced horror hulking in front of them. "Rich," said Dwayne, "at the Pentagon Sanctuary, you ever took on one of them? 'Cause we had an encounter once. It wasn't as big or freaky as this ugly bastard, but even then we chose not to fight and ran away from it."

"We did," Richie answered.

"And ..." urged Dwayne.

"One of our military generals killed it with a grenade launcher—after it killed a dozen men on the team. Everyone shot at the faces—they were big easy targets—but there was only one core face with the brain that the grenade launcher luckily caught. We don't have a grenade launcher, Dwayne; we can't risk taking it on."

"We don't have to," Dwayne said. "We're going around it."

"That's insane," protested Violet. "It'll still follow us. And let's not forget there will be more zombies ahead to worry about."

"Welcome to Dead-Ville County, Violet, where you can only keep pushing forward. Ain't no alternatives," Dwayne declared.

"There is one," stated Richie. "We turn back."

"That alternative means giving up on all hope ... on Edna's life, on a cure! *There ain't no alternatives.*"

"Guys, hurry up, it's getting closer," Elliot warned. The longer they argued, the closer the cluster's distorted shadow came.

"Edna wasn't one-hundred-percent sure this 'cure' could even work on zombie bites, Dwayne," Violet said. "If we can't get through the cluster, there will be no cure."

"There will be no *us* to save Edna," Richie added. Then added to himself, *Hopeless ... we're as dead as Edna is if we take on the cluster.*

"Would ya make up your goddamn mind, Dwayne?" Lamar roared. "We need to turn back or step on it!"

"Step on it," Dwayne ordered and Lamar obeyed. He pulled the handbrake and stomped on the gas pedal, letting the engine boom and tires screech. The three in the flatbed fell backward at the sudden acceleration. For a heartbeat, it seemed Lamar was about to drive the truck right through the cluster head first. Seconds before the expected collision between flesh and metal, Lamar swerved the truck to the right, avoiding the cluster's many grubby hands while crashing into three limpers. The zombies went down, swept under the tires that ground their spoiled flesh and weak bones. The truck drove over them as if they were a speed bump—only, that speed bump had a sinkhole that caught the back tire on the left. The three corpses piled up, as that left wheel kept ruthlessly spinning around, drilling through the ruined bodies of the undead and spitting out dark red chunks of their innards everywhere.

The rear tire refused to budge from the pile of eviscerated corpses, regardless of how hard Lamar's foot kept stomping on the gas pedal. The rubber spun without advancing, producing gore instead of distance. The cluster approached on five distorted feet. Oddly enough, one of the five resembled a horse's hoof, and another looked like a dog's hind leg. As for the rest, they were more like stumps than feet: they were hardly of any use. They could not support the mass of decomposed flesh, which made the cluster's movements very clumsy.

It was when Lamar had swerved the truck to the right, out of the cluster's reach, that the monster was thrown off balance, but to their misfortune, other zombies roamed the path. The mass of living flesh used its seven hands to claw at the earth, turn around, and seize the trunk's bumper with three of its strongest hands while extending the other four to grab at the figures lying in the flatbed.

Despite their shaken bones, they sat back up and set their backs against the sliding window. The truck was resisting, trying to wheel forward, but the cluster kept hold of the back, stretching out its four grotesque ruins of arms before its twelve faces wobbling on torsos and shoulders. Two of the twelve faces were of canines with teeth fully bared, eyeballs dangling from their sockets, and skin sloughing off beneath the molded fur. One face was of a horse, pushing out through the abdomen like a spear thrust out from a belly. The rest of the faces were … well … human, as human as any normal living dead.

"Get out your guns!" Richie had commanded. "Aim at the mouths and don't miss a single shot." And without warning, Richie fired first with his shotgun, followed by Violet with two shots from her pistol and Elliot's sniper rifle, silent but deadlier.

BAM! … BAM-BAM!

Each shot hit a different target, and there were plenty of spurts of blood, seeping pus, and splashes of gore but no kills. That was the work of the lumps of extra flesh surrounding the faces, thickening the mass around them to keep them protected. More firepower was needed to cause actual damage. The soldiers in the flatbed kept on squeezing the trigger, again and again, a graveyard of empty shells landing at their feet. The more they shot the same area, the frailer the mass got, and then a groaning mouth finally shut up. Richie had already taken out the canine over the chest, and Violet got one of the smallest faces. Elliot was still working on the face in the stomach, the snarling horse, believing it might be the core face with the brain since it was the largest of the twelve.

The shotgun blasts converged on the horse target along with the sniper rifle; both firearms fired off shot after shot until the entire face finally burst. The wheels of the truck still spun forward, but it kept going backward instead. Blowing the horse's face to smithereens had caused no lasting damage whatsoever. Elliot and Richie's hunch had been wrong: the horse was not the core face. Now four of the cluster's stretching hands were inching closer, as the three holding the rear of the truck kept towing the vehicle in reverse, bringing the three figures shooting at its faces within reach.

There was no escaping the flatbed for them: the dead already covered both sides of the struggling truck. If they were to escape the cluster's grasp, they'd only land themselves in a steeper tomb of grubby hands and grinding teeth. There was no way out of this other than finding the fiend's core face to shut down its swollen, blackened brain and drive away.

Richie noticed something even more disturbing as he continued shooting: where the horse face was shot out, there the lumps of gore and flesh were spreading, making way for another face to emerge. This one was blazing crimson and smiling. *This one has to be the core face,* Richie thought, and when he'd aimed the shotgun aim at the smiling red-slimed face, he pulled the trigger. But nothing came out of the twin muzzles. The shotgun was empty, and the bag of shells was on the opposite side of the flatbed, which Richie couldn't get to because of the greedy hands blocking the path. He cursed his rotten luck and grabbed his ax out of the thigh scabbard, then banged on the glass behind him. "Lamar," Richie called. "Put the truck in reverse and step on the gas. Hurry!"

"You crazy, boy?" Lamar spat.

"Trust me!" Richie then turned to Violet and Elliot. "You two, duck down and shoot at the hands, now!" They asked no questions and quickly did what they were told. "C'mon, Lamar, go, *go!*" For the first time, Lamar followed an order not given by his older brother. The truck wheeled backward, knocking over the cluster, loosening its triple grip on the flatbed. Richie seized his chance and lunged between the hands with his ax, double-fisted. He buried it within the smiley face and let go of it before the truck climbed over the thing, caught in an angle that made it a kind of a slipping-slide, where Richie's body was sliding back to between his firing troops.

His body abruptly stopped sliding. One of the four hands had grabbed hold of Richie's left ankle. "Richie!" Violet cried out. Lamar had shifted the truck back into drive. Rear tires were digging into the cluster like a construction driller on muddy grounds, splashing a fountain of foul-smelling bile behind them as the truck moved slowly forward. As soon as the trunk was in descent level again, Violet scooted up to her disarmed boyfriend and, with her machete, chopped off the arm tugging on him, leaving the corroded hand still coiled around Rickie's ankle.

Another hand snaked its fingers through Violet's tousled hair, tugging her towards the edge of the flatbed. Richie embraced his girlfriend in a bear hug to tug her back, but her hair felt like it was being yanked out by its very roots. She hissed and squealed from the awful stinging pain.

The rear tires reached the surface again, at last, free to drive forward. It peeled away belching out smoke and leaving its black-and-red tire tracks, reeking of charred rubber and undead flesh. However, the cluster hadn't released its grip on Violet, and the couple seemed likely to be snatched off the truck as it sped forward.

Fortunately, Elliot fired and hit the spot right between the joint of the wrist and forearm, freeing them from the cluster's final hand and giving them yet another trophy to keep of the monster itself. Spattered in gore and blood, the orange truck raced through the extended zombie hands on each side, as Richie fell on his back with Violet on top of him, still in the trunk.

50

PARADING AROUND

DAY 547

The hands were slimy with gore from when they'd first burst out of the cluster's young forming body, still attached to their rightful arms. The touch of the grasping hand felt clammy on Richie's ankle, while the other one was dangling in Violet's wind-swept hair. The two dislocated hands clung with gruesome fingers around new places where they did not belong, any more than they had belonged on the cluster.

Richie wrenched his ankle away with one furious yank. Violet took her time unlocking the bony fingers from her dark brown hair so that she could avoid yanking out a palm full of her own hair. Thus the cluster trophies were hurled out of the moving truck, and Violet learned to always keep her hair in a bun to keep it away from grubby hands when battling the undead fiends, especially after it grew longer over the past months, falling inches below the middle of her back.

Richie drummed angrily below the open window to get the brothers' attention, though really his frustration was directed solely at the so-called "leader" of this suicide mission, Dwayne. "What the hell, Dwayne!" Fury touched Richie's voice. "You almost got me and Violet killed out here!"

"But you *didn't* get killed," Dwayne said, "and you managed to take out that thing, so kudos to you." He didn't even turn back to look at Richie during his outburst. Dwayne watched the road his younger brother was driving along, with its colorful suburban houses on the right, rolling hills on the left, and corpses roving in all directions.

"We told you to go back; you should've listened to us," Richie ranted. "It's too risky to be taking on a cluster in a place like this. We don't have much ammo as it is, and we've already wasted a lot."

"And we're 'bout to waste some more, 'cause we're almost there," Dwayne said.

He's so fixated on the idea of a cure from some old woman's herb book that he's risking it all. "You're risking everything, and I'm afraid we might be too late to save her, or we might never make it back at all," Richie stated the hard truth. "There're just too many to take on here, Dwayne, and they keep on coming. We're rushing into this without even our full strength after our last encounter, man. We've had no time to rest, eat, or even drink some water."

"Drink from this if you're thirsty." Dwayne offered Richie his canteen. "We're almost there," he repeated, still looking out front. But the presence at the sliding window ignored the offer, so Dwayne drew back his canteen and slid the window shut to avoid any further complaints. Cowards' complaints, he considered them to be. He'd welcome none of them any longer; they would either come along or walk down the hill and back to the ranch on foot, putting their lives at a greater risk.

"What did he say?" Violet asked Richie, as he sat down next to her. She was counting ammo, as was Elliot, sitting opposite to them.

"The man's in way over his head," Richie answered. "But so long as we stay together, we can make it out of this alive. And if we have to do it by leaving them behind for doing something stupid again ... we should, shouldn't we?" Richie was not too sure of what he was saying.

"Take the truck and leave them to die, you mean?"

"No ... not like that, we can't do that. I mean like a ... we-don't-have-another-choice situation. Should we do it? God, I feel like an ass. But that's what I feel like they'll be leaving us with—no other choice. Dwayne's just too stubborn to listen to what I have to say, and Lamar just follows his big bro's orders."

"Like a dog, of his master's," Violet teased. A slight smile crossed Richie's face, not necessarily at her mockery, but more at the fact that Violet was being Violet, even after all she'd been through recently. "You're not an ass, Richie. You don't have the ass gene in you, unfortunately, or else you would've kicked that canteen to pour the water all over his stupid face. But I think what you're suggesting is right. When there's no other choice, best if *someone* makes it back to the ranch rather than no one. I wouldn't be surprised if they pull it on us."

"All the more reason we should stick together through this suicide mission," said Elliot. "It took just the three of us to take down the cluster; zombies should be less trouble after that, right?" Elliot's confidence had taken a boost from winning the ordeal, Richie saw.

Not if there are too many for us to take on. The words were itching to roll off Richie's tongue. *"Too many" as in enough to make twenty more clusters.* But he refrained from saying it, wanting to have hope on their side. "We've made it out of situations like these before ..." Richie made his answer very short and incomplete.

For minutes the truck swept past bothersome groaning wretches without any interfering with its course. The undead were scattered about everywhere, though not so much *in* the way. The ones that did get in the way, Lamar had no trouble evading, as though they were simply slowly moving traffic cones. Alas, a violent rattle began coming from the engine, and the truck began to slow on its own. Smoke puffed out, and when the truck came to a complete stop, it gave a signal for the dead nearby to limp over to where the smoke was rising higher and higher.

Lamar and Dwayne got out to inspect the problem. When they opened the hood, a hot haze immediately hit their faces. The engine had overheated, they decided, and the truck wouldn't run for a while no matter how many times Lamar tried to restart it. Some parts needed cooling down with water, and Lamar knew how to handle this. Dwayne was studying the parading zombies itching closer to the truck. "Edna's apartment building is not far from here—only a block away," he announced. "Some of us can sneak behind the small stores while the rest stay here with Lamar and draw their attention away from us."

Who does he mean by "we" and "us" if Lamar's not going with him? Richie wondered.

"C'mon, Richie, let's get goin'."

And there was his answer. *So typical of him to think that I'll just go with him without even consulting me first.*

"Wait just a minute, Dwayne," Richie said, as he climbed out of the trunk. "I'm not going anywhere without Violet. I can't leave her fending off zombies by herself."

"She won't be by herself," Dwayne pointed out. "Lamar and Elliot will be here with her, fending off the zombies till we get back with Edna's herbs."

"Lamar will be busy taking care of the engine while the rest keep the zombies off his back. Elliot's best role would be to stay in the flatbed, keeping a lookout and shooting heads through his sniper, so Violet can't possibly look after Lamar all by herself. There should be at least two people to stay as close as possible to Lamar, which means close combat, a specialty of mine and Violet's."

"Elliot is more than qualified for close combat with the dead. Now, let's get goin'," the brick-headed leader insisted, thinking that Richie would obey in the same way his younger brother always did. *Like a dog to his master.* As Dwayne gathered his gear from the front passenger seat, Richie remained standing, gathering nothing. "What are you still standing there for? Get moving!" the master barked.

This dog, however, had a mind of his own and would not obey the master's demands because he wasn't *his* master. Richie belonged to no one but her, and he intended to keep belonging to Violet—and she to him—till the bitter end that would likely to befall them sooner or later. "I'm not moving anywhere," Richie said. "If it wasn't for Violet back there with the cluster, I'd be dead, and if it wasn't for me, she'd be dead. And if it wasn't for Elliot, we'd both be dead. Like I told you before, your mission is too risky, Dwayne, and you plunged us in gut-deep. Now, I wanna make sure we get out of this alive ... all of us. And plunging deeper into this mess will not achieve that."

"Cut the crap! You just wanna stay here to play bodyguard to your girlfriend. To make sure that *she* doesn't get herself killed. I warned you 'bout her being a liability, didn't I?"

"She's not a lia—" As Richie was about to defend Violet, the girl in question leaped forward, machete in hand. The metal still carried the dark red of the cluster's blood, and Violet charged and swung it with brute force, spilling black blood from the zombie's head that had come too close to the truck without either Dwayne or Richie noticing.

The rest were not far behind, but Violet didn't charge at them just yet. She turned around to look at the two men arguing. "This live example should be more than enough an answer." Her machete pointed at the corpse. "Now, you either stay or you go," she told Dwayne. "We have zombies that need killing, so stop wasting our time."

Dwayne glowered at Violet and her fresh kill for a moment, not sure whether she was threatening him or trying to impress. No matter, Dwayne knew better than to argue more and could see the dead were edging close enough that he could almost hear their teeth, along with their groaning. He handed Richie a walkie-talkie and said, "I'm goin' all right, but when I radio for help ... you better come running, or else we lose Edna and the cure."

Like there ever was any hope for either of those things in the first place, Richie thought, as he accepted the walkie-talkie and nodded. *But if it comes down to not having another choice ... I'm running back.*

51

GUESS WHO'S BACK?

DAY 547

The sounds of clobbering and slashing made a song of bloodshed as the army of living corpses sang their verses of death when meeting their enemies' instruments of harsh metal and spiked wood. The instruments played over the verses of each undead groaner till their last incomplete verse. Yet they kept on coming.

The gore-covered instrument belonged to no other than the maiden slayer of the dead, Violet, throwing the long stretch of metal sideways at her pursuers, slashing their faces. One of her latest works made a half-naked, bearded zombie stand, quivering with nothing but its lower set of rotted teeth and a lolling tongue. The rest of the head had departed and crashed into another, smaller, corpse skulking nearby.

Richie had picked up Lamar's spiked club since the loss of his ax to the cluster. It was lighter than the ax and pierced the targets easily. Richie left his attackers with skulls ornamented with holes that oozed black pus. Two zombies limping towards Lamar, who was busy pouring water in the engine, did not anticipate the spiked club when Richie bested them. He swung the club with such speed that, one could barely see it till collision. Both attackers fell down with deeply dotted temples and slices of forehead skin peeled off like moist, smelly cheese.

They hacked and thrust continually, with an occasional shove to keep the aggressors at bay, before delivering the killing blow. Sometimes a solid kick to the knee took them down and spilled their brains, slimy and blackened. Exhaustion was beginning to run its course through during their tiring battle against the steadily approaching dead. Big Lamar was running back and forth, climbing in and out of the truck, turning the key in the ignition to get the engine started. But all it did was make revving sounds that made him climb out to inspect the engine some more.

Gazing through the rifle scope, Elliot was tireless in scanning 360 degrees, informing the fighters of how many were coming their way and from which side. He pulled the trigger when trouble arose with two or more advancing biters, but his main role was to remain in the truck and keep a lookout.

Elliot regretted the limitations of his role, but he knew that his close combat skills were not as strong as Violet's and Richie's. They would walk back-to-back, get close to the creatures, and strike them down—sometimes individually but mostly together, where one would deliver a blow that would bring the limper down and the other would shut its groans off for good.

Violet executed a takedown by cutting at one limper's frayed leg with her machete, trusting Richie to land the final blow. He was in a bit of a jam, tugging on the club that was embedded deep into a corpse's skull. Violet took a leap at another limper, her machete raised up high. Instead of going for a takedown this time, she sheathed the machete between its milky white eyes, and then she heard the *THUK!* That was the spiked club being driven into the head of the zombie she'd set up for Richie. In the space of a breath that Richie did not even consider taking, he left his club nailed to his recent kill and charged at the next one.

The zombie had its skeletal hands out to grab the glowing figure of a female armed with a machete. One second, it almost had her: the next second, it was on its back gawking at the sky with its static vision, and a glowing figure of a man appeared.

Richie had tackled it and pinned it for Violet. "Do it, Vi!" he urged her. She instantly swung the blade down horizontally as she would chop a tree log that had soft flesh and frail bones instead of splintering wood.

They needed to catch their breath after the grueling nonstop kills, but no, there was one more to go before they'd have a few seconds to spare until the next throng streamed in closer. Like the spiked club Richie abandoned in the skull of his kill, Violet's machete was wedged in solidly as well. The walking groaner was edging closer with dirty old sandals scrapping the floor. Richie gripped the machete's hilt along with Violet, doubling the power that pulled the trapped blade back and forth, sawing its way free. They could hear the sticky sounds of grinding flesh and the cracking of a bone as they pulled it out, but they could also hear the shuffling sandals inching closer. Its jaw dropped, mouth opened wide, teeth threatening to pierce the skin. The only piercing, however, was done *to* it. The zombie's hollow abdomen met the pointy, curved end of the machete once they freed it in the nick of time and used it as a shield to stop the famished corpse from taking the bite.

With the machete planted halfway into its core, the corpse persisted on, squirming to bring its clamping teeth closer to the stabbers and inadvertently wedging its body further onto the blade. Richie and Violet had other plans, though.

They stayed close and rocked the machete left and right this time, slowly loosening it. When the last few inches were still inside, they tugged it with a slicing motion that opened the belly horizontally, spilling its spoiled organs out onto its sandals. Repossessing the machete, Violet reared back and gutted the groaner, stabbing the blade in the back of its head, shutting it up for good.

A new report came from Elliot that a parade was heading their way from the south, where they'd driven in from. He took a closer look and saw calamity at the head of the living dead parade. *It can't be,* thought Elliot. *Richie killed it with his ax. He struck the core face, and it fell back!* Elliot took another look, hoping he was just seeing things. He saw the ax wedged in the middle of the crawling amalgam of carcasses, and that was enough to confirm it. The cluster was not dead.

"Oh, crap. Guys," Elliot called, "guess who's back?" Violet and Richie looked up but only got a head tilt from Elliot to come see for themselves, and by then they were able to see it all too clearly.

Violet swore. "What the hell do we do now?"

"We leave," Richie said simply. "Lamar, how's the truck doing?"

Lamar was cussing worse than Violet, trying to start the ignition, but to no avail. "Probably needs more water," he answered, "but I'm almost out."

"Save the last few drops then," said Richie. "The cluster's back."

"*What?* I thought you put your ax in that damn thing"

"I did, but it appears the 'damn thing' didn't die. We need to move, now." The undead were closing in on them. Lamar ignored Richie's previous command and went back to the hood to use the final ounces of water in an attempt to revive the broken engine.

Richie saw an opening: if they were going to escape notice, they must hide. Multiple shops were just a few yards away. Richie grabbed Violet's hand and drew out his shotgun with the other. "Over there, let's go!" He started to jog, forcing Violet to do the same.

Elliot was about to follow them, but as he tried to leave the flatbed with his rifle and all three ammo-bearing backpacks, a backpack strap got caught on the corner, making him tumble.

He quickly picked himself up, gathered everything, and ran. Half a dozen limpers blocked the path that Richie and Violet had chosen, and more were circling—plus the cluster and its horde were not far behind. Panic took Elliot. *I'm not a coward*, he told himself, and yet he was backing away, tossing the backpacks onto the flatbed again and climbing up behind them. He didn't make it up, though. His shoes were caught on something, or rather, caught *by* something.

52

RETREAT

DAY 547

Lamar held the canteen upside down as he used the last drops of water on the engine. The big reckless man had completely ignored the walking dangers approaching him—as well as Richie's retreat plan—to do whatever it took to fix the overheated engine. In return for his final attempt, there came a slithering tickle that touched the moist back of his neck as he was closing the hood. Like the soft scratchy brush of the tip of a fingernail, with a puff of hot breath that made the sweaty back of his neck shiver.

Lamar swung around and thumped the empty canteen against the open jaw of the living corpse that was fingering the back of his neck. Its jawline cracked, and yellow teeth spilled out with a clatter before the fall of their former possessor. He turned back to the engine to finish closing the hood but then jumped back in surprise when a zombie leaped from the driver's door.

A swift jab from Lamar's calloused fist brought it down easily enough, but to get to the driver's seat he'd need more than just a couple of knockout punches. That was where the AK-47—slung over one of his

FEAR IN FLESH

massive tattooed shoulders—came into play. Lamar shot at what appeared to be an endless train of zombies, which made him realize how bad an idea it would be to get back into the driver's seat and test the engine when there was so little chance of it working.

Shotgun blasts boomed. BAM! BAM!

Lamar dashed away from the truck to where the blasts were coming from and followed the rest of the group in retreat. One zombie intercepted the big man and got its ribcage kicked in. Another path-blocker almost got its head struck clean off with just a smack from Lamar's assault rifle. Its neck snapped back so far that the bones poked out.

Keep pushin'. They're not far ahead, Lamar kept telling himself. *Keep pushin'!*

He slowed his pace as soon as he realized that he was surrounded by oncoming corpses from every side. Lamar focused on his right and left flanks, unloading shells repeatedly into the heads of his carnivorous hunters. *Gotta push through or else I'll waste all my bullets.*

His AK-47's onslaught rattled on. The big man's fear was starting to show on his sweat-soaked face, for his tough-guy persona was being overwhelmed by the outnumbering fiends that sought him for a meal. Lamar was fighting all alone, fending for his life with nothing but his assault rifle to protect him. His eyes and mouth were tense as the ammo poured out, and he tried to hide his fear from the blind eyes of the groaners. He thought about ramming through the front column while shooting, but what would he do when his rifle stopped shooting? He wouldn't be able to make it through to the end of the column without at least one small bite. Yes, he had a stone-hard, muscle-built body, but his skin was not impenetrable to teeth.

The front column seemed to be closing in on Lamar for a moment until they stopped advancing when shotgun blasts began booming once more behind them. The loud shots were closing in faster than it took the two zombies at the head to turn. They got their faces blasted to smithereens, coating Lamar's clothes with the aftermath of the corrupted faces.

Richie stood behind the gruesome scene with his shotgun aimed at the two semi-headless bodies, which fell down, gushing blood. Violet was by his side, swatting at zombies with her no-longer-recognizable machete. Lamar stepped forward to join them before the pursuers at his back could grab hold of him.

They made it to the stores, panting from all the running and whacking they had to do to get there. Unable to escape quietly to the back of the buildings like Dwayne had, for all the undead senses were on them, they were trapped. The Cluster and its army were passing by the truck with nothing to halt its path.

All the stores seemed to be locked up, blocked and barricaded from the inside or infested with the walking dead, which they were able to see through the glass storefronts. Time was running out, with the cluster crawling over the groaning limpers, crushing their decaying bodies under its own mass of odorous decay. They passed shop after shop until they found a store with no undead roaming within. It was a jewelry store and had a steel cage front drawn down over the glass and locked.

In the blink of an eye, without pausing to think, Richie aimed his shotgun at the rusted lock and pulled the trigger, releasing the lock from the cage. "Lift with me, Lamar," Richie said. And for the first time, Lamar obeyed without offering brick-headed resistance. He slung the strap of his rifle over his shoulder and helped Richie pull the steel cage up as high as their upper body strength permitted them to.

Violet was the first one to crouch down, slip to the other side of the heavy cage, and hold it up from the inside. Richie went after her as quickly as he could to add his strength from the inside and allow Lamar to come after them. Lamar wasn't moving, though, just holding the cage up with trembling muscles. "What the hell are you waiting for? *Get in!*" Violet shouted. Lamar seemed dazed but finally slid in, and the moment he released his grip on the cage, it went crashing down on the hand of a zombie trying to grab his foot before he could make it. The zombie was then left with just a stump of an arm.

The small gaps in the cage were soon filled with extending hands, and some were stuffed with teeth-gnashing jaws. Luckily for the survivors, they had a narrow space between the glass wall and the cage to keep them out of reach. The plan, however, did not involve them sitting around like zoo animals with spectators who wanted to eat them instead of taking pictures. "We need to get into the store," Lamar said, with exhaustion. "Someone shoot the glass—I'm outta ammo. This place is too damn tight and 'bout to get tighter when the cluster gets here."

"I spent my last shot on opening the lock," Richie said. Then he and Lamar both turned to Violet.

"Don't look at me," she said. "I ran out of bullets way before the both of you did. That's why I've been using the machete this whole time."

"I thought I saw Elliot climbing down with the ammo bags," Richie recalled.

"I saw him going back in," Violet added. "There were too many around him. It's safer for him to stay in there, out of sight. All the zombies around the block by now know we're here. That can make an opening for Dwayne to get back to the truck. Between the two of them, they'll figure something out to get us outta here."

"Yeah," said Richie, "besides, this glass is thick enough to be bulletproof." He knocked on the glass with his knuckles. "There's a chance that our bullets wouldn't do jack to break through it."

A hysterical laugh burst from Lamar's throat. "That's great. That's just great. The cluster will just come by, ram through the gate, and eat us up for lunch. *Hell no!* I ain't sitting here waitin' for some big pile of ... dead faces t' gobble me up! I'm breakin' through this damn glass." He took his AK-47 and rammed the butt of it against the glass repeatedly, barely even scratching it.

"Heads up," warned Violet. "The big pile of dead faces is here."

"Get back, backs against the glass," Richie told them.

The crunching sound of bones, followed by the rusty screech of bending steel, was enough to drop all three survivors' hearts down to their stomachs. The cluster forced itself against the steel cage with its snaky fingers squeezing through the unoccupied gaps.

Just then, Richie's walkie-talkie started crackling.

53

NO OTHER CHOICE

DAY 547

The dead were scattering when Dwayne made his way back to the truck. He saw that there was little need to hide on the return journey since there were hardly any groaners paying attention to him. He still trod carefully, though. Dwayne speed-walked with a gore-wet sickle in one hand and a large black bag full of herbs in the other. An AK-47 of his own was slung over his shoulder, but he hadn't resorted to it yet. Inside the apartment building, there weren't so many dead that the curved sickle couldn't handle them, slicing and dicing. Now, out on the street, it wasn't that much different.

Dwayne kept his distance, pacing the edge of the cliff. He ran into one wandering limper and took the crown of its head off with the curve of the sickle, leaving the body bleeding and squirming. The ruckus made by the sickle when it tore through skin and cleaved bone caused some heads to turn. More bloodshed would attract more attention, so Dwayne decided to take them on skillfully. He set the bag of ingredients aside, along with his unused assault rifle, retaining the sickle as a last resort. His plan was to not involve any weapons but use his own bodyweight and bare hands. One after another, they approached Dwayne, who edged them closer to the cliff. Once they hit the border rail, they suddenly made a one-way descent from the top of Hill-Ville County.

There was something luring all the zombies away. It had to be something loud, Dwayne figured, or else why would they be so motivated? He quietly followed them back to the block on which the truck had broken down on. *Somethin' bad must've gone down*, thought Dwayne warily. *I don't hear any gunshots.* Neither did the zombies, but they kept scurrying onward, following the groaners that had heard the gunfire earlier.

The truck was still at a standstill when Dwayne returned on the tail of the zombie parade that continued off towards the stores, not paying any mind to the handful of their own kind shaking the empty vehicle. They followed the louder crowd instead. Dwayne snuck quietly to the truck and climbed into the front seat without being spotted. No fogged eyes gazed at him yet, but the truck was shaking slightly from the few angry corpses bumping and clawing on one side.

During his return journey, he'd considered radioing Richie through the walkie-talkie several times, but he didn't want to draw any attention. Alone in the truck, Dwayne had no choice but to radio the rest of the crew to see where they'd gone. He couldn't leave without them, whether the truck was fixed or not. First, he needed to make sure that the sound he'd make wouldn't be heard by the zombies currently wrestling with the truck. He turned his body to close the sliding window, and that was the moment when a pair of eyes finally met his.

Dwayne thought he was all alone in the truck—that everyone had fled when the situation grew dire—but he'd thought wrong. One had stayed behind with all the ammo bags with him in the flatbed. Elliot was staring back at Dwayne in panic. "Where is everyone?" Dwayne merely mouthed the words to avoid being heard. Elliot shook his head tremulously in the answer and gestured with one shaking hand at Dwayne to stay quiet and keep low.

Something big was coming.

A massive shadow was cast over the truck, swallowing the flatbed with its bulging, swollen lumps and multiple faces as the creature that bore them lumbered by. Dwayne ducked down just in time. Elliot held his breath as if he were underwater so that his shaking would be kept at bay.

The cluster moved alongside the truck with the ax embedded somewhere between the center and the lower left side of its carcass. Lumps of decay scraped onto one side of the truck, rocking it and squishing the few zombies that were groaning after Elliot. It continued on its pursuit of whatever the rest of Hill-Ville's residents were after.

Dwayne twisted the keys in the ignition, but grinding sounds echoed from the engine. Twisting once, twice, thrice—revving and quieting again until the engine suddenly roared back to life. Dwayne quickly sat up and drove away with a pack of the undead turning their attention toward the getaway vehicle. Luckily the uptick in attention didn't extend to the cluster's, for it was set on three nearby prizes.

Dwayne was steering with one hand and pressing the button of the walkie-talkie with the other. "Rich, you there? Where are you guys? Over."

The wait was nerve-wracking, but in reality, it did not take too long. "D ... wa ... yne, we're trapped here ..." The signal was full of static, but Richie's voice was understandable. "A ... jewlla ... ry s-store. Cluster ... ... z-zombies ... we can't ... get out."

"All three of ya are together?"

"Y ... es,"

"Stay put then: Me and Elliot will think of something. We'll get you guys outta there."

"Hu ... rry!"

Dwayne drove the truck back down the hill. "What are you doing, Dwayne?" Elliot asked through the window. "We're supposed to be helping them."

"Let me break it to you, Elliot. The two of us ain't much of a help with just our rifles against *all* that you saw back there. Which I guess you already know 'cause you were hiding from it all, am I right?"

"I couldn't catch up with the rest," Elliot said. "But still, we can't leave them behind."

"We're not," Dwayne said with a slightly scolding tone. "We just need to make it back home in time with the herbs, that we all risked our lives for, to save Edna. Then we're comin' back for them with the explosives." Dwayne paused for a moment to let that sink in. "It's the only way to fight through this many dead, so they'll have to wait. We got no other choice."

54

CAGED

DAY 547

The air was heavy with the stench of death. Caged within that small, confined space made it difficult not only to breathe but also to remain calm with all the mournful groans and snapping of teeth, along with the cluster's bony fingers scratching through the steel gaps of the cage. It felt as though they were in a zoo where they were the wild monsters, the visitors came to see locked safely away in their cages. Only here the cage was not a sanctuary to keep the visitors safe from the little monsters: it was to keep the visitors away so that they didn't eat the poor defenseless animals.

The true monsters were on the other side of that cage.

There was nothing but an unbreakable glass wall behind them, which they leaned on—away from the skinless, fleshy hands reaching for their sweaty faces to claw out whatever they could grab through the gaps. Richie, Violet, and Lamar were truly trapped. It was a prison in hell. All the groaning demons emitted heat from their decomposing bodies, trapping the three survivors in hell's lowest circle to drown them in their own sweat. Soon … it was only a matter of time, and they didn't have much of it.

Steel was bending slowly from the weight of the cluster, with a rusty shriek that made the bones of the imprisoned tremble. Lamar was trembling the worst of the three, by far. He was breathing hard and had an unsettled look on his face; no one could tell whether he was extremely angry or whether fear had taken over. He was soaked with sweat, and his black sleeveless shirt was sodden and sticky against his upper body.

Though Violet was always full of hope, despite all she had been through and survived, she felt very little of it in their predicament. At least they were together. That made Violet and Richie seem stronger and less tormented than Lamar, had for the past … time was lost. It might have been less than an hour for them, but it sure felt like more. Longer even, as the day went on and they could not see it from the mountain of twisted carcasses that blocked the light and made it seem like night time inside that cell.

The unending noises coming from the dead's lungs were unbearable, but they could still live through them. Those noises would undoubtedly cease once the cluster broke through, crushing their bones and devouring their flesh down to their broken skeletal forms. Still, they clung to one last hope: that Dwayne and Elliot were coming back to rescue them somehow.

No response came from Dwayne through the walkie-talkie, nor were there any attempts at communication from his side. Richie's attempts kept bringing the same results, though he kept the walkie-talkie next to his dried lips and pressed his finger down on the button, calling, "Dwayne …? Elliot …? Anyone there …? Over." They only heard radio static for an answer. "Dwayne …? Elliot …? We're still trapped here. Anyone else? Angie …? Jerry …? Kermit …? Anybody …? Help us."

"Ain't no one comin' to help us," Lamar wheezed. "We're gonna die out here."

"Well, not technically out, but in," said Violet. "We're trapped inside, so we're gonna die *in* here." It was no time to be making petty jokes, Violet knew, but she couldn't help it. "And we're not going to die here, Lamar. Your brother is on his way. He'll get us out."

"She's right," agreed Richie, still clinging to that last thin thread of hope. "He'll probably be back with some of the grenades Gunter had left us after he passed away. Blow up the horde and clear the path for us to get out, that's what he'll do."

Gunter Waters had, a day before being savaged by the undead bear in the middle of the hunting grounds, blown up his car with a hand grenade to get rid of the dead herd on their tail, back at the gas station. There had been six grenades in total in his backpack, and now there were five left. How many would Dwayne use for this reckless rescue mission? A better question was *if* Dwayne would make it back on time.

A rattle of steel sent a shiver down Lamar's spine, and he punched one of his rough fists into the ceramic tile flooring with all his might. The ceramic squares were a part of the jewelry store's outer design: milk white with glitter that made them sparkle like diamonds. Lamar didn't manage to break the squares with his fist, and, though his knuckles were raw and darkening, Lamar showed no sign of physical pain. Still, the agony was pouring out of him—through his wide-open eyes, his trembling lips, the sweat streaming from every inch of his exposed skin. The big man was deathly terrified—that was plainly obvious—and his terror was tampered with wrath.

As the steel cage bent more and the skinless hands reached out closer to the trapped meat, the air grew worse. Lamar lurched to his feet, forehead dripping sweat onto the diamond-white ceramic floor. "Ain't no one comin' back," the big man blurted out in a heavy puff of breath. "We're dead. They left us here fo' bait."

"Did you sweat the last drops of your brain out, Lamar?" Violet shot back. "You're his brother. There's no way he's leaving you here to die like this."

"Then where the hell is he, huh? Where's the big brotha that's comin' to save us all? All I see is that goddamn pile of shit groaning at us, no Dwayne. He left us … fo' good."

"Calm down, Lamar." Richie intervened. "We're all sacred here, and—"

"Scared? I ain't scared!" Lamar snapped. "Don't you say I'm scared, boy. If only I had bullets, I'd bust our asses outta here. It's just that … this place … it's too tight up in here." His breathing sounded labored as he spoke. He banged the back of his fist against the firm glass wall behind him twice. "You just had to trap us in the smallest place you could find!"

"Sorry, but our options were limited," said Richie, irritated. "Either get in or get eaten."

Lamar felt as though the walls were closing in on him. He unslung his empty AK-47 and started thumping the butt of it against the glass wall. He knew well that not even bullets could break through the glass, but desperately he continued his useless attempts, only scratching the transparent surface. "I can hardly breathe," the big man huffed out. "I need …" THUMP! " … air," he managed to say between breaths and. THUMP-THUMP-THUMP! THUMP-THUMP! THUMP!

The noise was exciting the cluster's many faces. Heads started bobbing more frantically, teeth clamped on steel with a shrill sound, and the groans grew ever louder. Violet stood up and tried grabbing Lamar by the arm to put a stop to his mad rampage. "Lamar, calm down already!" Though her words were clear, the hulking prisoner refused to listen. Her tugging at his arm ended abruptly when he turned and shoved her away with one hand as if she were a soft cushion, sending her nearly crashing to the ground. Richie caught her halfway.

"*Hey!*" Richie exploded. "I don't care what kind of crazy you're going through, but you don't *ever* put your hands on her like that again, understand?" He stepped close, face-to-face with the mad six-foot-tall beast of a man, staring into his fearful and angry eyes.

In that very small prison with all the skinless hands extending outward, Violet stood still inside. Richie had gotten between her and Lamar, which ignited one heated-looking standoff that might just stir up the pot of their current predicament from scorching hot to hell. Lamar twisted both hands into the front of Richie's shirt, ripping it, and spoke gruffly. "If it weren't fo' me, you and yo girl would be inside that thing by now back when it caught the truck."

Richie gripped both of Lamar's wrists and squeezed as he struggled to pull them off. "We wouldn't be in all this mess if it wasn't for your brother's orders and *you* listening to him instead of taking our side, *knowing* that we were making the right call." He put more pressure on his wrists and forced him to draw back his hands.

The big man would not be overpowered so easily. He twisted his massive hands over Richie's to grab him by the neck, but Richie managed to keep himself at a safe distance, by deflecting with his hands and tucking his head back. "You sayin' this is my fault?" Lamar demanded during the struggle. Richie surprisingly managed to overpower the big man using his agility to dodge sideways and push Lamar away to almost stumble onto his backside.

The action had taken aback Lamar so much that Richie could now see more anger than fear in his perspiring face. Yet Richie could not hold back the urge to answer Lamar's question. "Your fault and Dwayne's. The way I see it, we saved your ass twice. You should be more grateful."

"Grateful fo' what? Trappin' us in here to get eaten inside rather than out? Small places do me no good, son, and this place—it just ain't big enough to keep us all safe."

"Relax, Lamar." Richie tried lowering the tension, as Violet stood there with a jolt of memory surging through her, forming a picture of a familiar dark place and a small battle ring of clawing hands, red glowing eyes, and gnashing teeth. The white knight in a shining armor and the ebony armored behemoth. *No, no, not this ...*

"There's only one way I can relax," Lamar said. "I'll need more air. So I'll have to make more room for it, and the only way to do *that* is to make our numbers less. I don't share my goddamn air with no one!" And with those final words, Lamar charged at Richie like a raging bull, lifting him up in the air with his brute strength.

Violet wailed in dismay. *"No!"* For one moment, her partner stood before her, and then he was swept off his feet and slammed into the crack-resistant glass wall with bone-jarring force. The dual had begun, and the cheering groaners were bursting with excitement. Richie was pummeling at Lamar's upper back with his elbow, and he wrapped an arm around his damp neck in a reverse headlock, as the big man swung Richie's entire body left and right in a mockery of a bear hug till he wrestled him to the floor.

Violet's pleas for Lamar to stop were all ignored, so she saw no other way but to throw herself into the heart of the skirmish. She yanked Lamar's head backward by his afro with both hands, yelling, "Get off!"

However, the out-of-control man would not budge, except to slam one of his tattooed elbows into Violet's ribs, knocking her to her knees, fighting a gag reflex. That distraction cost Lamar his grip on Richie, who broke free of the big man's hold and jabbed him in the face.

Once Lamar's weight was off Richie, both men still struggled, unwilling to let go of one another. Lamar had a chunk of Richie's shirt in one fist, and Richie kept his punches coming, right and left. The big man took the punches while tucking his head down low and, with a well-timed move, was able to block a left hook from Richie and deliver it right back to him. Richie began seeing dark spots and hearing ringing in his ears, for Lamar's punches really did a number on his face. The more the hooks and the jabs connected to Richie, the further he was forced to step back until he felt the back of his shirt being tugged. He felt unsettlingly long, pointy fingers brushing against his back, and Lamar kept on pushing.

At that time Violet jumped back in by leaping onto Lamar's back and hanging onto his neck in a choke hold, stabilizing her position by wrapping her legs around his waist. It lasted no more than two seconds when Lamar took a few quick steps backward and rammed Violet against the glass wall. The back of her skull thudded against the wall. Then her head swam in a sea of unsteadiness, causing her chokehold to loosen and the sparkly floor to come rushing up to her when she fell, half-conscious.

In his dazed, beaten state, Richie somehow found the strength within him after witnessing what Violet just took from Lamar to pull out of the cluster's grasping fingers and charge. The distance was short, and Richie extended his arms, causing his black shirt to rip in half and dangle about his waist. He was freed from the skinless clawing fingers and free to attack like a dog with a loosened leash. A leap and a hook took Lamar by surprise because his scruffy left cheek went numb, and he felt a stab of pain rush up his head. It was time for Richie to lead the dance, and he was leading Lamar away from the glass wall and into the deadly hands.

Being the brute specimen, he was, Lamar did not allow his strength to be turned against him. His large booted feet had put on the brakes. The big man was coming to and trying to turn the tables on Richie again, but Richie pushed himself even harder to maintain his position, matching Lamar's strength. He could feel the cluster's fingertips poking at his back. That's when Lamar truly started to panic, thrashing around and shouting in fright. As Lamar got desperate, the power of his smaller opponent began to overwhelm him. He looked down at Richie and knew that he had to regain control no matter what.

Richie's face was hurting; blood was seeping down one of his brows and out his nose too, but he saw that he was winning the fight. Richie had to do whatever it took to survive, to keep himself and Violet safe from the monster that was trapped with them. The cluster was waiting for a big meal, teeth snapping, drooling for the big man's sweaty flesh.

Richie's eyes gazed at Lamar one last time before he would leave him to the cluster. He saw the amount of fear in the big man's face with one eye and briefly saw a thumb with the other—then blackness. Richie's left eye went blind when Lamar's desperation led him to shove his fat thumb deep into the socket. A scream of agony found its way out of Richie's mouth but was shut off in seconds when Lamar turned him over to the skinless hands.

Big or medium, the cluster had caught itself a meal, and Lamar made sure that this meal would not escape its grasp again. He kept pummeling Richie's face with his bloody fists until it was no longer handsome. His teeth were broken, as were his lips; his cheeks were enormous, his nose twisted, his right eye bloated, and the left eye gone. It was then up to the cluster to finish the job.

Violet was still only half-conscious during the struggle, but the scream of anguish rang in her throbbing head, and she managed to look over. *It's only a dream, a freakin' nightmare is all.* She tried convincing herself, but she saw Lamar as the black armored behemoth with two gigantic horns, beating the light out of her knight in the shining armor. The hands assisted the horned demon in detaining her knight, pulling his wrecked body towards the cage as the behemoth kept on pummeling his face bloody. *It can't be Richie; it wasn't his face ... not his beautiful face.*

When Lamar finally stepped aside, Violet saw a face that did not look like Richie's. It was a ruin from the beating, just like that of the knight in her dream. As she watched, the cluster dug in. Richie's naked upper body poured blood when the long fingers scraped away his skin to paralyze his movement. Mouths fed on whatever part of him they could sink their teeth in through the steel holes of the cage. Arteries burst and skin split, as Richie's lifeblood was drained out of his broken body and chunks of his flesh were caught in the cluster's teeth. He screamed his lungs out till a couple of sharp fingers punctured his throat, destroying his vocal cords. Richie made a gargling sound from choking on his own blood that oozed down his neck and bubbled out of his mouth. The one eye he had left was wide open and looked very much in pain, for there were teeth right next to it, gnawing the skin off. Bones could be heard cracking as the hands pulled his body against the cage until it almost seemed his bare back was being shredded like cheese, crushing his spine and ribcage as well.

Violet's big green eyes kept on staring in horror till Richie was reduced to a bag of dripping blood and entrails. She bellowed from the moment she regained consciousness and caught her boyfriend's suffering to the moment she drove her machete into his crown to end his excruciatingly slow slaughter. The last light faded out of her knight in the shining armor.

All went silent afterward; there were only the chewing sounds made by the cluster's mouths burrowing into Richie's corpse. Lamar—the culprit in Richie Morey's inhuman murder—stood frozen, watching the cluster feeding. Violet went back to the glass wall with a machete bathed in the brains of her life's love. She set her blazing eyes on the behemoth while his gaze was still locked on the feasting filth. He did not even notice Violet moving back, hardly acknowledging her existence after the shock of the atrocity he had just committed. Suddenly he remembered her after a biting sting went through his abdomen.

When Lamar lowered his head, he saw his own blood coating a long metal object that was razor sharp. In the dream, both the knight and the demon dueled with elaborate weapons, whereas in reality there were only fists of fury, but all the same, it ended equally horrific.

Violet stood behind him, her eyes glowing beneath the damp hair that half covered her furious face. She twisted the hilt of the machete so that it would sink deeper and immobilize Lamar. The big man found himself on his knees, which he could no longer feel. His breathing was labored, and his palms were open under the blade, sticky and red from his trickling blood. "I should've used this on you the moment you went crazy on us," Violet said in a volatile whisper. "I wasn't thinking. It ... it all happened so fast. I thought I could calm you down, but that was a mistake. That escalated everything, and I saw it all coming, but I was ... I was blind to it. I should've driven this machete right through the top of your head instead of Ri—" She started to sob, unable to finish saying his name. "I should've ended you the moment you put your filthy hands on me, and then fed your worthless corpse to this messed up abomination instead of Richie!"

"So t-tight ..." Lamar exhaled, "... it's t-too tight up in h-here."

"It should've been you!" Ruthlessly Violet kicked him in the back of his head. She could not bear listening to the sound of his hoarse voice. Lamar's face dropped and hit the ceramic floor, as did his entire body. At the moment of impact, the machete was driven back out halfway. He screamed a desperate cry of pain, but Violet wanted him to scream louder—as loud as Richie had been screaming before the cluster got to his throat and damaged his vocal cords.

She pressed on the hilt with one palm to keep him wailing in torment, as the other palm snatched up his head by his hair so that he could see the feast he had hosted by killing Richie and making him the main dish for their unwanted guest. "You see what you've done? *You see?* Now you'll have to pay for it, you monster!" Violet transferred her other hand to Lamar's hair and smashed his face down into the ground. The thud of the impact was awful to hear, but his scream was too satisfying. By the second thud, Violet heard a cracking noise that turned out to be Lamar's nose popping. By the third and fourth thuds, Lamar's face was painted red. The fifth thud cracked the ceramic tile on which his face was being repeatedly smashed into. The sixth thud shattered the ceramic, which cut Lamar's right eye badly. By the seventh thud, cement began showing beneath the glittery ceramic, and when Lamar's face was lifted up for the eighth hit, his eye was dangling from its socket.

An eye for an eye, and a life for a life. As Violet went for the eighth, she heard and felt a quaking explosion that rumbled just on the other side of the cage. Too angry to care, she smashed his face in for the eighth time as a tremble of exhaustion ran up and down her arms. No more shouts came from Lamar; he was either dead or unconscious. From the looks of how his face was rearranged, he seemed more likely to be dead, but Violet couldn't tell from her fuming rage so she kept on smashing.

A second, closer explosion hit and blew Violet off of Lamar after obliterating the cluster. Only the leftovers of many carcasses remained. The explosion also brought the cage halfway down in a twisted bend. Violet was underneath the cage now, and right next to her was Lamar's motionless body facing up, both showered in the cluster's gooey substances.

When the smoke cleared, Violet thought she was free to escape, but first, she had to roll Lamar's corpse over to pull out her machete. She looked up to find two screeching monsters outside the cage waiting for her with long, sharp claws; cruel fangs; and red glowing eyes. Behind them, a cloaked shadow of a creature stood holding a scythe taller than her.

55

OUT CAME A MONSTER

DAY 547

The truck stopped where the horde was gathered behind the cluster, swarming around the jewelry store. Dwayne stepped out of the driver's seat with a grenade in hand. Elliot was out of the passenger's seat, too with his sniper rifle, as usual. Both weapons belonged to the deceased marksman, Gunter Waters. Five grenades remained after Gunter used one at the gas station, and Dwayne had brought two with him.

He had Elliot by his side in case of any small intrusions from the side of the roaming dead. Dwayne needed to stay focused because he had to make each grenade count. After all, it was his first time using one, and he only had two. One would follow the other: the first would blow away the horde, and the second would be designated for the cluster, but both, the trigger extraction point and the tossing distance needed to be carefully considered. They didn't want the imprisoned survivors to come to any harm.

Getting Lamar, Richie, and Violet out of there was the mission; therefore, Dwayne brought in reinforcements. Jerry and Kermit were the best he could do, and he gave each his own firearm and left them standing on the flatbed to shoot at any dead faces focusing on Dwayne, Elliot, or the truck.

Dwayne pulled out the trigger needle with his middle finger and then threw the grenade, watching it roll on the ground like a bowling ball that would blow up the pins instead of striking them down. It rolled and rolled between many wobbling feet till it hit one and stopped ... BOOM! The undead were eviscerated; parts of them went flying and raining down like a downpour of blood. The ones that were only caught in the wave of the explosive were dispersed, opening the path for the second grenade to roll down and strike the biggest remaining pin in the pile.

BOOM!

The result was the eerie sight of a roaring fireball mixed with enormous lumps of rotten meat that exploded out of the creature's body when it popped like a balloon, dispersing the remnants of the cluster all over the front of the store and about twenty yards back, where the living dead minions had been massacred. The smoke of the blast spread as far as the gory aftermath but did not take long to blow away, unlike the everlasting mess and smell that would surely draw in Cliffroyce Bay's entire population of flies and crows for the feast stinking up the hill.

Carefully placed footsteps advanced towards the store after the smoke had cleared up. Aside from the zombies that were staggering to their feet, there were ones who could not stand up because of a missing leg or two—or the whole lower body—but still, despite their disabilities, they persisted in trying to capture Elliot and Dwayne.

Jerry and Kermit did their job as best as they could to keep the milky-eyed groaning wretches away. They shot from a slightly awkward angle, given where the truck was parked in the middle of the road, so they couldn't place every bullet in a rotted brain. Still, they managed to keep them away anyhow so that Dwayne and Elliot could check the jewelry shop for their trapped teammates.

When they were standing at the footstep of the broken security gate, the smoke was still fading. At first, they saw their teammates beneath the steel gate as just shadows lying on the ground, and there seemed to be only *two* figures behind the curtain of haze left from the explosion. One was lying flat, unmoving while the other moved next to it, fumbling at something.

As the smoke grew thinner, and the two figures were at last revealed to be more than just fog creatures, Dwayne and Elliot saw them with strange colors that seemed almost less recognizable than the shadows had been. The cluster's inner liquids that covered them both certainly hid some of their human features, but one of them had no features to speak of. His face was a deformed ruin; one eye hung down to where his ear would be, as the rest of the face was a fusion of torn skin and battered bone covered in dark blood. The stature still looked the same—big—even as he lay dead. Tattoos on the arms showed beneath all that blood and confirmed his faceless identity.

The second identity did not need much confirming, though the long hair was soaked in blood and grime. There was still only one that possessed hair that long.

Violet was fumbling for something on Lamar's corpse—well, more *in* Lamar's corpse. She dislodged the machete from his spine before their very eyes, and then she stepped out and stood right in front of them with a weapon that dripped with the blood of Dwayne's little brother. "What the hell!" Dwayne managed in spite of his shock at witnessing the post-death image of his brother.

"V-Vi ... w-what happened?" Elliot spoke timidly. "What did you *do?"*

Violet did not answer; her unblinking eyes glowered with dark fury.

"Put the machete down." Elliot lowered his rifle and stepped forward. "C-come with me." He extended a hand to her.

The machete-wielding hand flinched; Dwayne caught the movement with his teary eyes. "No, Elliot, step back!" he warned. And that shifted Elliot's attention away from Violet to Dwayne. In that brief moment, Violet lifted the blade overhead and let out a garish battle shriek that dragged Elliot's gaze back to her. When the machete cut down, it rang against the sniper rifle, as Elliot was quick enough to raise the firearm sideways to block his friend's attack.

Repeatedly the machete rose and fell with relentless speed. The sheer ferocity of her strikes caused the ringing of metal on metal to ignite sparks, and Elliot fell down. "Violet, stop, it's me!" He tried talking to her, but to no avail. Violet was blind with anger and madness, just like Lamar had been when they were caged in, but she could not see it. She was too angry to stop and think. Elliot was a sharp-clawed, razor-toothed, red-eyed monster to her. All she wanted to do was kill this monster, as she had the horned one back in the cage before he could kill her like he did Richie.

Dwayne was having no more of this lunacy. He stepped in and grabbed Violet by her swinging arm in the middle of a cut. "*Enough!*" he rumbled, and she reacted swiftly by twisting her entire body around, her arm still in his grasp, and biting him with the machete. The blade gashed Dwayne's right shoulder. With a hiss and a few swear words, Dwayne released his hold on her arm and started to back away. His left hand was covering his right shoulder, as the mad woman came at him with the machete dancing left and right. He dodged and dodged as he backed away one step at a time until he tripped and fell over a stack of carcasses.

The machete followed swiftly to cut Dwayne right where he sat, but his legs split open so that the descending blade penetrated the carcasses instead while getting caught in the process. Violet's hands never left the hilt; she frantically tried breaking the machete free, which gave Dwayne an opportunity to shove her roughly away with his foot, breaking her contact with the machete.

She got back up as fast as she'd fallen down. Her speed caught Dwayne off guard as he tried to unsling his AK-47 from his back. Once he started to fumble with the strap, Violet surprised him with a quick close-range attack. He tried keeping her away with one hand so that he could prepare the firearm with the other, but she retaliated by biting down on the hand that got in her way.

No matter how robust a man is, there is no mystical force on earth that will make him not feel the pain of teeth sinking into his flesh. Dwayne bawled out in pain and gave up on using his firearm for the moment. He instead used his free hand to grip the side of Violet's head by the hair; Dwayne had a fist full of her rank hair and pulled so hard, he felt as if he would snatch out chunks of her hair by the roots.

Being faster didn't do Violet much good this time; she gave out from the pain faster than Dwayne had. She unclenched her teeth and was shoved face first into a shallow pool of blood, almost as dark as seawater at night. She floundered around to keep the taste of more blood out of her mouth and the sting of it out of her eyes so that she could see the monster she needed to kill, but with all that wallowing in blood, it coated her whole face before she could get out.

Not even halfway up, Violet fell back down, face first into the puddle again. This time she flailed less wildly. She hardly even moved because this time Dwayne was the one who sprinted faster, acting unmercifully aggressive, though not as deadly as she was. It was time for him to strike harshly and put an end to this madness. He unslung his assault rifle and bashed the butt of it into Violet's head.

After she got bashed in the head with a heavy assault rifle, her thoughts and memories began to scatter. She plunged into the pool of blood and sank deeper in the endless pitch-black mouth of darkness that seized her consciousness. Until she would awaken from this terrible nightmare full of monsters, Violet had only felt one thing before the world blacked out ... fear.

EPILOGUE

DEMON-MAN

Marvin Conley had been a man of fun, comical attributes with a lovable persona during the days before the undead virus broke out upon the world. The plague had taken his Daily Comics shop from him, along with his friends Richie Morey and Violet Turner, and eventually what remained of his witty personality.

All was lost after he miraculously survived Cliffroyce Bay's airstrike bombing on the fourth day after the breakout. Since then, Marvin Conley had fallen into the mouth of darkness.

Moments after Marvin had seen the broadcast announcing the airstrike on his store's television, he'd gathered as much food and bottled drinks as he could and fled the store. His only weapon, he'd donated to Richie, who went off looking for Violet. Marvin ran outside not long after Richie had left, looking for an escape vehicle for himself, but the dead still roamed the maze of jammed vehicles, making it difficult for Marvin to go unnoticed. He ran across from car to car, looking for a key inside until he ran across three of the undead in the lane nearest to the west sidewalk.

Going back would mean running into the dead that had pursued him earlier. Marvin could only move forward, so he tackled the first groaner with the molded face, using his body weight. He then took out a beer bottle from the plastic bag he carried and smashed it against the head of an elderly-looking zombie, leaving him with an obese zombie. Marvin used the broken bottle he had in his fist and stabbed it repeatedly into the third zombie's eye until the overweight corpse collapsed.

That was when Marvin found his opening. Right behind those three, there was a car blocking part of the sidewalk with a key still in the ignition. He let himself in and locked all four doors. He turned the key in the ignition but all he got was the engine struggling to start.

The two zombies he had taken down momentarily were back up and clawing at the windshield with more of their friends swarming the vehicle, clawing, and groaning. If the engine would not start, Marvin would be stuck there till the airstrike blew him up along with the rest of the district.

VROOM! The engine finally revved to life.

Marvin could not have been happier. He adjusted the vehicle and drove along the sidewalk he'd seen Richie zoom down on his motorbike. Unlike Richie's vehicle, Marvin's was bigger and wider: he couldn't just zigzag around obstacles of all kinds. He carefully bumped along so that no harm would come to the engine. The car was moving fairly slowly for some time, as Marvin looked for an opening to get back on the road. The entire avenue was blocked from the abandoned traffic jam; Marvin had to keep the car on the sidewalk until he reached the end of the avenue.

Time was running out: he could hear engine sounds roaring louder than those of the car he was driving. The airstrike was on its way. Marvin sped up. The car hit a dumpster and it flew against the front windshield, and then a bench went up and cracked it into a glassy cobweb.

FEAR IN FLESH

Marvin was losing control over the vehicle after he lost sight of what was in front of him. A zombie came bouncing against the bumper and over to the hood. Another zombie went under the tires, forcing Marvin to swerve left and right until he hit a fire hydrant and water came bursting out from the underground pipes. The car could not take any more damage after that, stopping right there, near the end of First Avenue. Marvin saw no choice but to get out and keep running.

The airstrike had deployed the missiles that whooshed across, and the whole district was catching fire in great explosions that could be seen miles away. Marvin was hardly even one mile away, puffing desperately as he tried to escape the oblivion devouring his town. There was no escaping it, so he took shelter in the back seat of a van and put the seatbelt on, holding tight.

The van that held Marvin had been abandoned at the crossroads between First and Second Avenues for a few seconds and was thrown to Second Avenue from the force of the waves of the explosions. The van hit a few smaller vehicles on its way and landed on two tires before crashing to a stop. Marvin was dazed, bloodied, with gashes on his face and bruises throbbing across his arms and legs, but he felt very lucky to be alive.

Once he exited the van and wondered haggardly around Second Avenue for a few moments, a group of survivors found him—a very odd group of survivors, who looked dangerous with their multitude of weaponry—melee and machine—and faces hidden beneath Halloween masks. After those miraculous hours of Marvin's escape, he was taken in by the league that became known as the "Masked Rebels." Not knowing exactly what he was getting himself into by accepting the helping hand, all he had in mind at that time was to survive.

Since then, Marvin had donned his own mask, like all the other rebels, gaining a new look and nickname to distinguish him from the rest of the growing league's members. He wore a scarlet demon mask with white rubber fangs and black twin horns jutting out from the forehead, earning him the name "Demon-man" for almost the two years since he'd joined. While the living dead continued to defile the world with their disease, the Masked Rebels encountered them multiple times, only to overcome them by the sheer power of their numbers.

However, their brutality was not only limited to the living dead, but the living had also become their enemies, their competitors for resources, hence they showed them, too no mercy when they crossed paths. Lately, those encounters always ended with a raid and a slaughter. It was a cruel new world, and that was how the Masked Rebels became a force to be reckoned with. When it came down to the priority of staying alive, all rules were gone, aiding the dead more than the living in spreading terror across the ruins of Cliffroyce Bay.

This Demon-Man that had replaced the jolly Marvin Conley was as ruthless and selfish, a killer as the rest of the crew he rode with for over a year till they conquered the Royce Pentagon Sanctuary.

The day they entered the Royce Pentagon Sanctuary, Marvin weighed significantly less than what he had before the plague, wearing a medium T-shirt and shorts.

A ginger ponytail hung to his shoulders, and his beard grew as bushy as the undergrowth taking over the abandoned streets. He had just woken up, though the day began hours ago outside his lonely tent. Still wearing the same dorky glasses he'd always had didn't make him less of a badass once he put on the demon mask. As Demon-Man, he was well-known and respected among his criminal colleagues.

FEAR IN FLESH

Demon-man stepped out into the daylight, armed with a sheathed machete and a machine gun strapped to one shoulder, making his way up to one of the six watchtowers. On his way, a man wearing a zebra mask greeted him. "Morning, Demon-Man."

"Hey, Donkey-Stripes, how's it going?"

"It's *Zebra*-Stripes, man. Won't you ever get it right?"

"Donkey, zebra—they both look the same to me, and I bet they'd taste pretty delicious too if we could find any to hunt. Anyhow, watcha need, Stripes?"

Zebra-Stripes glowered under the mask, but he answered anyway. "We found two survivors today near the E-shop downtown: an adult and a kid."

"Please tell me you put them both down painlessly."

"Well, we did for the adult. We found med-kit supplies on him, and the kid, well, he was a cripple, and no one had the heart to shoot him down."

"Tsk-tsk-tsk." Demon-Man was not pleased with Zebra's answer. "See, there are only two choices you could've made if you didn't shoot that poor, crippled orphan. One, you left him out there to survive by himself with the zombies, or two, you brought him here. So which is it, Stripes? Did you leave him out there to be eaten alive? Or did you bring him here for Pig-Face and his group of rapists to defile him?"

"We ... brought 'em here with us, but Pig-Face still doesn't know about him. No one does except for you now."

"Good, then you need to do that poor boy you just orphaned a favor and put him out his misery. And do it outside the sanctuary's territory. We don't want anyone whispering about you trying to go all Abraham Lincoln, freeing Pig-Face's slaves and what not."

"But Pig-Face already killed all his slaves because we're running short on supplies to feed our own. Can't we bring in the kid, give him a mask, and train him to be one of us?"

"Two results will come of that, Stripes. One: Pig-Face finds out about this new masked member, calls him in, finds out he's a child, rapes him over and over till he's bored, and then slits his throat open. Two: All that happens, plus they find out we're involved with sneaking him in, so we end up with *our* throats cut open too. There's no way out of it, and you said it yourself: we hardly have enough supplies to take care of our own. One extra mouth to feed is still a big deal, so do him and us a favor …" Demon-Man put the muzzle of his machine gun against the side of Zebra's head. "All it'll take is just one squeeze, and the problem will be solved. Spill his brains out and sleep it off, Stripes, or it'll be your brain instead. You got me?"

Zebra-Stripes gulped and nodded. That meant they'd come to a solution, and Demon-Man was finally relieved to pursue what he'd been after in the first place. He went to stuff his belly with food and a morning beer since they didn't have coffee and then approached one of the watchtowers looking to the west, where Cliffroyce was mostly in ruins—the ruins that Marvin Conley had luckily escaped.

One guy was up there with a pumpkin face mask on, sitting on a lawn chair with bullet holes in the cloth. The pumpkin-faced man was snoozing, and his sniper rifle, which he was supposed to be using to scope out the grounds below, was on the floor.

Demon-Man picked it up and dropped it into the sleeping rebel's lap. He woke up with a snort and, in confusion, said, "It wasn't me!" Then he saw Demon-Man standing before him.

"I'm sure it wasn't," said Demon-Man, "and even more sure you weren't the one keeping your eyes open at your post, Pumpkin brain. You were snoring instead."

"I've only been out for like five minutes." The rebel yawned. "I was waiting on you, and it's Pumpkin-*Head*."

"Whatever. You can go back to your tent now, Pumpkinseed; I'll take it from here." Demon-Man exchanged his machine gun with the sniper rifle. Pumpkin-Head accepted the exchange and was about to leave the post. "Any strange activities take place last night?" Demon-Man felt the need to ask.

"Nah, it was a very quiet night, actually. Not a single—" Pumpkin-Head stopped talking right then when a loud trumpet sounded, echoing across the ruins below. Pumpkin-Head was not interrupted by just any random noise from far away: it was an actual elephant's trumpeting that they heard coming from the destroyed parts of the town. When the roars of the animals died down a little and the sounds drew closer, it was then that they heard slithery, hisses and whispers of some words being chanted. But they couldn't understand the chants.

Demon-Man lifted the sniper and started scoping out the area of the former home of Marvin Conley. What he saw down there was an utter freak show. Legions of the living dead were limping in unison like an army, and within that legion trooped a small zoo. Animals were limping among the dead, and Demon-Man's eyes could just make out the middle rows of the marching army of the dead—he couldn't even find where the rows truly ended.

It may have been the largest group of zombies he'd ever seen. There were giraffes at one end and elephants on the other, and in the center was a bizarre herd of lionesses, tigers, and black panthers guarding a white horse in their midst with a long-haired rider on its back.

"What are you seeing, man, tell me!" Pumpkin-Head pleaded.

"Pumpkin-Breath, I think this might be a good time to put the whole pentagon on alert for an approaching attack," Demon-Man answered. "Would you like to do the honors?"

"I'm not going anywhere till you tell me who's attacking," Pumpkin-Head protested. "Is it the dead? Scavenging survivors like us? Or ..."

Demon-Man handed him the sniper rifle. "Take a look for yourself 'cause I'm not even sure what to call it. But whatever it is, it doesn't look good." He stood at the edge of the tower with Pumpkin-Head next to him. Gazing through the scope, Pumpkin-Head easily spotted the marching horde on its path of destruction, but it was the peculiar middle rank that caught his eye, just as it had Demon-Man's.

Pumpkin-Head managed to adjust the scope to zoom closer and paid closer attention to the words that were being chanted.

"Conquest ... Pestilence ... War ... Death ... Apocalypse ..."

"It's the names of the four horsemen," Pumpkin-Head said. He was shocked because the reality was now presenting him a picture that he had, very long ago, refused to believe and turned away from. Pumpkin-Head used to be a devout Christian until he repudiated Christianity for atheism.

"What is this, a marching Bible study group?" Demon-Man joked nervously. "C'mon, man, we have to put the whole pentagon on alert." Too late, though, for another masked rebel had already beaten Demon-Man to the punch. The blow horn sounded. "*What the hell is wrong with these idiots?*" Demon-Man exploded. "We need to keep it quiet till the horde passes along, and they're blowing the freakin' horn!"

"I don't think the horn will make any difference," Pumpkin-Head said ominously. "They know we're here."

As the approaching army of the dead got closer, he was better able to see the rider of the white horse. He had long hair, as messy as his horse's, and seemed to be naked. He looked very human. Pumpkin-Head could not be sure of the expression on the rider's face, but it almost looked like a grin. "You have to take a closer look at this guy, man." Pumpkin-Head handed the rifle to Demon-Man, shaking.

As he looked through the scope, Demon-Man asked, "What am I looking at—the naked guy on the horse in the middle?"

"Yeah."

No more jokes came from the blabbermouth Demon-Man afterward. What he saw was enough to knock him into a state of silent shock. After Pumpkin-Head had worked the zoom, the rider became much clearer, but it still remained a mystery as to whether he was human or a zombie.

This naked, unusual rider had exposed arms, one of which was half covered by some green, moldy-looking substance, and the other was holding the reigns of the horse.

All Demon-Man felt on the sight of that man was utter, agonizing fear. He knew that the sadistic and evil grin etched across the face of the rider would be the harbinger of nothing but annihilation.

It was then that Demon-Man realized what they were, it was the sensation that their sight evokes, that elicited a name for the existence of this army of living dead, they were ... *Fear in Flesh.*

THE END TO ALL IS COMING

AFTERWORD

How it all started

Before I dive into the messy topic of how I decided to write my first book in the zombie apocalypse genre, I'll explain how a guy like me, who barely had the ambition to finish his bachelor's degree in a field he had no interest in, ended up writing a novel.

For starters, I was already neck-deep in this major: two years enduring endless reports and essays about the same boring topics over and over again—"transportation that blah" "logistics that blah." I never pictured myself becoming a corporate slave, though I was for a short period of time post-graduation. A man's got to earn a living: that's how life works, and I was rolling with that, and still am. Halfway into my major, I stumbled upon two elective courses: "*The Hero's Quest* and *The Alchemist*" and "Writing Lives." Two signs that I might have some purpose in life other than living and dying as a corporate slave.

The first course made me explore Paulo Coelho's work *The Alchemist,* which was the first official book I've finish reading that had no pictures on the inside. We were told to write reader responses as we read, and in one of those responses I mentioned that maybe I could do something like that with just typing words in a document. Hell, I'd been doing that from the moment I got into collage, but just once, maybe I could write thousands and thousands of words that were exciting to me.

"Writing Lives" came the semester afterward, in which we were instructed to write an autobiography including our past, present, and you guessed it—future. By that time, we were approaching the year 2014, and I was barely twenty-one. In the autobiography assignment's future part, I added a New Year's resolution. In January 2014 I began fulfilling that resolution from day one. Two years and two months later, I finished my first novel, *Fear in Flesh,* which I had no idea would turn out so long or even get a title that didn't have the word "dead" in it!

Why zombies?

Well, why not? I was always into zombies, ever since I started switching the lights on at night after watching a horror movie at God only knows what age!. The year 2013–2014 was the year of the zombies for me. I was already hooked on AMC's *The Walking Dead* (God bless you, Robert Kirkman). Also, I was playing two zombie genre videogames on my Playstation3: *Resident Evil 6* and *The Walking Dead Season 1.*

Before those two, I was also busy playing the Naughty Dog's *Last of Us,* plus, the movie *World War Z* was just coming out.

I had those decaying bastards on my mind 24/7 that year, so I figured why not just write about them. What if a bunch of ordinary characters living in a fictional town in New York City suddenly underwent a siege of a spreading disease that made people eat each other till only a few remained, trying to survive. Simple. Didn't even make up a reason as to how the zombies came into being, just like most zombie stories out there. It just happened!

At the time I was just in a hurry to get started, or "practice" as I called it. I reached a point where I was struggling to keep my eyes open reading some chapters. It was no different from any other cheesy zombie movie I'd seen, and I'd seen *a lot* of zombie movies! So I took some time to think of a way to spice things up, and that was when the idea of the prologue hit me. The story kept changing drastically and ballooning from there on out. It became something more than just a zombie horror flick; the zombies got an upgrade by having a far bigger backstory that dated to millennia ago.

As for now, try not to get killed off while you wait, because all the answers to your questions regarding Violet's dreams and the Grim Reaper's role in this timeline will be revealed in the second installment where Fear invades reality.

Hesham N. Ali

Born and raised in a minuscule Middle Eastern island known to man as the Kingdom of Bahrain. His entire life, Hesham had traversed through the infinite cosmos and amidst the time of the dinosaurs, falling all the way down the rabbit hole. When he finally emerged on the other side into the backward world of fiction writing where he battled his greatest demons in a multiverse of genres—that was when his reign of madness began.

2014 was the year he was diagnosed with the infamous "Writer's Bug". By 2016 he debuted with two novels: {Fear in Flesh} and {A Portrait of Memories}. Hesham was 23 when he published both titles, and as his passion for making up stories keeps on growing, so does his love for creating fictional worlds then tearing them asunder.

Find out more and stay in touch with the author through . . .
Instagram: @h.rex92/@madrex.92
Amazon: @Hesham N. Ali
Goodreads: @Hesham N. Ali
Email: hesham_nasser@outlook.com

1st EDITION

Sold on Amazon.com @Hesham N. Ali

OTHER PUBLICATIONS

Sold on Amazon.com @Hesham N. Ali

A PORTRAIT OF MEMORIES

Where Devils Dance, Angels Fall

Made in the USA
Columbia, SC
15 December 2022